AF417990

WOMEN OF A CERTAIN RAGE

A CHARMING COZY MYSTERY

EILEEN RENDAHL

Copyright © 2020 by Eileen Rendahl

Print ISBN: 979-8696721385

All rights reserved.

No part of this book may be reproduced in any form or by any electronic or mechanical means, including information storage and retrieval systems, without written permission from the author, except for the use of brief quotations in a book review.

MORE COZY MYSTERIES

EMPTY NEST MYSTERIES

#1 Women of a Certain Rage

#2 She Looks Good for Her Rage (Coming soon)

More *Cozy Mysteries* by her alter egos:

KRISTI ABBOTT

Kernel of Truth

Pop Goes the Murder

Assault and Buttery

or LILIAN BELL

A Grave Issue

If the Coffin Fits

ALSO BY EILEEN RENDAHL

Romantic Suspense

Veiled Intentions

Hold Back The Dark

Vanished in The Night

Thriller

Veiled Intentions

Cover Me in Darkness

Petals on the Pillow

Paranormal

Don't Kill The Messenger (A Messenger Novel #1)

Dead on Delivery (A Messenger Novel #2)

Dead Letter Day (A Messenger Novel #3)

Payback for a post-mortem (Messenger Series)

Dreidels and Demons (Messenger Series)

Tinsel and Temptations (A Holiday Anthology)

Petals on the Pillow

Chick Lit

Do Me, Do My Roots

Dancing Naked Under The Moon

Un-Bridaled

Un-Veiled

ACKNOWLEDGMENTS

There are always a lot of people to thank when I finish a book, but this one has more than usual. Women of a Certain Rage was a hard one for me to write. After spending quite a few years merrily writing one or two books a year while wrangling part-time jobs, school, teaching, and family, I hit a wall. The creative well had run dry and I wasn't sure it was ever going to fill back up or where I was supposed to drill for a new one. People held my hand and listened to me whine, they brainstormed with me, they read pages and gave me feedback, and they assured me that I hadn't forgotten how to write a book. Then there are also the amazing women who inspired me to write about the friendships in this book. I really don't know if I would have been able to write this and end up with a book that I like and think is worth your time, dear reader, without them. They are (in no particular order) Andy Wallace, Marian Ullman, Diane Ullman, Spring Warren, Tilly Rodrigues, Tamsen Shultz, Lisa Nalbone, Kris Calvin, Catriona McPherson, Janice Peacock, Beth McMullen, Carol Kirshnit, Ellen

Shields, Shelly Hebert, Deb Van Der List, Kelly Safford, Donna Ward, Ellen Chesler, Maureen Muldoon, Tai Farnsworth, Lisa Trahan, Michelle Barney, and Emma Burcart.

*To Teddy and Alex who made me a Mom
and seem to have forgiven me for every way I screwed it up.*

ONE

"WHAT DID YOU DO?" Lillibeth Ocampo jabbed an index finger into Brady Atkinson's chest with each syllable.

Brady backed away from Lillibeth until the wall made it so he couldn't get any farther away from her.

I'd walked into the assisted living area of the Caring Hands Retirement Village (our motto: Get the Best Care at Caring Hands!) in Darby, California after entering the code to open the door (it's kept locked to discourage unsupervised wandering) and nearly got bumped over by Gabriel, the floral delivery guy from Happy Blossoms as he hurried out. I swear that guy found a way to come here every chance he got. I suspected it was because he had a bit of a crush on Christy, our receptionist, but it was getting kind of ridiculous. He didn't stand a chance with her anyway. I didn't even have time to shoot him a nasty look for not watching where he was going, though, because of the flurry of activity down the hall.

Brady slumped against the scuffed wall. I picked up my pace to get to him. I'd been planning on cutting through the assisted living unit to the multi-purpose room where I held my art classes.

I wouldn't have even slowed my steps on my way if I hadn't seen Brady standing in the hall, looking whiter than even a blond-haired, blue-eyed white boy should look and being accosted by Lillibeth. She was short enough to have to crane her neck to look up at him, but it was pretty damn clear who was the alpha dog in that scenario. It was, after all, all about the size of the fight in the dog and Lillibeth was all fight.

Fighting was one of the few things that Brady hadn't gotten in trouble for. Yet. I'd known Brady since he was nine-years-old and he'd ended up on the same soccer team as my son Tyler. They'd been friends forever and Brady's mother Rayna was one of my best friends. Back then, Brady was at my house so much that he kept a toothbrush, pajamas, and a change of clothes there. Those days were gone. The boys had graduated from high school and Tyler had left for UC Santa Barbara. Brady, however, hadn't quite managed to launch yet. At least, we all hoped it was yet.

Brady attracted trouble the way a white pair of pants attracts black cat hair. I honestly didn't think he did all that much that the other kids didn't do, but he seemed to always be the one who got caught. Which was why he was at Caring Hands. I'd helped get him a spot to do the Community Service the court had sentenced him to for disorderly conduct. Or maybe possession of some small amount of weed (he was only nineteen so it still wasn't legal for him) or possibly public urination? I couldn't keep it all straight. Something. He'd done something wrong and our lawyer friend Sharon — mother of Max who had been on that same aforementioned soccer team — had managed to get him community service. I'd smoothed the way for him to do the community service here, taking the library cart around, helping people to the multi-purpose room, and assisting during music therapy.

"Tell me what you did," Lillibeth poked Brady again. Lillibeth had taken a clear and instant dislike to Brady, complaining to Dionne Gordon, the retirement village administrator, about Brady's clothes (his pants sagged too low), his punctuality (he'd been ten minutes late on one occasion when a train coming through town had stopped traffic), and his voice (he was a mumbler). She was right about that last one, but still. It's possible that she was just voicing what everyone else was thinking, however she and Dionne were friendly with each other and I knew she had Dionne's ear. Let's hope Lillibeth wasn't bending it about me, too. I was more than happy to do anything I could to help Brady and Rayna, but I wouldn't be happy if it cost me this job.

I walked toward them to see if there was some way I could help in the five minutes I had before a stream of seniors would be filing into the dining to make glass gem suncatchers to sell at the Spring Fling Craft Fair. I don't like to keep them waiting. I knew I only had a minute or two to spare, but I was definitely going to spend them with Brady if he needed me. He might be a young man now, but when I looked at him I still saw the sweet nine-year-old who would snuggle up next to me when we watched *Ghostbusters* because the Stay Puft Marshmallow Man was too scary.

Brady held his hands up as if a cop had told him to, something he unfortunately had a bit of experience with. "I didn't do anything. I swear. I came in to say hello and maybe read to him. He was gone."

"Well, he wasn't 'gone' this afternoon at one-thirty. He was fine then. I took his vitals. Absolutely one hundred percent fine. Temperature. Heart rate. Oxygen. Blood pressure. Blood sugar." She poked his chest with each word.

What she said was patently untrue. If Floyd had been one hundred percent fine, he wouldn't have been on this wing of the assisted living area. He'd have been over in the independent living cottages or maybe even home. Even I knew that and I didn't know much when it came to health care. My expertise lies elsewhere. I just have to figure out where that is.

"Something must have happened between then and now," Brady said, his voice sounding like it was getting clogged in his throat. I knew that sound. He was trying not to cry. It was how his voice sounded when he missed the penalty kick that would have moved the soccer team up in the regional tournament back in seventh grade.

"That's what I'm saying. Something happened," Lillibeth snapped back. "What did you do?"

I waved to Camila Diaz, on duty at the nurses' station, and walked up next to Brady and stood shoulder to shoulder with him, looking down at Lillibeth. It wasn't too difficult. I'm a solid nine inches taller in my bare feet and even more wearing the boots I had on. I glanced into Floyd's room. I couldn't see much besides a television set and a vase of flowers on the table next to it. "What's going on?"

She looked at me through narrowed eyes. "I'm not sure, but I'm sure as hell going to find out." She stomped off toward the nurse's station, the floor trembling beneath her tiny feet.

I turned to Brady for an explanation. He swallowed hard and said, "Floyd Winstead died. I found him."

Poor kid. I doubted he'd ever seen a dead body before, much less the dead body of someone he knew and cared about. Brady had started his community service stint with a sneer on his face and a drag in his step, but he'd ended up connecting with some of the seniors he was helping. Floyd was one of them. Brady would read to him, take him on walks, and sit next to him at music therapy, shaking little egg-shaped maracas and singing "When the Saints Come Marching In" with real enthusiasm. The sneer had vanished and while his steps might not be bouncy, they were definitely not the reluctant gait of someone forced to be where he definitely did not want to be.

Finding the lifeless body of someone he'd come to respect and care about explained Brady's pale face, shaking hands, and trembling chin. Who wouldn't be upset that someone they had connected with passing? I felt a pang about Floyd myself. He had a dry wit and sweet temperament that I would definitely miss. It didn't, however, explain Lillibeth's finger poking, though.

I opened my arms and Brady stepped into my hug. I patted his back, but I could feel how straight and still he was holding himself, trying like hell to keep it together. I let him go. "I'm so sorry, hon. Floyd was a great guy. We'll all miss him. But why is Lillibeth so hot under the collar?"

"I swear I don't know. The second I realized Floyd wasn't asleep I hit the call button. I don't know what else I was supposed to do." He kicked at the floor with the toe of his untied sneaker. Definitely fighting tears. Poor kid.

Malachi Donnelly, the Physician's Assistant for Caring Hands, came out of the room, stripping off plastic gloves and tossing them into the orange-lidded container by the door. "You did exactly right, Brady," he'd said, his voice deep and resonant. He clapped Brady on the back.

Brady's shoulders relaxed. "Do you think so?"

Malachi looked as Irish as his name with dark black hair and bright blue eyes. Scrubs hung on him like the ones actors wear in hospital shows, which, trust me, is not standard issue, and he smelled a little like something citrus. His voice, rich and calming, made everyone slow down a bit. Whenever I saw him, he seemed to always be taking a moment to say hello to people, to pat them on the back, or to give a compliment. He was relatively new. Not as new as me, but not an old timer at Caring Hands, either. I hadn't worked with him much. He'd been on the night shift and had only recently transferred to days. No one does arts and crafts during night shift so we hadn't really crossed paths before now.

"Absolutely. You did everything you were supposed to do," Malachi said. "Lillibeth was frustrated and looking for someone to take it out on. I'll talk to her. She shouldn't be taking her anger out on volunteers."

I'm sure no nurse wants to lose a patient, but she had to be at least a little used to it considering where she worked. "What had her so upset?" I asked.

Malachi rubbed his chin for a second before answering. "I stopped her from doing CPR. Floyd had a DNR on file. She probably would have done the CPR anyway if I hadn't gotten there first."

Ah. A Do Not Resuscitate order. Also not uncommon around here. I peeked into Floyd's room. He sat slumped over in his wheelchair. A bright bouquet of flowers sat on the counter next to him, their cheeriness completely out of place and contrasting with the gray of his face. Tears welled up in my eyes. I hadn't been just talking when I said Floyd was a great guy. He was. I'd enjoyed getting to know him. Now, just like that, he was gone.

"Lillibeth thought she could have saved him," Malachi continued.

"Could she have?" Brady asked. A jumble of emotions passed over his face. Hope. Defeat. Sadness.

Malachi shrugged. "Maybe. Probably not. Maybe she would have saved him, but he would have had brain damage. Maybe he would have been fine. It's a moot point. He made his wishes very clear. No CPR. No heroic efforts. It probably didn't help that it was the second one in as many weeks. Harvey Cornish died last Tuesday. He had a DNR, too."

Brady's head slumped again.

Harvey had had a stroke a few months ago and had gone from being a fairly active resident to being unable to move or talk. While that may have been why he put the DNR in place, the majority of residents had DNRs, actually. Most didn't want heroic efforts. CPR doesn't really work like it does on TV. Success rates are alarmingly low even with young healthy people and even if the person survives, they often have deficits. "Shouldn't Lillibeth be accustomed to people having DNRs?"

"Oh, she hasn't been here that long and before here she worked at an emergency room. The focus was different." He shifted from one foot to another, clearly a little uncomfortable. I understood what he meant. He didn't spell it out, but it was pretty clear to me. People show up at the emergency room wanting to be saved. People checked into Caring Hands not expecting to leave unless it was feet first. Malachi glanced up at the clock and then turned to Brady. "Why don't you go home for the day? Take a little time for yourself."

Brady kicked at the brown carpet for a second. "Okay." Then his head came up. "But I'll be back tomorrow."

"Of course you will." Malachi rested his hand on his

shoulder again. "I know this is hard. You never get used to it, but it does get easier."

Brady nodded as if he didn't quite trust his voice and walked toward the exit for the unit. Malachi and I watched him go. I could tell with each step how much he was hurting.

"He's a good kid," I said.

Malachi grunted. "Not completely good or he wouldn't have ended up doing community service here."

I turned sharply. The comment seemed at odds with the kindness he'd shown Brady moments before and it worried me. Too many people were ready to write a kid off for minor offences. I didn't want anyone to write Brady off. I also didn't want them to write me off. I was the one who'd brought him into the facility. I needed this job. I didn't need people looking at me funny because of my association with Brady. "Kids make mistakes. It doesn't have to define who they are."

He took a step back and held up his hands. "Sorry. Just an observation."

I glanced up at the clock. "I've got to go. My group is probably already in the dining hall tearing things apart. I hope no one's gotten into the hot glue guns again." That had been an epic fiasco. I thought I was never going to get Tessie Arthur's fingers unglued. I started down the hall.

"Leah?" Malachi called after me.

I turned. He leaned against the wall, rubbing at the stubble on his chin that had formed over the course of his shift. "Brady must be okay if someone like you believes in him. He's lucky to have you to stick up for him."

I'd turned away before the flush went all the way up to my scalp, but I was way too aware of his eyes on me as I'd walked down the hall.

The unit was set up like four spokes on a wheel with the nurses' station as the hub. The entrance to the unit was at one end of the most eastern pointing spoke along with the physical therapy office and the director's office. The most western spoke was all patient rooms, which were a cross between hospital rooms and studio apartments. Not quite as utilitarian as a hospital room, but not quite as home-like as a studio. The rooms summed up where most of the people who lived here were in their life stage. They weren't ill or incapacitated enough to be in the hospital or skilled nursing area, but they couldn't really live on their own anymore either.

The multi-purpose room where residents ate and had music therapy and did art projects and watched movies was at the tip of the northern pointing spoke. It was shaped like an octagon with one flattened side. The rest of the walls were mainly windows looking out onto banks of oleanders that lined the sidewalk. It was light and bright. I liked that about it. I could have lived without the slightly buckled linoleum flooring and the faint smell of stewed vegetables, but beggars can't be choosers and I was happy to have a big light space to do crafts in.

There were lots of reasons to do crafts with seniors. Being creative helps them keep their brains sharp by making them focus and concentrate. It gives them a way to communicate their feelings, something that many of them have been taught not to do. It can help them connect with each other. A lot of times, moving to a senior facility like Caring Hands means leaving friends you've had for ages behind. Not to be too blunt, but at their ages, sometimes those friends aren't around anymore anyway. Doing an activity together helps break the ice and makes it easier to make new friends. And it gives them goals. Like today. We needed to finish up a pile of suncatchers to sell at the Arts and Crafts booth at the Spring Fling, one of Caring Hands' big fundraisers for the year.

The group was indeed waiting for me. "There you are," Waylon Langston grumbled. "We were supposed to start five minutes ago."

"Something came up, Waylon." I didn't let it bother me too much. Waylon was always cranky. Based on the deep frown lines on either side of his mouth, he'd always been cranky, too. He'd been a big man in his day and he still took up a lot of space both physically and emotionally. His hair was snowy white and thin on top, but it wasn't totally gone. His blue eyes weren't warm. They were more like ice than water or sky. I set my box of supplies down and pulled out the plastic lids they'd be using. I set one down in front of each one of them.

"What's this for?" Gladys Smalley asked, poking at the lid. She was so hunched over in her wheelchair that she was nearly eye-level with the table. The baby doll she toted around with her was jammed into the corner of her chair, momentarily forgotten. Caring Hands had been giving dolls to some of the female patients with dementia. It seemed to soothe them. A few of them treated those dolls as gently as if they were real babies. Gladys, apparently, not so much. Her doll often looked a little worse for the wear.

"I'll explain in a minute, Gladys." I pulled out bags of colored glass beads to set around the table.

"It's for the suncatchers, Gladys," Tessie Arthur said, her voice loud. "She told us about it last week. Don't you remember?"

Gladys looked over at her, eyes watery. "Remember what?"

Tessie rolled her eyes and shook her head, making the

tight gray curls on her head bounce against her brown skin.

"That's right," I said. "We're making suncatchers. I'll pour some glue into each of these lids and you choose which glass beads you want to use and what pattern you want to make. After it dries, we can take them out of the lids and put some hangers on them. They look darling hanging in a window."

I pulled out my demo suncatcher and held it up so the light shone through.

"Oooh," Gladys said, like she was at the fireworks.

I smiled. "Exactly. Ooh. Let's get started."

———

It was two days later at a little after seven on a Friday evening, when Rayna called me. When I saw her name on the Caller ID, I expected an invitation to meet for a glass of wine or to go for a walk or just to chat. I snatched up the phone. I was up for any of it. I'd done a pretty good job of adjusting since Tyler left for college, but sometimes evenings stretched before me like a giant maw of silence. Okay. They pretty much all stretched that way.

None of it mattered because instead of an invitation, she said, "Leah, the police have picked up Brady."

Great. He hadn't even finished his community service for littering or peeing in public or smoking weed before he had another run in with the law. Again.

I bit back a sigh, but let my eyes roll. Rayna didn't call me for judgment. She called me for support. She couldn't hear an eye roll, though, right? "Do you want me to come with you to the police station?"

Rayna's husband traveled a lot. Like all the time a lot. The chances that he'd be in town early on a Friday night were somewhere between slim and nil. This wouldn't be the first time I was Rayna's emotional back-up when George was out of town. It was only fair. She'd been mine about eleventy bazillion times in the decade I'd known her. I'm not sure I would have managed to raise Tyler as a single mom without the help and backup of my Mom friends and Rayna was the cream of the Mom friend crop.

"Please?" she asked. "George is in Portland. I called him. He's trying to get home, but I don't know how long it will take him and I don't want to go alone." A loud bang on the other end of the line made Rayna gasp a bit.

"Of course I'll come with you. You know I don't mind. Don't be ridiculous. Did you call Sharon?" Sharon had been the one who'd gotten Brady community service for his last misadventure instead of something worse. Maybe she could work her magic again.

"Yes. Yes. Of course I called Sharon." Rayna sounded almost out of breath. Was she starting to hyperventilate? "She's going to meet us at the station."

I smiled. She'd known I'd offer to go with her. She'd been counting on it. It felt good to be someone she could depend on. It had been the other way around all too many times. "Good. I'll be at your place in . . ." I glanced up at the clock and down at the pajamas I'd already put on even though it was only seven-thirty because that's the kind of rock-and-roll-party-all-the-time lifestyle I led these days. "Fifteen minutes."

"Thanks, Leah. Thank you so much."

"It's no problem." I hesitated a second before I asked my next question. The answer didn't really matter. I'd be there no matter what, but I was curious. "What did they pick him up for?"

"Murder."

TWO

I'D GOTTEN DRESSED SO FAST, I was amazed I didn't have
my shirt on backwards. Rayna was outside her house
waiting for me when I pulled up. She was only on the other
side of the park from me, but her neighborhood looked like a
totally different town. Darby isn't huge. I lived over in the
river streets (my house is on Danube Avenue) among adobes
from the 1930s and Eichlers from the 1970s with slightly
cracked driveways and the occasional crooked gutter. My
neighbors were teachers and managers of retail stores and
administrative assistants. Rayna resided on the bird streets
(her house was on Quail Terrace) in a neighborhood of two-
story stucco McMansions with professionally landscaped
yards that managed to look both natural and lovingly
tended at the same time and pristine driveways. Her neighbors were doctors and lawyers and accountants.

Thirty years or so ago, Rayna's neighborhood had probably been a tomato field. Or possibly a corn field or a
sunflower field. They grew all that stuff around here in the
Central Valley of California. That and almonds and
walnuts and avocados, and well, just about everything else.

We aren't what people generally think about when they think of California. There's no ocean or lake or beaches. No mountains and no skiing. We could get to all that in an hour or two. We were close enough to the Bay area, though, that real estate had started to get more expensive and houses were more profitable than farming. There was no way I'd be able to afford my house now. I was lucky to have bought it when I did.

Right now, though, Rayna's house didn't look like a mini-mansion or an agricultural enterprise. It looked like a crime scene. Two police cars and a van lined her driveway and curb. The police cars had their red and blue lights swirling, casting weird shadows on the rough stucco. Every light in her house blazed and people in uniforms buzzed in and out. She stood out front to one side of all the vehicles.

I hit the unlock button on my Frontier and Rayna slipped into the front seat. If you didn't know her, you might not know how upset she was. Her blonde hair was pulled back into a smooth ponytail. Her make-up was flawless. Like me, she had on jeans with a scoop neck top and a jacket and boots. She looked like something from a magazine. Me? Well, I looked clean. I had that going for me.

I knew her, though. I knew her well enough to see the slight tremble in her hands as she folded them in her lap. She gestured out the window at the activity. "They had a search warrant. A search warrant." She bit her lip. "That's never happened before."

Down the street, Eva Wentz came out of her front door. It figured she'd be the first one out to witness the drama. You could count on Eva having her nose in anything going on in our town, whether it was any of her business or not. Eva also had a kid the same age as Tyler and Brady. She was one of those moms who couldn't wait to tell you what your kid was doing wrong.

We'd tried to make friends with her, inviting her for coffee and including her in conversations as we stood around waiting for the kids after school or at whatever event we were all attending. She never reciprocated, though. None of us had ever seen the inside of her house. Nor had our kids. None of them had ever been invited for a play date. After a while, we got the message. She didn't want to be friends. She didn't want to play nice. I was surprised Eva hadn't brought a lawn chair out to settle in and watch all the drama unfold. Schadenfreude was definitely her thing.

"Can we go, Leah?" Rayna asked. "Now?"

"Buckle your seatbelt." Once she did, I put the truck in drive and pulled away from the curb.

We started rolling and Rayna started talking. "We'd finished dinner, right? Brady was loading the dishwasher while I put away the leftovers and there was this knock at the door." She rubbed her hands over her face. "A hard knock. More like a bang. You know what I mean?"

I nodded, my imagination conjuring up jackbooted thugs pounding on the door with clenched fists.

"I answered the door and there were two police officers there. They were so big. They filled up the doorway. I couldn't see past them. They handed me the search warrant and came in. There must have been a dozen more right after them." Her hands twisted in her lap. "They put him in handcuffs." The last word came out on a squeak.

My own heart clenched at the thought of seeing one of our babies in cuffs. Brady might be the consummate screw up, but handcuffs? I reached over and put my hand on hers. "I'm sure it's some kind of crazy mistake. They have the wrong Brady Atkinson or some stupid clerical thing like that. Who are they even saying was killed?"

"Someone named Floyd Winstead." She shook her head. "I don't even know who that is."

I returned my hand to the steering wheel as my stomach lurched. "I do. He was a resident at Caring Hands. He died two days ago. Brady's the one who found him. He didn't say anything?" Adolescent boys weren't the most forthcoming, but the death of someone you knew seemed worthy of making it into a conversation, especially one with your mom.

She shook her head. "He didn't say a word. He came home, changed clothes, and went out to play basketball at the park."

I turned onto Manor Street to cut across town to the police station. I counted to twenty as I sat at the red light. We were the only car at the intersection, but I somehow always managed to hit it when it was red. Rayna leaned back in her seat and pinched the bridge of her nose as if she was trying to ward off a headache.

The light changed and I started forward. All in all, going down to the park to blow off steam didn't sound like a completely unhealthy way to deal with the shock and trauma Brady must have been experiencing. I glanced over at Rayna. "He probably wasn't ready to talk about it. One of the nurses wasn't very kind to him about it."

"Was it Lillibeth? She's had it in for him from the day he started." Rayna rubbed at her chin with the back of her hand.

There was no way to argue with that. She wasn't crazy about any of the kids who came through doing community service, but she had especially disliked Brady.

None of this pointed to Brady having anything to do

with Floyd's death, though. What had happened that the police thought he had been murdered and why on earth would they think Brady knew about it? Had Lillibeth been angry and frustrated enough to accuse Brady of having something to do with Floyd's death? And convincing enough to get the cops to believe it?

"What did Brady say to the police?" I asked, swinging into the roundabout on Everest Road.

"Nothing," Rayna said. "I told him not to say a word until Sharon got there. He knows, though."

Neither of us said anything for a second. This wasn't Brady's first rodeo and we both knew it even if we didn't want to acknowledge it right then. I angled my truck into a parking place in the lot behind the police department. The lot was quiet with only two cop cars parked in it. Maybe all the officers were over at Rayna's searching her house. There'd been enough cars there. Darby isn't all that big. It was probably the most excitement they'd had in a while.

We got out of the truck. I tugged my jacket straight and Rayna straightened her ponytail and we walked into the low two-story building. Sharon was waiting for us. She stood as we walked toward her. She held out her arms and she and Rayna hugged.

Sharon had on lawyer armor and was in full-on lawyer mode. She'd coiled her long brown hair up in a complicated twist on the back of her head and she had on perfectly creased black trousers with a black jacket, a purple shirt that made her tawny skin glow and a pair of well-shined heeled black boots. There was a solidness to her. It wasn't about her body type, it was how she conducted herself. Confident. Professional. Sound.

Her son, Max, was yet another one of the crew of boys that had run like a wolf pack together during the summers, played soccer together through the fall and basketball in the winter. Of all of our boys, he'd gone the farthest away, attending Brown back east where Sharon had grown up. Jayden, Tamika's son, was the fourth of the quartet. He was at Cal Poly. Brady, of course, hadn't gone anywhere except, well, here to the police station.

Rayna stepped back, still holding Sharon's shoulders. "Thank you so much for coming out like this. I know it's late."

Sharon shrugged. "It's fine. It's not like you interrupted some big thing. We hadn't even figured out what movie we wanted to watch."

"Still, tell Mindy I appreciate her letting us disrupt your evening." Sharon's wife, Mindy, was a lecturer in the Biology department at the University and had been more than patient during moments like these over the years.

"Mindy understands," Sharon said, waving Rayna's words away. "Listen, I've got some good news and some bad news and they're kind of the same thing."

"Hit me with it," Rayna said to Sharon.

Sharon gestured to a set of chairs off to the side and I settled into a hard seat across from her. "They haven't arrested him. They've only brought him in for questioning."

"That sounds like good news, right? How is it bad?" Rayna asked, brushing off the chair before she sat in it.

"It means he's a suspect. A person of interest. That's never good. It's especially not good when we're talking about something as astonishingly serious as murder." Sharon sat also and leaned forward, bracing her forearms on her legs. "They won't arrest him unless and until they feel they have a solid case against him. But Rayna, he's not a juvenile anymore. If they decide to arrest him, he'll be going through the regular court system."

And the regular prison. Yikes. I had an idea of what that meant. I'd seen *Shawshank Redemption*. My stomach lurched and I shook my head. Rayna's lips were pressed so hard together that they had entirely disappeared.

The door of the station whooshed open. We all turned to look and let out a collective sigh of relief when Tamika walked through the door. Now our quartet was together and somehow that made me feel a little easier. The four of us had weathered an awful lot over the decade plus that we'd known each other. Parents getting ill, spouses losing jobs, kids applying to college, and a very memorable burst pipe in my laundry room, to name a few of the disasters we'd helped each other survive. Tamika bent over to put her arms around Rayna, her braids swinging forward, the beads on the ends clicking. "I'm so sorry."

After a brief squeeze, Rayna leaned back. "What do you know?"

"Enough." Tamika made a face. "Eva is all over social media. Do NOT look at your mentions. She must be spending 100 percent of her time posting."

Of course Eva was posting madly about it. We should have expected that.

"Freaking Eva," Rayna muttered. "It's not like her kid is so darned perfect."

That was true. Eva's son Nick did stupid kid stuff on occasion like they all did. We could have pointed his errors out the way Eva pointed out our kids' screw ups, but none of us did. I won't lie. I occasionally wanted to get back at Eva, but not enough to do something to hurt her kid. "What is she saying?" I asked.

"So far it's mainly pictures of the police cars in front of Rayna's house, but with some commentary about someone being taken away in the back of a cop car. It's not going to take rocket scientists to figure out who she's talking about." She sat down across from me. "What can I do?"

Sharon shook her head. "Not a lot at the moment. Can you keep an eye online to see what chatter there is?"

Tamika nodded. Tamika is a computer programmer and the IT consultant for all of us. If something needed to be done on a computer, she was definitely the person to turn to. It certainly wasn't me. I'd had to have Tyler give me a tutorial on how to use our TV remote before he left for school. "One hundred percent."

"He gets to come home tonight, right?" Rayna rubbed her thumb along the ridge that had formed between her eyes.

"Probably. I think so. It could be a while, though." Sharon frowned and reached for her purse. "Do you have a headache? Do you need some ibuprofen?"

As Sharon and Rayna conferred, Tamika turned to me. I filled her in on what Brady was being questioned about in a low voice.

"Was Floyd the old guy who always tipped his hat? Or was he the one who was handsy?" Tamika's mother had been a resident at Caring Hands for a short time after a fall so Tamika knew the people there pretty well. She was the meat in the caretaker sandwich of her family, trying to hold together three generations at once while still having a life of her own. She was also the one who'd clued me into the art therapy job there, which had been a life saver both financially and personally. I needed the distraction of a place to be a few times a week nearly as much as I needed the money and I definitely needed the money.

"The hat tipper," I said.

"Oh, no. He was one of the cute ones. And one of the

ones who wasn't one hundred percent bonkers." She put her hand on her heart.

That might not have been how I would have put it, but she was right. Floyd had had all his faculties. Not everyone in the Caring Hands Retirement Village was that lucky, even in Assisted Living. Or maybe they were the unlucky ones, stuck in a reality that wasn't always pretty. I could never decide. "I know. He was so sweet. He wrote me the nicest thank you note for helping him make a bracelet for his granddaughter's birthday. Brady was pretty broken up."

"So he found him? That's not enough to charge someone with murder. There's got to be more to it." She took a small bottle lotion out of her bag, squirted a little in her hands and then offered it to me.

I took the bottle. My hands were always rough. It was all the crafts I did, yet somehow Tamika was the one who always had the bottle of lotion. "I don't know that there is. This is all some kind of crazy misunderstanding." It had to be.

Tamika did that slow blink thing she does when she doesn't want to upset me with whatever she's going to say next like when she had to explain to me that my five-year-old laptop was no longer 'new' and I was going to have to buy a replacement. "If the police are involved, then someone did something, Leah. Something more than misunderstand." She kept her voice low and glanced over at Rayna and Sharon as if she maybe didn't want them to hear what she'd said.

I handed the lotion bottle back to her, momentarily wordless.

Sharon glanced at her phone to check the time. "I think you should all go home and get some rest. You're going to need it. I'm going in. They'll probably start questioning him soon. I think they wanted to wait to see if they turned anything up in the search."

"What did they think would be there? Do we even know how Floyd died?" I asked.

"I don't know on both those questions, but I'll definitely be finding out. Let's all check in tomorrow morning at coffee." Sharon stood up, squared her shoulders, and then gave me a weird grimace. "Anything in my teeth? We had spinach omelets for dinner."

"All good." I pulled a protein bar out of my purse and handed it to her. "Just in case it's a really long night. A spinach omelet is an awfully light dinner." I pulled out a second one and handed that one to her, too. "In case, Brady's hungry."

Sharon took both bars, gave us a little salute, and then walked over to be buzzed into the back of the station. The door opened and a nice-looking Asian man in a suit stepped out to usher her in. Before he followed her through and shut the door, he gave the three of us a complete up and down. Not in a pervy way. More like a careful assessment. For a second, my gaze locked with his. My face flushed, but I didn't look away. He gave me a brief nod and then followed Sharon through the door. Tamika snorted. "He certainly thinks he's the last Otter Pop in the freezer." Then she turned to me and gave me an appraising look. "Or maybe he thinks you are."

"What?"

She rolled her eyes. "Never mind."

We walked out into the parking lot. I shivered as we hit the night air and a breeze rustled the elm trees planted around the lot, tossing their naked branches around. Spring was right around the corner, but it wasn't here yet. At least not at night. You could almost sense how ready nature was to burst into bloom. Pent up energy seemed to pulse in the air. Or maybe that was the tension rolling off Rayna. "Call me if you need anything," Tamika said as she got into her Acura. "Anything," she repeated before closing her car door.

Rayna and I got back into my truck. I drove back to her house, but drove right past it. The police cars were still there. They must not have finished searching. Rayna's house was so neat and organized, I couldn't imagine it taking more than few minutes to go through every drawer and closet. She had at least three-quarters of the stuff labeled so you didn't even have to guess what was there. I hoped they wouldn't leave too big a mess for her to clean up. "Let's go to my place for a bit," I suggested.

She nodded, reaching up to pull her ponytail tight.

I pulled into my driveway and we walked past the lavender, sage, and rosemary that dotted my front yard and up the path to my house. I undid the dead bolt and the knob lock. We went inside and I deactivated the security system.

Rayna sank down on the couch and put her head in her hands.

I pulled out a bottle of old vine zinfandel that was part of a case I'd gotten from a winery in Paso Robles in exchange for a painting they could use on their labels. I handed Rayna a glass. She took a sip and set it down, then reached for her phone.

"Are you texting with George?" I hoped he'd managed to get on the next plane home.

She looked up surprised. "Who? What?"

"Your husband. George. Tall guy. Slightly gray at the temples. Father of your children. Is he on his way home?" I poured myself a glass, too.

She gave her head a little shake. "Yes. Of course. But no. That's not what I'm looking at." She held the phone up for me and I saw a grainy picture of her front yard. "It's the security camera on the garage. We had it installed after we kept getting vandalized last year."

Ah. Yes. Hard to forget the giant penis that had been spraypainted on their garage three times. Not exactly conforming with the Homeowners' Association CC&Rs. "Did you ever catch who was doing it?"

"No. I think whoever it was saw the camera and backed off." She tapped a bit more on the phone.

"And you can access it from your phone?" The wonders of technology often amaze me. And baffle me.

"Mmhmm," she murmured, looking back down again, seemingly forgetting how to have a conversation, but not forgetting how to take a fairly substantial swallow of wine.

I tucked myself into my favorite corner of the sectional couch, the one where I kept a pillow I'd made from one of Travis's old flannel shirts. I ran my fingers over the soft fabric as I tucked it behind my back, then picked up my latest crocheting project. I crochet blankets and scarves with names and words and phrases woven into them and sell them online. I'll crochet an afghan with a bride and groom's names and their wedding date worked into it or a baby blanket with words like 'darling' or 'snugglebunny' as part of the design. One more of my brilliant ideas of how to create a revenue stream. By the time I paid for yarn and postage, it didn't exactly net me a bundle. At least it kept my fingers busy in the evenings. Without it I'd probably eat all the ice cream and at least half of the potato chips and weigh 300 pounds. Besides, I crochet when I'm nervous. I made an entire poncho while the boys were taking the SATs for the first time.

Rayna finally looked up. "I don't know whether or not to tell Harrison." Harrison was Rayna's older son, the one who successfully flew out of the nest and whose easy successes I suspected might have something to do with Brady's penchant for screwing up. Little bro has to carve his own place in the family and Harrison didn't leave a lot of space to stick a chisel in. "Eva's got a shot of the police cars up on Instagram, hash-tagged from here to kingdom come."

Figured. "Then you have to tell him. Imagine how he'll feel if he sees it on social media first."

She nodded and hit the button to dial Harrison. She waited a few seconds. "Call me," she said. "As soon as you get this, please." She hung up, shaking her head. "It's no guarantee. Half the time it takes him two or three days to return one of my calls. At least I'll have tried."

I fired off a text to Tyler with the same urgent message.

George arrived on my doorstep at eleven o'clock. I opened the door, he gave me a nod, then rushed past me to take Rayna into his arms. She melted against him, tears she'd been holding back for hours now leaking slowly from beneath her closed lids.

I felt a momentary pang. It had been a long time since I'd been held like that. A really long time.

My husband was diagnosed with a brain tumor on a Sunday afternoon in June thirteen years ago. He'd been doing some work in his study, then came out and started speaking to me, but nothing he said made any sense. I mean that literally. There was a string of words and sounds, but there was no logic to it. I thought he was having a stroke.

We should have been so lucky.

Eleven months later, he was dead. Tyler was five. I was thirty-four.

I'd dated a little since then. You would not believe how many people were chomping at the bit to fix me up with someone. Co-workers, brothers, cousins, old friends. Maybe part of the problem had been I wasn't ready. None of them seemed good enough to introduce to Tyler. Then, after a while, people stopped setting me up. Most of the time it was fine. I had Tyler. He was my focus.

But moments like this, when I saw the strength Rayna drew from George and him from her, I hurt a little. It didn't help that it wasn't Tyler and me against the world anymore. Tyler had gone, launched. He'd come home for all the regular holidays, but I knew from my own life experience that leaving for college was a watershed event. Nothing would be the same. Home would never be home in quite the same way again.

"Let's go," George said.

Rayna nodded against his chest. "I think it's safe. I checked the camera. It looks like the police have all left."

I locked the door behind them, set the security alarm, and spent a few minutes rinsing out our wine glasses. Then I poured on more glass, lifted it high and said, "To you, Floyd," and poured it out in his honor. I grabbed the flannel pillow from the couch made from my late husband's favorite flannel shirt and climbed into my bed alone.

THREE

Saturday coffee started the first fall all the boys were on the same soccer team. I think it was Sharon who started it when she showed up carrying one of those little cardboard carriers with four lattes in it. Tamika laughed and said we were becoming clichés, sipping our lattes on the soccer sidelines. That didn't stop her from drinking it, though. Or being the one who brought it the next week. The week after that was Rayna. Then me. Then it turned into a regular rotation.

Since none of us were spending Saturdays shivering on soccer sidelines or crowded into claustrophobic gyms now, we usually met at a coffee shop on Prospect Avenue. I'd already started gathering my stuff up when Rayna texted me: Can you pick me up?

Me: Sure.

Her: I'll be on Vale Way.

Me: I can come to your house.

The next text was an image. It was the street in front of Rayna's house. I could see Eva down the street pretending to do yardwork.

Her next message said: I'm sneaking out the back gate.

I replied: Got it.

I locked up behind myself and went to my truck. The day had dawned bright and clear, although it was still a little chilly. I wouldn't need the jacket I had on in a couple of hours, but I was glad I had it on now. It was almost time to abandon my winter uniform of jeans, boots, blouse, and blazer to transition to my summer uniform of capris, sandals, tank top, and cardigan. I save my imagination for my art projects.

Tyler called as I drove to pick up Rayna. I tapped the button to activate the hands-free device. "What's up, Mom? What'd you need to talk to me about?" He sounded sleepy. He probably was. I tried really hard not to imagine too much about how my son spent Friday nights. I knew what my college years had been like. He's always had more sense than I had so I had some hopes he wasn't following in my footsteps, but I wasn't fooling myself either.

"Brady is in some trouble." I signaled and turned onto Forrest Avenue.

"Not exactly a news flash, Mom."

Definitely my kid. "This is worse than usual."

"How much worse?"

"They're questioning him about a murder."

There was a gasp on the other end and then some gulping noises. "Did you say murder?"

"I did. It's already hit the Internet. Eva Wentz had it online before Rayna and I even got to the police station." I grumbled. "I wanted to tell you before you found out from social media."

"Who was murdered?"

"An old man at Caring Hands. A really nice old man." For a second, I couldn't say more. Not without crying.

"Not Floyd!" Tyler said.

I paused. "How do you know about Floyd?"

"Brady talks about him all the time. They were like buds."

"How often do you and Brady talk?" I turned onto Vale Way.

He sighed. "I don't know, Mom. We text or whatever a couple times a week."

"And he didn't say anything about Floyd dying?" Hmmm. What did that mean? Was he too upset to even text about it? Or was he keeping it to himself for a reason?

"Yeah. No. But I haven't heard much from him this week. I figured he was busy and so was I so . . ." Tyler's words trailed off.

"He didn't do it, Tyler."

"Of course he didn't do it! Geez, Mom! Brady's a screw-up, not a murderer." There was a pause. "Do you want me to come home?"

I swerved a little and got beeped at. "What? No! Of course not. Why?"

"If you needed me, I'd be there. You know that, right?"

"Back at you, kiddo."

I promised to keep him posted about what was happening and we hung up.

It had been Tyler and me against the world for thirteen years and while I would much rather it had been Tyler, Travis, and me against the world, I loved how close we were. What I didn't like so much was where lines had begun to blur. Tyler had always been protective of me. Lots of kids feel protective of their moms. That's fine. Tyler's inclinations had taken another step beyond that, though. Sometimes – like when he offered to come home if I was upset – I was worried he felt responsible for me. I didn't want that. I wanted him to count on me, not the other way around. I was the mom. I wanted it to stay that way.

I almost drove past Rayna. She had on a hooded sweatshirt and sunglasses and was standing half behind an almond tree that had begun to blossom. I pulled over and unlocked the door so she could get in.

"What's with the get up?" I asked.

"I'm trying to be incognito, right?" She slid into the car, brushing a few errant pink petals from her sleeves..

I waited until her seatbelt was clicked, then pulled back out onto the street. "You look a teeny little bit like the Unabomber."

She flipped the hood back and took off the glasses. "Better?"

It wasn't really. The glasses had hidden the deep dark circles under her eyes. She clearly hadn't slept the night before. I nodded anyway.

"How's Brady doing?"

"Asleep right now." She rubbed at her eyes with the palms of her hands. "But as of last night, I would say scared. And angry. And confused."

It sounded about right to me. It was how I felt, too.

Sharon and Tamika were already at our regular spot in the back corner of Espresso Yourself, the area with the leather couch and armchairs. In the rest of the place, they'd gone for an industrial feel with a long single table under carefully spaced pendant lights with outlets for laptop charging every couple of feet. About five people were scattered along one side or another, tapping away at their novel or their business plan or their legal brief or whatever it is that they all do. The back of the shop was still cozy, though, with armchairs and couches and a few tables scattered around for coffee mugs and newspapers.

Sharon looked considerably more relaxed than she had the night before. Her hair was still pulled back, but in a long braid rather than a twist, and she had on jeans and a tank top under a cardigan. The shadows under her eyes were nearly as dark as Rayna's, though. Of course, she'd had a late night, too. Tamika might be the only one of us who looked rested, curled up in her armchair in yoga pants and a long-sleeved T-shirt, even though Sharon and I were the ones who actually did yoga. We spent at least an hour every week lowering ourselves into Chataranga Dandasana, balancing on one leg in Vrksasana, and twisting ourselves into Patita Tārāsana and trying to find inner peace while warding off osteoporosis. Tamika and her husband had started ballroom dancing classes instead, which frankly sounded like more fun, but only if you had a partner.

Rayna and I ordered our coffees and joined them.

"So we have more information than we did last night," Sharon said. "Although I'm astonished they were able to get a search warrant for your house based on what it is they know."

Tamika set her mug down. "Let's hear it."

Sharon glanced around to make sure no one was close enough to hear. "Floyd Winstead died of fentanyl poisoning."

"You mean the patches?" Tamika asked, twisting her braids back so they didn't get in her coffee as she leaned forward.

"Exactly." Sharon wrapped her hands around her coffee mug and took a sip. "Except not in patch form."

"Wait. Explain that to me." I wasn't following. I also still didn't have my coffee. Maybe that's why my brain wasn't quite functioning.

"Fentanyl is an opioid. They use it for pain management. The patches are supposed to deliver a slow steady amount of the drug over a few days. It's strong. It's stronger than morphine. Hell. It's stronger than heroin," Sharon said.

"My mom had the patches after she fell." Tamika's mother had a spinal column with the consistency of sidewalk chalk. She'd taken one tumble and almost every bone had cracked and shifted. It was why she'd done her stint at Caring Hands. She'd recovered, but not fully. "Could he have been on it for pain?"

"Floyd had an astonishing amount of fentanyl in his system. Significantly more than he'd need for pain management even if it had been prescribed for him, which it wasn't." Sharon turned her mug in little circles on the coffee table in front of her.

"Could it have been some kind of accident?" The nurses were generally really careful with prescriptions, but I'd seen mistakes happen. Most of the time they were caught before they could become big problems. Maybe this had somehow slipped through the cracks. "Maybe somebody read a chart a little bit wrong and gave it to him by mistake."

"At this point, no one's owning up to that," Sharon said, but she made a note on her legal pad.

The truth was no one would unless they were backed into a corner. A person could lose their license for a mistake like that.

"Plus it wasn't administered in a patch. It's pretty hard to OD on those. They're designed to deliver the drug slowly over time. Someone injected Floyd with it." Sharon looked grim. "Someone did this deliberately."

"Coffee for Rachel," the second barista called and Rayna got up. I shot her a look.

"Keeping a low profile, okay?" She shrugged, going to pick up her coffee. Sharon nodded her approval.

"So how was it administered?" I asked.

"Syringe," Sharon said succinctly as she took a big gulp of her coffee. "The good news is they didn't find patches or needles when they executed the search warrant at your home," Sharon said when Rayna returned with both of our coffees. As good news went, that sounded a little lame.

"What do they have? Do you know why they zeroed in on Brady?" I asked.

Sharon pursed her lips. "They became suspicious about how Floyd died because of the nurse." She checked her notes. "Lillibeth Ocampo. She's the reason that they suspected anything about Floyd's death at all. She was convinced that someone had . . ." She paused there, but we all knew which someone she was talking about. Someone had done something untoward."

Rayna made a noise in the back of her throat that was close to a growl. Mama Wolf was not pleased.

"If she hadn't pressed, they wouldn't have done an autopsy. I guess they don't always do them, even if the death is somewhat unexpected. The whole thing would have gone unnoticed." Sharon carefully didn't look over at Rayna. "Floyd's death would have been an old man dying in his sleep. No one would have questioned it. They might have even been grateful that he didn't suffer."

I didn't know what to feel. It was good that Lillibeth had figured out that someone had killed Floyd. I didn't care that people might call it a "good" death or a mercy. It wasn't right. But what wasn't so good was having it end up with Brady being suspected of having anything to do with it. Speaking of which. "So what does that have to do with Brady?"

Sharon said, "There was a piece of paper with Brady's name on it in Floyd's room."

"I'm not sure I follow," I said.

Sharon shifted on the couch and pulled her braid over her shoulder. "Sitting on Floyd's bedside table, there was a piece of paper that looked like it had been torn out of a notebook or something. It had Brady's name on it in Floyd's handwriting. Nothing else."

Tamika shook her head. "So? That could mean anything or nothing."

"The police think it was Floyd's attempt to tell people who killed him. Like writing a murderer's name in blood." Sharon looked over at Rayna who had gasped. I reached over to take Rayna's hand. She grasped mine, her fingers cold as ice. I tried to rub some warmth into them.

"A name on a scrap of paper doesn't mean anything." Although why Floyd would be writing Brady's name on anything escaped me.

"It's obviously not enough to make an arrest, but it was enough coupled with him being the one who found Floyd to get that search warrant and bring him in for questioning." Sharon sat bolt upright. "Ay Dios mío!"

She stripped off her cardigan and fanned herself frantically with one hand. Her face had gone beet red and a little drop of sweat appeared right by her ear and trickled down her jaw line.

"Hot flash?" Tamika asked, pulling a little rectangular battery-operated fan out of her purse and handing it to Sharon.

Sharon pointed the fan at her face and neck and then pulled out the neck of her tank top to blow air straight down on her chest. "When do these things stop? I was up three times last night, absolutely drenched."

That explained those dark circles.

"Mindy got up and went to the guestroom to sleep. She said it was like sleeping next to a blowtorch." She lifted her braid off the back of her neck and blew the fan on her nape.

"My mom says she still gets them on occasion." Rayna made a face. "Sorry."

"And she's how old?" Sharon stopped and looked at her.

"Seventy-eight." Rayna shook her head.

"I won't make it." Sharon sat back down, her face already starting to return to its normal honey brown tones.

"You will," I said. "It's like labor. Once it's started, you can't stop it. You don't have a choice."

Tamika snorted. "Well, aren't you a little ray of sunshine?"

I ignored her question and asked one of my own. "Have you told Jayden and Max what's happening?"

Sharon and Tamika both nodded. "We didn't want them to find out from someone else," Tamika said.

"I felt the same way." I turned to Rayna. "Did Harrison call back?"

"This morning, but it was too late. He'd already seen it online." She looked down into her coffee and then shrugged. "If he'd answered when I called or returned my text, he could have heard it from me instead of from Eva."

"I'm sorry." I gave her hand another squeeze.

"All right, then." Sharon clapped her hands. "Rayna, you keep Brady off social media. The last thing he needs is to get panicky seeing posts about this and he definitely mustn't reply to anything. Not positive things or negative things. They'll be watching. All of you, tell your boys not to comment on anything regarding Brady no matter how much they're provoked. Tamika, you stay on it and keep an eye on what's online. Let me know if there's something you think I should know about."

Tamika looked at her phone. "I've got to go. See you all at movie night tonight?" Movie night was another tradition that had started when the boys were little that we hadn't stopped. Once a month, one of us picked a movie and ordered take-out food for the group. Our movie selection had gotten a little wider and sometimes we actually cooked instead of ordering pizza, but otherwise it hadn't changed much.

"Can I bring anything?" I asked.

Tamika snorted. "You know what Jamal's like when he starts cooking."

I did. No one would need to bring anything except an appetite.

Tamika would help with anything computer-related. Sharon had the law stuff all covered. "What about me? How can I help?" I asked.

There was a pointed bit of silence. My skill set, such as it was, didn't lend itself to doing a lot of good in urgent situations. Drawing you a sweet little picture of your cat didn't solve a lot of problems.

"Keep your eyes and ears open around Caring Hands," Rayna said, finally.

"Keep her eyes and ears open for what?" Sharon seemed honestly curious.

Rayna tapped her foot on the floor for a few seconds and then said, "I'm not really sure. Anything that doesn't seem quite right."

Anyone who has ever spent any time in a retirement village knows a lot of things don't seem quite right. That list was going to be long.

I dropped Rayna back on Vale Way so she could slip into her house through the back. My phone rang as I drove home. I didn't recognize the number so I didn't answer. I figured if it was a real person, they'd leave a message I could understand. As a result, the first time I heard Detective Daniel Park's voice was in a voicemail after I got home, asking me to call him as soon as possible. I called Sharon instead. "What do I do?" I took off my jacket and kicked off my boots and sat down in my comfy place on the couch. I looked around for my Travis pillow. Cops made me nervous. I needed all the comfort I could get, but then I remembered it was still back in my bedroom.

"You return his call, Leah." Sharon sounded weary, even more weary than she'd looked at Espresso Yourself.

I put the phone on speaker and picked up my crocheting. "Is there anything I should or shouldn't say?"

"Tell him the truth, but only the truth and only about what he asks. Don't tell a story to illustrate your point. Don't make it into a metaphor for something else. Don't do an interpretive dance."

That stung a little. I'd become a bit more of a chatterbox since Tyler left home. There wasn't anyone to talk to at home. I didn't even have the cat anymore. Mr. Fluffbottom (a blessed memory) had shuffled off this mortal coil a few weeks after Tyler left. He (Mr. Fluffbottom, not Tyler) had been sixteen years old and his kidneys were failing, but I still thought it might have been a broken heart that took him. Or perhaps I was projecting. "Got it," I said, trying to keep my voice neutral.

Apparently, I failed. "I'm sorry, Leah. I'm tired. I know you like to make things into good stories to keep everyone entertained. Resist those urges. Be as close to monosyllabic as you can. Don't make things any more complicated than they already are. Okay?"

I considered pouting some more, but decided against it. The important thing was to protect Brady. The kids came first. Always. "Absolutely."

"Call Detective Park right away. It'll look good that you're cooperative."

I did what she asked, and called him. He answered on the second ring. "I'd like to ask you a few questions about Brady Atkinson."

"Of course." I waited. That was close to monosyllabic, wasn't it? Only one itty bitty extra syllable.

"I'd rather we do it in person."

Great. Now I'd have to worry about breaking into that interpretive dance. Once Sharon planted the idea, it was hard to get it out of my mind. "Sure. What time would you like me to come down to the station?"

"Oh, that's all right. I'll come to you."

"You mean, at my house?" I hadn't realized that police officers made house calls.

"If that's okay." It was phrased like a question, but it didn't sound like one. It sounded like I'd have to give a reason I wasn't okay with it and that could lead to other explanations and – damn it – we were right back at the interpretive dance.

I looked around. I will say, with Tyler gone, my house stayed clean a lot longer. When he'd been home, I'd barely been able to keep up with the piles of shin guards and cleats, books and papers, dishes that somehow made their way out into the living room, but never back to the kitchen. Without those, I had time to actually, well, clean. My ceiling fans had never been this dust-free. "Sure. When?"

"How's now?"

It would be better to get it over with. I told him my address and then realized he probably knew that and a whole lot more about me already. Feeling foolish, I hung up.

He was on my doorstep ten minutes later. Darby isn't that big, but even Sharon, who drives like a bat out of hell, can't get from the police station to my house in ten minutes. Had he been lurking somewhere, waiting for me to call? Or worse yet, watching me?

It turned out that Park was the nice-looking Asian man who had let Sharon into the back of the police station the night before. He had high cheekbones, glossy black hair, and broad shoulders. He was clean-shaven with short hair and a decent suit.

If he wasn't what I expected, the look on his face made me think that I wasn't what he expected either. I invited him in and offered him water or coffee. He declined both, while looking around my place as if he was mentally measuring it. His head swiveled back and forth like a camera panning across a scene. He walked over to the shelves that lined one end of my living room and picked up a snow globe with the Santa Cruz boardwalk in it, gave it a little shake and then put it down. Then he picked up a Day of the Dead figure and inspected it. Then a Hopi wedding vase.

The inspection made me bristle. "Are you looking for something in particular?" I asked.

He looked up, a smile on his face. "Sorry. No. Just curious."

I didn't trust that smile. It was a cop smile. It didn't mean anything. "About my tchotchkes?" I crossed my arms over my chest.

"Your what?" His face stayed carefully blank, but he blinked a few times.

"My knickknacks. My gewgaws. My trinkets." Damn it. So not monosyllabic. I had to brace myself not to do a pirouette.

"Got it." That smile didn't move. I still didn't buy it.

I sat down on the couch. "You wanted to talk to me about Brady?"

He lowered himself slowly into the armchair across from me, hitching his pant legs up as he did. "Yes. How long have you known Brady?"

"Since he was seven." I bit back the explanation of how he'd been on the same soccer team as my kid and how I was friends with his mother and, well, everything else. Just the facts, like Sharon wanted me to.

He nodded at a photo of Tyler on the shelf. "Is that your son?"

"Yes." I was getting good at this.

"How old is he?"

"Eighteen. Why?"

"Is he friends with Brady?"

That one was harder to answer succinctly. They'd been best buddies for a long time. All through grade school and into junior high. Then something happened. Brady wasn't over at our house after school as often and Tyler wasn't at his place. They chose different after-school clubs. I asked Tyler if something was wrong and he always said no. About six months after I noticed that, Brady was suspended from school for the first time. It wasn't a big deal. They found a pipe in his locker. Still, Rayna was mortified. She didn't say much about it to me. It didn't help that it was the same month that Tyler was named Student of the Month by the local Elks Lodge. The boys drifted farther apart after that and I didn't ask why. I didn't want to know and I didn't want it to put any wedges between Rayna and me. That didn't mean Tyler and Brady weren't friends, though. Just not best buds like they'd been in elementary school. Then again, Tyler said they still talked a couple of times a week.

"Ms. Glaser?" He prompted.

"Yes," I said, perhaps a little too emphatically. "They're friends."

"And you're friends with Ms. Atkinson?"

That was easier. "Yes." I wanted to tell him how great Rayna was, how many times she'd been my co-parent, how often she'd helped me out of scheduling jams, how kind she was, how efficient and organized she was. I was pretty sure that wouldn't be following Sharon's instructions, though. It felt like it could turn into a jeté or a glissé or something.

"You helped set up Brady's community service."

It wasn't a question, but he seemed to be waiting for an answer. "I did."

"How'd that happen?" He relaxed back into his chair.

How could I relay this as simply as possible? How could I explain how my heart ached for Rayna as she told me that Brady was in trouble again? How I wanted to do something to make my friend's life easier and helping Brady connect with Caring Hands was one of the few things within my nearly useless skill set to do? "I knew Brady was looking for a good place to do community service and that Caring Hands can always use more volunteers."

Park nodded. "I see."

There was something in his tone that made me want to explain more about how innocent the whole arrangement was. I bit my tongue. A silence stretched between us. I wanted to fidget. Instead, I picked up my crocheting and focused on that. Finally, he said, "I understand you were there when Mr. Winstead was found."

I shook my head. "No. I was there a few minutes after."

"How many minutes?" That caught his attention. He shifted forward on his chair.

I thought for a second. "I really don't know."

"Who did you see in the area when you got there?"

"Well, Brady and Lillibeth Ocampo were standing outside the room. Malachi Donnelly was inside it, but came out a few minutes after I walked up."

"No one else, though?" he pressed.

I replayed it in my mind. "Like who? There are always people around. Other nurses. Delivery people. Service people. Visiting relatives."

"Can you remember which ones?" he asked.

I shut my eyes and focused. "The flower delivery guy was there, but I don't remember anyone else in particular."

He shut the notepad he'd been using and tucked it into his jacket pocket. "Thank you for your time."

"That's it?" It didn't seem like enough questions to have made the effort to come over here or have given me a chance to make sure he didn't suspect Brady of anything.

"Is there something else you'd like to tell me?" He sat very still.

I couldn't help it. I couldn't contain myself anymore. "Brady didn't do it."

"Do what exactly?"

"Whatever it is you think he's done."

Park sat back down and took his notepad out. "What makes you think that?"

I dropped the scarf I was crocheting and threw my hands in the air. "Because I've known him since he was a teeny little boy. I've driven him to soccer practice and baked cookies for his birthday. Because I've seen him be a consistently kind kid for over a decade."

He shut the notepad. "Those aren't things you can present in court."

"It doesn't mean they're not important." As far as I was concerned, they were the most important things.

He stood back up. "That's it?"

"What did you think I was going to say?"

He rubbed the back of his neck. "Something more definitive. Something less . . . squishy."

"Squishy?" I stood to walk him to the door even though he was only about two steps away from it. My house isn't that big.

"I need something factual."

"What factual things do have that are making you ask questions about him?" I countered.

"I can't comment on an ongoing investigation, Ms. Glaser." He crossed his arms over his chest.

"It's Lillibeth, isn't it? One nurse's unfounded suspicions don't sound all that non-squishy to me."

"Her suspicions have been pretty spot on so far." He took a business card out of his pocket and handed it to me. "If you think of anything else you'd like to tell me, give me a call."

"But only if it's not squishy, right?"

This time his smile seemed genuine. "Yes. The less squishy, the better, but anything you think could help us figure out what happened to Mr. Winstead would be appreciated."

"Is that why you haven't arrested Brady yet? Because everything pointing to him is squishy?" I asked.

And there was the careful cop smile again. "Thank you

for your help, Ms. Glaser," he said as he turned back to the door and left.

I watched as he walked down the sidewalk, got into a sedan, and drove away, leaving me standing alone in my doorway wondering what to do with myself once again.

FOUR

Tamika and Jamal lived on the eastern edge of Darby, a little shy of where everything turned into farmland, but only a little, in a two-story white wood-framed house with a wide front porch. I knocked on the front door and Tamika opened it almost immediately.

I sniffed the air. "Taco night?"

Tamika smiled. "You got it in one."

"I should have worn stretchy pants." I handed her a bottle of wine and walked into the house. "Am I the first one here?" Of course I was. Everyone else had other things to do, other people to be with, other things to occupy them.

Jamal was in the kitchen presiding over a truly ridiculous number of dishes. I went up on tiptoe to give him a kiss on the cheek.

He was a big man, taller than me by easily six or seven inches, with a mustache and a round face and a close-cut Afro. "You do remember that it's just us grown-ups now, right? You're not trying to feed three or four teenage boys anymore."

He laughed. "Can't seem to get out of the habit."

There was a satisfying pop as Tamika uncorked the bottle and poured us both glasses and handed me one. "To Saturday."

"To Saturday," I repeated, but with a bit less enthusiasm. I wasn't sure what I was supposed to do with them anymore.

"Let's go sit in the living room and get out of the way of the chef." She indicated Jamal with a head nod.

"That detective interviewed me about Brady when I got home," I told her as I got settled in my usual seat under the lamp in the corner.

Her eyebrows went up. "How'd that go?"

"I'm not sure." I rubbed my feet together. "I hope I said everything right and didn't say anything I shouldn't have. Sharon told me not to do an interpretive dance."

Tamika glanced down at my feet. "Probably pretty good advice."

I stopped fidgeting. "Are Max and Brady still in touch?"

"I'm not really sure. Why?"

I took my crocheting out of my bag as I tried to put into words what I wanted to ask. "Tyler says he and Brady text a couple times a week, but Brady never said anything to him about Floyd dying. He didn't say anything to Rayna before the police showed up, either."

Tamika took a big sip of wine. "And?"

"And I'm not sure. Tyler said Brady talked about Floyd a lot. Enough so that Tyler knew his name. Why wouldn't he have told them something that big?"

The doorbell rang and Tamika went to answer it. I heard the sounds of Sharon and Mindy coming in and saying hello to Jamal, then coming into the living room. Mindy stopped to give me a kiss on the cheek. She was a small woman with wavy gray hair whose blue eyes lit up when she talked about Max and nineteenth-century Transcendentalist poetry.

"How'd it go with Park?" Sharon asked, sitting down on the loveseat with Mindy next to her.

I shrugged. "Fine, I think."

"You kept it simple?"

"Reasonably." I counted some stitches on my crochet project to avoid looking into her eyes.

"What does reasonably mean?" she pressed.

Mindy tapped her on the shoulder. "Don't cross examine her. This is a social call. Remember?"

Sharon sighed and leaned back into the couch. "Sorry. Apparently I'm a little too prosecutorial these days."

I shrugged. Hadn't she always been? It was one of her charms as far as I was concerned. There wasn't a kid whose story could stand up once Sharon started taking it apart. It looked like Mindy might not think it was so charming at the moment. "He came to the house and asked some questions. I answered them."

Sharon picked up Mindy's hand and gave the back of it a little kiss. Okay. Maybe I was reading too much into Mindy's comment. "He came to your house?"

I nodded. "Why?"

She made a face. "Nothing. That's not all that typical, though."

Tamika gestured at me with her wine glass. "Neither is she."

Sharon turned toward Tamika. "You think?"

Tamika shrugged. "Did you see him give her the once over at the police station?"

Sharon shook her head. "I missed it."

"Well, I didn't," Tamika said.

"Stop talking about me like I'm not here." I picked up my wine glass and took a substantial sip.

"Fine. Is that it then? He came to your house, asked questions, and then left? And you answered them as simply as you possibly could?" Sharon asked.

"I may have told him that Brady didn't do it." I crocheted a little quicker.

"Leah!"

"I couldn't help it!"

The doorbell rang again and Rayna and George arrived. Talk about being saved by the bell. Jamal announced that dinner was ready and we all went to fill our plates with the ridiculous number of dishes he'd made. There really isn't anything you can't put in a taco and he made sure that we had a wide selection: roasted vegetables, beef, chicken, and shrimp. Plus sour cream and guacamole and salsa and cheese. The room filled with a happy buzz of talk and laughter and I shut my eyes for a moment to give thanks for being surrounded by such good friends. When I opened them, I surveyed what was left after we all had heaped our plates. "You're going to be eating this for a week," I told Jamal.

He shrugged. "I've suffered worse fates."

We all sat down. "I got an email from Caring Hands. Floyd's funeral is going to be on Wednesday," I announced.

"Brady can't go," Sharon said without a second of hesitation.

"I told him it was a bad idea," George said, reaching for another tortilla.

Rayna twirled a lock of hair around her index finger and tugged at it. "He wants to say good-bye."

I could understand that. There was a reason we had

rituals like funerals. We needed to stop to process our feelings and let what different events meant sink in.

"It's a terrible idea. Astonishingly terrible." Sharon shook her head hard enough that I thought her teeth might rattle.

"Could he send a card?" I asked.

"No." Sharon's answer was definitive.

"Flowers?" I suggested.

"No." Sharon's voice got a little louder.

"An Edible Arrangement?"

"Leah!"

I shrank back in my chair. "Sorry."

"Brady has to sit tight until we have this figured out. Understand?" Sharon said.

George waved his fork at Rayna. "Told you so."

I let it drop.

The evening ended early. Rayna was uneasy about leaving Brady alone in the house. George thought she was overreacting, but none of the rest of us did.

————

On Sunday, the house was quiet. Too quiet. The only noise came from a phone call from Judy Gordon, another recent empty nest mom, asking me about my pet portrait business and making an appointment to meet her dog, Sugar Pop. All the anxiety about Brady and having a cop in my house left me with nervous energy to burn off. Crocheting simply wasn't going to cut it and yoga wasn't for hours yet. I still hadn't adjusted to my weekends not being filled with driving to games or helping with homework or chasing after Tyler in one way or another.

It happened a lot, that feeling of not quite knowing

what to do with this Tyler-sized gap in my life. I wasn't sure what to fill that mental space with.

So I baked. I love baking almost as much as I love painting and crocheting and crafting. Unfortunately, I also love eating baked goods and they, in turn, love my thighs. So I bake and then send it all to Tyler at school. Not exactly finding something to do that wasn't kid-centered, but baby steps toward a goal. Stretching that emotional umbilical cord out one tiny inch at a time still got me a tiny inch closer.

I looked at the calendar. In February, I'd made heart-shaped pink cookies with white chocolate chips. January had been heart-healthy oatmeal raisin cookies. I'd made white and blue-iced dreidel-shaped cookies for December. What to do for March? Hamantaschen for Purim? Why not? It's not like anyone would want gefilte fish for Passover through the mail. Or really ever.

I let myself get lost in the rolling of the dough, the cutting of the circles, the filling of the cookies. By the time I was done, there was flour everywhere and I had about three dozen triangular cookies filled with jam. Do not get me started on filling a perfectly lovely cookie with prunes. Not gonna happen. Not on my watch. Three dozen, however, was a lot of cookies, even for a college kid living in a dorm. I had enough to spread the love around and I knew someone who could probably use a whole bunch of love. I cleaned up the kitchen and packaged up two dozen of the cookies to put in the mail to Tyler, put the other twelve on a plate, and called Rayna.

"Hey, I made some hamantaschen to send to Tyler. I saved out a few. I thought I would bring them over to Brady to cheer him up. He always loved them."

"Sure. Come on over. You might want to park over on

Forest Avenue and come in through the back, though, unless you want Eva broadcasting it everywhere that you brought undisclosed items into the house." She laughed, but not a normal laugh. It sounded like a whinny from a spooked horse. "You still have the key, right?"

"Of course and let Eva post whatever she wants. I've been accused of worse than smuggling baked goods."

"Haven't we all?" Rayna sounded defeated. Maybe the slightly hysterical whinny was better? This tone made me sad.

I did as she suggested, though, and slipped in through the Atkinson's back gate. The pool cover undulated under the slight breeze that came in through the plum and pomegranate trees along the fence line, the leaves scattered on top of it skittering this way and that. Last year, the boys had all been dipping their toes into the water by this time, waiting for it to be warm enough to swim and play wild games of water basketball. Would those long afternoons by the pool, watching the kids play, making endless sandwiches and snacks, applying coat after coat of sunscreen, feeling lucky to be surrounded by so much fun and friendship happen again?

Rayna met me at the kitchen door. "Stress baking, right?" She gestured for me to enter.

She knew me too well. "A little." It wasn't the first time I'd turned to the glories of butter and flour and sugar to calm my nerves. It was highly unlikely that it would be my last.

"Lucky us." She took one cookie from the plate and took a minuscule bite of one of the three corners.

Rayna's kitchen looked like a photo layout in a home improvement ad. It was light and bright with an island/breakfast bar in the center, copper pots hanging from a rack, and an herb garden growing in a bay window over the sink. It smelled like coffee and buttered toast. There was only one coffee mug out on the counter, though.

"Where's George?" I asked.

She sighed and took another nibble. "Golfing."

That surprised me, but I supposed there wasn't really much he could be doing here. No reason he shouldn't get some exercise. "You doing okay?" I asked.

She sat down on one of the stools at the breakfast bar in her kitchen. "As well as can be expected I guess."

I sat down next to her. It wasn't only Brady who needed some TLC, apparently. George should have stayed home.

She took a slightly bigger bite of cookie and then put her head down on the counter on folded arms. Her breath made little puffs of fog on the highly polished granite. "How did I screw this up so badly?"

"What did you screw up?" I asked, honestly confused.

She tilted her head toward me, but still kept it down on the counter. "Motherhood?"

"You're a wonderful mother. You've done everything right." Okay. Maybe not everything. There was that one time she forgot to bring soccer snack, but that was pretty minor and it was only once. Penny Manderson forgot soccer snack practically every time she was assigned to bring it. She forgot it so many times that I used to keep an emergency snack in my car just in case.

"Then why is my kid in constant trouble?" Rayna asked.

I sighed. I honestly didn't think Brady did much that the other boys didn't do. The other boys just seemed to know when to stop. "Bad luck? Worse timing?"

"Whose? Mine or Brady's?" She turned her face back to the counter. A ray of sunlight made her blonde hair glint.

That I didn't have an answer for. "Harrison is doing

fine," I pointed out. He was a junior at UC San Diego and was getting an engineering degree.

"You mean the kid who doesn't answer his mother's phone calls or texts? That one?" Her voice came out muffled, but that didn't keep me from hearing the catch in it.

"They're still young. He'll outgrow that."

"Sure he will." She didn't sound the least bit convinced.

I patted her back for a minute, but then she straightened up, wiped at her eyes, and gave me a smile. "Don't mind me. I'm just having a little pity party, right? Go on upstairs and take those cookies to Brady before I eat them all myself."

That didn't seem likely since she'd barely eaten half of the one she'd taken, but I did as she asked and carried the plate upstairs.

Brady sat on the couch in the bedroom that Rayna had made into a game room for the boys — her house had enough rooms for that and a guest room — wearing blue plaid pajama pants and a Golden State Warriors t-shirt, thumbs moving vigorously on the game controller while he swayed back and forth as if he could use his body to move the soldiers on the television screen as they fought off a horde of zombies. I waited until he set the controller down with a disgusted thud.

"Not going so well?" I asked.

He looked up, surprised it seemed to see me standing in the doorway. "Leah, hi."

I lifted up the plate. "I brought hamantaschen."

"Sweet." He held out his hands for the plate.

I handed it over and sat down next to him. Neither of us said anything for a moment. Of course, part of that was because Brady was busy chewing.

"How are you doing?" I asked.

He shrugged and took another cookie.

"Do you want to talk about it?" I picked up the afghan on the floor, folded it into a square, and hung it over the arm of the sofa.

Brady swallowed his cookie and then said, "I feel like I haven't done anything else since Friday night and there's nothing to tell. I explained it to Sharon and then to the cops and then again to a different cop and then to my parents." He shoved an entire cookie into his mouth, chewed.

I waited for him to finish the cookie. "Could you give me the broad strokes?"

His jaw clenched. Or maybe he was just chewing. He wiped the crumbs from his mouth with the back of his hand. "I had library duty when I first came in so I did that for about 15 minutes until that one lady came in."

"Which lady?" I coiled up the cord of one of the controllers on the floor.

Brady went pink. "The one who always forgets she's not in her room." He looked down at his controller.

Ohhhh. He meant Adriana Hancock. There'd been some issues with her getting undressed in places she shouldn't. She always seemed to think she was in her room getting ready for bed. "Gotcha," I said. "Do you usually start in the library?" I didn't remember seeing him in there very often.

"No. Nurse Ocampo asked me to start there when I first came in. She said it was a mess and someone needed to straighten it up." He made a little face when he said Lillibeth's name. "I thought if I did a good job, she might lighten up on me a little."

We knew how that had turned out. "Where did you go next?"

"I went to find Floyd. We were going to go out to the

courtyard and read some more of this book about the cold war with spies and stuff." He set the controller down and looked at me. "It's old, but it's like kind of awesome. I thought it would be boring, but it's not. Anyway, I expected Floyd to be out at the nurses' station waiting for me like usual. When he wasn't, I went to his room. I thought he was asleep, but then I couldn't wake him up and I pushed the call button. Then Malachi came and after him Lillibeth came and then she yelled at me in the hallway and then you got there."

I could take it from there, at least factually. That hadn't been the only thing I'd wanted to ask Brady about, though. "Brady, is there a reason you didn't tell your mom about Floyd dying?" Or anyone else, I added silently.

He picked at the seam of his pajama pants. "I . . . I didn't know what to say about it."

Now I felt stupid. Of course he didn't know how to talk about it. There was a perfectly rational explanation. "Have you ever had anyone you cared about die before?"

He shook his head and set the plate of cookies to one side as if he'd suddenly lost his appetite.

I put my hand on his arm. "It's hard. It never fully goes away, but I want you to know that it does get easier. Your heart won't always feel like this."

He stared straight ahead, Adam's apple bobbing as he swallowed. "He was such a nice guy. It was a bummer that he had that COPD stuff. It was making it harder and harder for him to get around. It really bummed him out."

COPD. I scanned my mental data bank to come up with what it meant. I'd learned an awful lot of acronyms since starting work at Caring Hands. COPD is Chronic Obstructive Pulmonary Disease. It meant that Floyd had started having trouble breathing and it was only going to get worse. They can help with some of the symptoms, but there really isn't a cure. Plus by the time people have symptoms, usually their lungs are already damaged. Short version? It sucked. "I didn't know about the COPD."

"Yeah. He was diagnosed with it about a month ago. He said it was kind of a relief because at least he knew something was really wrong and it wasn't only in his head. There didn't seem to be much they could do about it, though." Brady jiggled his knee, like he might be able to run away from the topic.

Poor Floyd. It couldn't have been fun to have that diagnosis staring him in the face, knowing he'd spend the rest of his days having a harder and harder time taking a breath. "So he'd been pretty sad lately?"

"Yeah. Between not feeling well and his bud Harvey dying, he was having a hard time. He was hella upset about Harvey."

Harvey had been in really bad shape. His death was not unexpected. I knew as well or better than anyone that that didn't make a damn bit of difference. It still hurt. "Harvey wasn't doing so great."

"That's the thing." Brady sat up straighter, turning toward me. "Floyd was convinced Harvey was getting better. He said Harvey was talking more and had started to use his right hand again. Then BAM. He was gone."

Sometimes people rally right before they take that final turn for the worst. Travis had. The night before he died, he'd spoken to me clearly for the first time in days. He had trouble finding words, but I'd figured out what he'd meant when he told me I was the cutest button on his coat and I still treasured those words. But the next morning he was gone. I'd had a bit of the same response that Floyd had had. He'd been improving. How could he die like that? The hospice nurses had explained it to me. There also could be some wishful thinking there. Sometimes we see what we want to see. It looks like someone is using their hands more because we want to think that they're getting better. Their speech seems better because we want it to be better.

"Floyd was trying to keep busy, though. He liked helping people. Even that scary old lady with the weird baby doll." Brady shuddered at the thought.

"Gladys?"

"Yeah. Her. He was going to fix her doll for her. It's always covered with bandages and stuff. And that really tiny lady who's in a wheelchair? They used to hang out together. And he liked to read and to go to your art classes. He wanted me to teach him some stuff about computers, too," Brady said.

"What kind of stuff? I asked. There was a small computer room with a couple of PCs and one Mac for the residents. It was almost always empty.

"He didn't really say. It seemed like internet stuff. How to do searches for images and that kind of thing." Brady picked up the game controller and fiddled with it. "I helped him create an account and set it up so he could do searches and send email."

"Do you know what he wanted to search for?" I asked.

Brady shook his head. "No. I just got the account set up and showed him how to use it."

Whatever it was, Floyd wouldn't be searching the internet for anything ever again now.

I left Brady with the plate of hamantaschen and a kiss on the head to get ready to meet Sharon at our weekly yoga class.

———

I was balanced on my left hand with my left leg extended in front of me, my right leg straight and my right arm reaching toward the ceiling.

"Don't forget to breathe," Sierra, our yoga instructor, called out as she walked through the forest of women in Fallen Triangle post, stopping to correct an arm or leg placement here or there and tripping once on Amelia Nguyen's outstretched leg.

I hated Fallen Triangle, Patita Tarasana. There was a reason Sierra had to remind us to breathe. It was impossible, miserable, torturous. "Why," I choked out. "Why do we do this?" I asked Sharon.

She groaned as we finally got to return to Downward Dog. "So we can take care of ourselves when we're old."

"I think I'm already old." We started the sequence on the other side.

"All the more reason to do this then," she said grimly.

I waited until we were in my favorite pose – shavasana or corpse pose – to talk again. "Does Rayna seem okay to you?"

"No, but I don't think it would be okay if she was okay. This is an astonishing amount of stress." Sharon answered, but kept her eyes closed and her face toward the ceiling. "Now stop talking and breathe."

"Do Rayna and George seem okay?" I whispered.

Sharon made a funny noise in the back of her throat. "How do you mean?"

"When I went over there this afternoon, he wasn't there. He'd gone golfing."

"So?"

"So I thought maybe Rayna could use some more support." I turned my head to look over at her. Her face still pointed at the ceiling.

"Finding a way to relieve stress is supportive. Let him whack at a golf ball instead of yelling at Brady." She adjusted her shoulders with a wiggle. "Better to get angry at a bad putt than at your kid."

"Why does he need to get angry at all?" I poked her with my toe.

Sharon turned on her side to look directly at me. "We all get angry. Not all of us know how to let it out."

FIVE

I PULLED into Caring Hands parking lot on Monday afternoon after taking Tyler's care package to the post office. It
was still sunny, but the wind had picked up. The sycamore
trees out front swayed like dancers and clouds scudded
across the sky, but it was still blue. So much for spring. I
parked my truck in front of the "Get the Best Care at
Caring Hands" sign. Malachi was over near the front sliding
doors getting on his motorcycle as I walked up. It was one of
those big old touring motorcycles made for the open road
with the giant panniers on the back.

"You might be the only health care professional I know
who doesn't hate motorcycles," I said. I'd heard some of the
nurses refer to them as donor cycles. "Aren't they a little
unsafe?"

He laughed. "There's something about knowing I can
hop on my bike and be gone in a minute that actually makes
me feel safe," he said, pulling on his gloves.

I felt safest at home, knowing I was secure with a roof
over my head and Tyler's. Different strokes, though. "We
might have different ideas of what's safe."

He put on his helmet and gave me a little salute and then he was peeling out, waving one gloved hand at me as he roared away.

The doors to Caring Hands slid open in front of me and I braced myself to walk down into the basement to get my knitting and crocheting supplies for this week's Yarn Circle. Not the catchiest name, I knew. I'd tried calling it the Fiber Arts Circle, but a lot of people showed up thinking it was a lecture on staying regular.

It was one of my favorite classes. The danger level was very low. No one can burn themselves on a crochet hook or cut themselves on a knitting needle and, so far, no one had used the needles to stab anyone. Our biggest issues were dropped stitches and miscounted rows. It was meditative and quiet, but not silent. I loved hearing the women (and it was almost always all women) tell each other bits and pieces of their life stories and seeing the photos of the children and grandchildren and great grandchildren items were being made for. I could feel the connection back and forth between the generations and all the love that was being poured into those snuggies and blankets and sweaters. I didn't have anything like that. No family heirlooms or items that had been passed down. Nothing my mother or sister had made especially for Tyler. I felt that lack. I hoped Tyler didn't. When — and I suppose if — Tyler had kids, the poor things were going to be inundated with handcrafted items. I wanted them to be able to feel that connection when they held those items in their hands and I wanted to feel that connection as I made things for them. For now, I settled for making small blankets to donate to the local homeless shelter.

To get to Yarn Circle, however, I still had to get the yarn and the hooks and the needles and the stitch markers. The door to the basement was right next to the front desk. Christy was, of course, not there. She was probably in the bathroom touching up her perfectly winged eyeliner or applying more lip plumping gloss. There was a sign-in sheet on the desk, but nobody — including me — ever used it except for some of the delivery people, especially Gabriel from Happy Blossom who used it as an excuse to talk to Christy. I'd seen him checking his hair in sideview mirrors of his delivery van out in the parking lot before coming in. He wasn't a bad looking kid. Thin, but not skinny. Teak-colored skin and jet black straight hair that fell across his forehead, putting his dark brown eyes into shadows. Christy looked right through him most of the time. She didn't brighten for him like she did when Malachi or one of the attending physicians walked in.

I hesitated at the door to the basement. No one would know I was down there. There was something about the basement that made the hair on my arms stand up. If there was any place at Caring Hands that would be haunted, it would be the basement. It was cold and damp all the time even though it had been years since they'd run the water in there. Everything echoed as you walked around making it sound like you weren't alone even though no one else was down there. The light didn't reach all the way into the corners so it always felt like there was something crouched there watching me. To top it off, there was a faint earthy smell of something about to decay.

They'd given me the old hydrotherapy room as a storage space. I didn't want to complain too much especially since my complaints didn't have anything factual to back them up. They'd put new shelves in it for me and there was lots of space. They kept a few other supplies and some old files down there, too, but it was rare that anyone went looking for those. No. It was my creepy domain most of the time. I took a deep breath and walked down the stairs one careful step at a time. The air got colder with each step down, clearly more proof that it was haunted.

The ceiling was lower down here and the pipes and conduits that ran overhead made it even more claustrophobic. Spare hospital beds and walkers and wheelchairs were stacked along the walls, casting tortured shadows onto the concrete floor and rough plastered walls.

I went around the corner to the hydrotherapy room and grabbed my box of yarn and needles and hooks and my book of patterns. A clicking noise from the other corner of the basement startled me and the hair on my arm and neck shot up to stand on end. I sprinted up the stairs as fast as I could, trying my best to convince myself that the sharp clicking sound was probably from a compressor or a transformer turning on and not the clicking talons of a monster or serial killer. I arrived back by the desk panting. Of course Christy was back, her liner and gloss looking freshly applied.

"You okay?" she asked, looking at me like maybe she smelled something bad.

"Sure," I said. "Just getting in my steps." She didn't need to know I was convinced that the zombie ghosts of old residents were waiting down there to do whatever it was that menacing ghosts did to innocent arts and crafts ladies. Chin up, I rested the box against my hip and headed to the unit where my knitters and crocheters would be meeting, stopping off at the employee lounge to lock up my purse and put on the white jacket I'd been issued to wear during my craft classes. Apparently having the whole staff wear white jackets or scrubs made things less confusing for the residents and it kept me from ruining too many of my clothes with paint or clay or glue.

The lounge wasn't huge and looked like a set from *That '70s Show*. It was a linoleum-floored square with a few tables, some plastic chairs, a coffee maker, a mini-fridge, a microwave, a soda pop machine, and a bank of banged up lockers. It smelled like burnt coffee and microwave popcorn. Always. Using the staff lockers was optional, but definitely a good idea. A few of the residents had busy hands and were confused enough to think everything was theirs. The first time I found Gladys making a little pyramid with the tampons from the bottom of my purse was the last time I left my purse out while I tried to lead a class.

I put my purse and sweater into the locker, shrugged my white jacket on, balanced the box o' yarn on my hip, and went to the unit. I entered the code and pushed through the double glass doors.

Tessie stood at the nurse's station screaming. "Give me back my phone!" Her face, usually soft and creased and close to the color of khaki, was tight and red. Her whole body shook.

Lillibeth said, "We don't have your phone, Tessie." Her tone was gentle, calm.

"Liar!" Tessie pounded on the counter, her cheeks quivering. "Someone stole it from my room. You were just in there. It must be you. You're lying. Now give it back."

"I'm not lying. Your daughter took your phone. Remember?" Lillibeth looked hopeful. "I was in your room to test your blood sugar, remember?"

Tessie looked down at her finger as if there would be some clue there, which there sort of was. Even Lillibeth left a mark when she drew blood and she had the deftest touch with a needle of all the nurses at Caring Hands, or so I'd heard.

Camila shook her head and said, "Thanks in old age—

thanks ere I go. For health, the midday sun, the impalpable air—for life, mere life. Walt Whitman." Camila was somewhere between me and Lillibeth, height-wise. Her skin was tawny and flawless. Her eyes were so dark it was hard to see the pupil sometimes, the lashes so long they brushed her cheeks.

Irma Warren wheeled up next to me in her power scooter. I had a soft spot for Irma. She was sharper than a fresh Xacto blade and had a dry sense of humor. Unfortunately for her, her body wasn't in as good a shape as her mind. Osteoporosis and arthritis had left her almost wheelchair bound, although she managed pretty well getting around on her Jazzy Pride scooter, only occasionally scraping the walls. She seemed to shrink on a nearly daily basis these days. I swear she'd gotten smaller since I started working at Caring Hands, taking up less and less space in her motorized scooter. Her elastic waisted pants in pastel colors with the matching shirts got bigger and bigger on her. Even her fluffy white hair looked too big on her head lately.

"Why did they take away Tessie's phone?" Irma usually knew the 411 on everything. It's like people didn't see her as she scooted along, almost literally below the radar. She heard a lot more than people realized and was always a good source of information.

She sighed. "Oh, Tessie got scammed. Somebody called her cell phone, claimed he was her grandson and was in trouble and needed her to send money right away."

I cringed. That was cruel. "And she did?"

"Oh, yeah. Whoever did this had done their homework. They knew her grandson's name and the city he lives in and that his parents were out of the country on vacation. They knew she'd just had her birthday. They knew that maybe she wasn't tracking things quite as well as she had not so long ago, but still had access to all her credit cards and stuff." Irma shook her head. "These identity thieves and scammers. It's a shame. That's what it is."

She sounded like she was speaking from experience. "Does it happen a lot?" I asked.

"Tessie's easily the third one in the last couple of months to have something like that happen," Irma said.

"The same scam each time?" I asked.

"No. They change it up. There's the grandkid needing money for a car repair or bail, there's the one where they claim they're from the IRS, and there's plain old identity theft when they get hold of people's credit card numbers and the like." She shook her head.

"That's terrible." Was anyone lower than someone who would pick on elderly people who were just trying to get by?

"It's got everyone's in a tizz. Those good-for-nothings don't care how much havoc they wreak." She straightened her slacks to cover the tops of her compression socks.

"There's already been more than enough havoc around here recently," I said, walking down the hallway toward the multi-purpose room. I could smell the spaghetti and garlic bread they'd had for lunch this far down the hall. I'd open a window once I got there. Irma put her Jazzy Pride in gear and wheeled along next to me.

"When you say havoc, do you mean Floyd?" she asked.

I nodded.

"I'm going to miss Floyd. He was one of the few men around here with something going on upstairs." She sighed and paused for a moment in the hall, letting Gladys scurry past clutching her baby doll to her chest. There were a couple of bandages on it as if the doll had gotten hurt. Tyler used to do that with his toys if they got damaged somehow, putting bandages on scuffed Power Rangers and banged up Pokemon. It was cute when a little boy did it. It was a bit disturbing when an old lady did. Life wasn't fair.

"Floyd had it together. Unlike that one," Irma said, pointing at Gladys. "I don't know what's going on in her noggin. I'll miss Floyd. Harvey, too. Movie night's going to be a lot less fun without them."

"You knew Floyd pretty well." It wasn't a question.

"Mmhmm," she murmured.

"Did you know about his COPD diagnosis?"

"Mmhmm."

"I hear he was pretty down about it."

Irma sat up and looked at me. "No one wants to learn that they're never going to be able to breathe normally again. You go for years taking that whole air-in/air-out thing for granted and all the sudden you have to worry about it all the time. It's no fun."

No fun was one way to look at it. "Do you think he might have been upset enough about it to . . . well, you know?" I didn't want to say the words, but it had been bugging me. What if Floyd had decided he didn't want to live through the last stages of COPD and figured out how to check out early?

Irma looked around furtively and then whispered, "Leah, are you asking me if I think Floyd might have killed himself?"

I leaned in and whispered, too. "Well? Could he have? Would he have?"

"Could? Probably. He wasn't a stupid man. Would? I don't think so." Irma sat back with a sigh. "Our worlds get so small, Leah. We lose one thing after another. It gets hard to see and to hear and eventually to walk and talk and maybe even breathe. Of course we get depressed. Who wouldn't?

But we also know how precious every minute and every person is. He would have known how devastated his family would have been."

"But maybe they wouldn't be so devastated if it looked like he'd slipped away in his sleep?" I asked. "Because if Lillibeth hadn't made a fuss, no one would have known that it was anything but that."

Irma froze for a moment and looked at me. "You're right about that. No one would have known or suspected anything. It would have been one more old man kicking the bucket. Nothing more."

"So you think he could have maybe taken his own life?" Because if he had, Brady would definitely be completely cleared. I still wasn't sure why Floyd would write Brady's name on a slip of paper like that, but that wouldn't matter if Floyd had killed himself.

"No. I don't. It wasn't in his nature." She squinted up at me. "You're close to that boy, aren't you?"

"Which boy?" This was not a conversation I wanted to have with Irma.

She waved a finger at me. "Don't be cute. You know who I mean. That boy who wore his pants down below his behonkus. The boy whose name was on the piece of paper in Floyd's room when Lillibeth got there."

I sat down on one of the benches that lined the hallway, hoping that if I was eye-level she at least wouldn't be shouting about Brady loud enough for everyone to hear. "Yeah. I know him."

She leaned in close enough for me to see the powder on her face. "Do you think he did it?"

"No. I don't." How many people was I going to have to say that to?

She leaned back in her chair and rubbed her chin. I made a mental note to stop by Irma's room to ask her if she wanted me to pluck those chin hairs. I'd slip a pair of tweezers in my jacket pocket later. I knew I would appreciate someone helping me tend to those stray chin hairs when the time came, but now didn't seem to be the moment. "I don't know about that kid. I didn't much like him at first, but once he settled in, he seemed all right. He definitely seemed to really be fond of Floyd. I'd hear them laughing out in the courtyard as they fed the birds and read old spy novels."

"I think the same thing!" I looked out the window at the courtyard she was talking about. A slight breeze ruffled the bird of paradise plants, making the orange flowers dance. Marty, the service guy from Let the Good Times Roll wheelchair repair, walked through, then stopped and hitched his pants up under his belly, jumping a little onto his toes as he did so.

"On the other hand, he could be a very clever sociopath. He could have convinced everyone he loved Floyd so no one would suspect him of being a killer." Irma raised her eyebrows at me.

I shook my head. Someone needed to check what Irma was watching on television. Maybe she should watch fewer crime shows and more home and gardening ones. "How likely do you really think that is?"

She shrugged. "When you get to be my age, you learn that people are capable of a lot of horrible things. Some-times it's the most innocent seeming people that are the most guilty."

"Not in this case," I said firmly.

She chewed that over for a second. "A lot of people don't think Brady seemed all that innocent anyway. Lillibeth was suspicious of him as soon as he walked through the door. Camila, too."

I waved her words away. "Lillibeth doesn't like anybody."

As if on cue, Lillibeth's raised voice echoed down the hallway. "What are you doing here?"

The response to her question wasn't clear because it was uttered in teenage boy mumble. Luckily, I was fluent in teenage boy-ese. Brady said, "It's time for my shift."

I patted Irma on the shoulder and walked as fast as I could with a box of yarn bumping against my hip back toward the nurses' station.

"You have a lot of nerve showing up here after what you did." Lillibeth stood in the middle of the circular station, hands on hips.

"I didn't do anything." Brady's voice had gotten a little louder and a little clearer.

I rounded the corner to stand next to Brady, who was keeping his very red face pointed toward the ground. "Lillibeth, I think you should keep your voice down," I said.

She rounded on me. "You are not the boss of me."

She had me there. "No, but you're not the boss of Brady, either. I think we should go talk to Dionne."

"Fine. Let's do that." Lillibeth tossed her ponytail behind her and stepped down out of the nurses' station. She marched off.

I followed and motioned for Brady to follow us, which he did, but with his feet audibly dragging against the industrial-grade carpet.

Lillibeth had already flung Dionne's door open when we got there. Dionne's big brown eyes had gone wide and then narrowed at the parade coming into her office. She was a thin woman with a very slight island lilt to her accent. I liked her. She was one of those people who always seemed to have an oasis of calm around her, no matter how chaotic things were getting. "What seems to be the problem?" she asked.

Lillibeth gestured at Brady with her thumb over her shoulder. "Him. What is he doing here?"

Dionne turned toward Brady for an answer. "It's court-mandated," he mumbled. "I didn't think I had a choice."

Poor guy. Here he was trying to do the right thing just to be pilloried publicly by the world's meanest Filipino nurse.

"I see," Dionne said. "So you came in for your regularly scheduled shift."

Brady nodded.

"He shouldn't be here. Not until we know for sure that he didn't have anything to do with Floyd's death." Lillibeth stamped her foot.

"Hey," I broke in. "What about innocent until proven guilty?"

Lillibeth whirled on me, ponytail whipping behind her like a figure skater doing one of those axel things. "What about protecting patients from a dangerous menace?"

"Who says he's a menace?" I countered.

"I do," Lillibeth said.

Dionne clapped her hands and we all turned toward her. She took a deep breath before she spoke and I could feel the temperature in the room shift down a couple of degrees. "Perhaps it would be okay for Brady to take a break from his community service until this is cleared up."

Lillibeth threw a triumphant look my way.

"Which doesn't mean that we in any way suspect Brady of wrong-doing," Dionne continued.

Now it was my turn to give Lillibeth a bit of side-eye.

"We want to avoid even the appearance of impropriety."

Dionne pulled a folder out of a rack on her desk. "I'll contact the county and let them know that Brady is taking a break for the moment so he won't get into trouble."

"Thanks," Brady mumbled. I looked over at him and he pulled himself up straighter and repeated, "Thanks," in a louder clearer voice. I nodded.

We shuffled out of the room. I looked at my watch. I was going to be very late for Yarn Circle. "Brady, do you need a ride home?"

He shook his head. "No. I rode my bike."

"Okay. Tell your mom I'll call her when I get home if she wants to talk."

He nodded and slouched off toward the front entrance.

As soon as he was out of earshot, I turned toward Lillibeth. "He didn't do anything wrong. Leave him alone."

"If he didn't do anything wrong, then why did Floyd write his name on that piece of paper?" Lillibeth stepped into my personal space.

"How should I know? You don't know either." I did not feel like backing down. Not one inch.

It paid off when Lillibeth stepped back, looking surprised. "Maybe I do and maybe I don't. I still don't want that kid around here."

She marched off to the unit. I followed more slowly back to Yarn Circle. Irma was still where I'd left her when I came back.

"So what was that about?" she asked, putting her Jazzy Pride into gear to follow along next to me.

"Like I said, Lillibeth doesn't like anybody." I didn't see a need to fill in the details.

"She likes a few people. Not you, though." She pointed at me as if she was making a gun.

I had suspected it, but wasn't super happy that other people had noticed. "I wish I knew why."

Irma snorted. She held her hand up and made a circular gesture in front of me. "It's all that."

"All what?" I stopped.

She rolled her eyes. "You know. The hair. The eyes. The . . ." Her circular gestures narrowed in on my chest.

I buttoned another button on my blouse. "Who around here cares about that?"

Irma chuckled. "I've seen Malachi watching you walk away and I've seen the way Lillibeth looks at him." She patted my leg. "You could do worse, you know."

It had been so long since I'd even considered if I could do better or worse that I didn't even know how to respond. My mother had brought a string of boyfriends through our house after my dad left. Since one of my main parenting maxims was to do the opposite of whatever it was that my mom did, I hadn't brought any men into our lives. Tyler got my full attention. But he wasn't here to pay attention to anymore. Was there room in my life for romance? In some ways, it felt too late to embark on that journey again. I shook my head. "I'm too old for that."

She laughed. "You're never too old." She hit the button on her chair and buzzed off. I cringed as she winged past the nurses' station, clipping the baseboard on her way by and nearly taking out Gabriel as he walked out of Betty Fisher's room. He had to leap out of the way to keep from colliding with her.

Getting old wasn't for sissies. Working around old people wasn't either.

SIX

Yarn Circle made good progress on the afghan we were making for the Spring Fling fundraiser. Each member was making a six-inch by six-inch granny square in whatever design and color they wanted and I was going to piece them together into a blanket that would be auctioned off to raise money for the Caring Hands' Foundation that helped out financially strapped seniors.

Everyone but Georgina and Miriam were done with their squares and some people had made more than one. That left me with close to enough to make something decent sized already and I could whip up some quick ones if necessary. I laid the finished squares out on one of the tables and let them all admire their work. "Very nice," Carmen said patting my arm with one hand while leaning heavily on her walker with the other. She'd made three squares, each one absolutely even with precise edges.

"You guys did all the work." I shifted two of the squares around to get the colors to balance out a bit better.

"Sure we did." She did a three-point turn, laboriously

lifting and smacking down her walker's yellow tennis ball-covered legs with each shift.

"See you next week," I called after her.

She waved one hand. "God willing and the creek don't rise."

I gathered the squares up, careful to keep them in the order I wanted them to line up in. I'd piece them together and do the edging at home. It would be something to do while I watched TV. I tucked the stack under my arm and waved at Marty as he came out of Miriam's room as I went past on my way to the employee lounge to get my coat and purse.

There were never more than three or four people in the lounge at a time since someone always needed to be on duty in case a resident needed something, but the room was full when I got there. Not with employees, though. Detective Park and two uniformed police officers - a man and a woman - stood at the bank of lockers. "Detective Park?"

He turned toward the door. "Ms. Glaser?"

"What are you doing here?" I asked. It felt a little bit like seeing your teacher at the grocery store when you were a little girl. He was out of place.

"We're here to search Brady Atkinson's locker." He glanced down at a piece of paper and pointed to the second one from the right on the bottom row. "That one."

He turned to Christy. "Could I have the combination, please?"

She checked the index card in her hand and rattled off three numbers.

He gestured at the two cops. The woman spun the combination and opened it. There wasn't much in there. A hoodie. A water bottle. Two granola bars. And a small square box with the words Duragesic Transdermal Patch across it. The uniform held it up, Detective Park opened a plastic evidence bag. She dropped it inside.

My stomach dropped faster than the box. Would that be enough non-squishy evidence for them to arrest Brady? A vision of him getting on a prison bus rose up in my head and nearly choked me. "Anyone could have put that in there," I blurted out. "You don't need the combination to get into these."

Park turned a degree at a time to look directly at me. I found myself wishing for the pleasant smile that I was sure masked something else. There was no smile at all now and his gaze was intense. "What do you mean?"

I pushed past him, grabbed the handle of the locker next to Brady's, jiggled it, and then banged the door with my shoulder. It popped open to reveal a stack of books, a book of poems by Mary Oliver on top. Somebody was a reader. "The locks are chintzy. They're a formality."

Park's jaw clenched. "How many people know how to do that?"

I shrugged. "How should I know?" I turned to Christy. "What do you think?"

She crossed her arms over her chest. "I didn't know how to do that and I've worked here three years."

I shrugged. It wasn't like Christy was the most observant person in the world. She definitely was no Irma.

"Do you break into these often?" Park's eyes narrowed a bit.

"Of course not. I had a little trouble remembering my combination when I first started here and I got tired of asking Christy for it." I gestured over to her. Not so much tired of asking, actually. More like embarrassed.

Christy rolled her eyes and inspected the ends of a lock of hair. "Because it was like every day for a while."

I gave her a bit of side eye and then turned back to Park. "Numbers aren't my thing."

Park rubbed the back of his neck. His two buddies watched with their mouths slightly agape.

"Did you figure that little trick out yourself?" Park looked up. The nice smile was back.

"Sort of. I mean I figured it out some place else and then used it here."

He didn't say anything. No one else did either.

I rushed to fill in the silence. "A couple of years ago, I was trying to get some soccer cleats that Tyler forgot at school. There was this tournament up in Rio Linda and there wasn't time for him to come with me for the cleats and still get to the field on time. I left him at the field with his team and went to the school. I got there and couldn't remember his combination. I couldn't reach him and I was frustrated so I jiggled the handle and bumped it with my shoulder and it popped open. When I got frustrated with these locks, I tried it and it worked here, too."

My words had picked up speed as I had gone through my explanation and my hands waved the afghan squares around like flags as I spoke and by the end of it I wasn't sure anyone had understood me and had a little bit of a better understanding about Sharon telling not to do an interpretive dance. The two cops' mouths had dropped a little farther open. Christy's head was cocked to one side like a confused puppy and Detective Park was still looking down and rubbing the back of his neck.

"Go. I'll catch up." Park waved the uniformed officers on. Christy followed them out. He leaned one shoulder against the bank of lockers.

"Who else might know that trick?" Park asked.

"I really don't know." I found myself leaning against the

locker opposite him, the cool of the metal locker felt good in the suddenly overheated room.

"Has anyone seen you do it?" He pressed. "Please think about it. It could be important."

I shifted so my back was against the locker, studying the pattern the sunlight coming through the vertical blinds made on the floor. I hadn't made a secret of opening my locker that way, but I hadn't exactly sought an audience either. "I'm not sure. Maybe." I snapped my fingers. "Definitely. I did it once when there was a birthday party in here for Camila. Probably three-fourths of the staff was here. I remember because Lillibeth made a kind of snarky comment about knowing who to suspect if things started going missing." She really didn't like me one little bit, did she?

"Do all the employees have lockers here?" he asked.

That I was more sure of. "Not the administrators and those type of people. They have offices with desks where they can leave their stuff. All the nurses and nursing assistants and people like Christy and me do, though." I turned again to face him and traced a line down the locker's edge with my forefinger. "Besides, Brady was here this afternoon. Dionne sent him home so he didn't work his regular shift, but he had plenty of time to come in here and remove anything suspicious from his locker. Why would he have left that in there?"

"He was here?" Park's eyebrows went up.

I nodded. "He was. I'm telling you, Brady didn't do it."

"So you keep saying." He pushed off the locker and straightened his tie.

"And I'll keep saying it to you and to everybody else until I can get you all to believe me." I straightened, too.

He opened his mouth as if he was going to say something else and then shut it. "Thank you for your help again, Ms. Glaser." Then he left.

The second he was out the door, I texted Sharon.

She texted back instantly. "On it."

I stepped out of the break room and almost tripped over Irma. "Hi, Irma. Do you need something?" I asked. She didn't usually leave the unit without someone to help her.

She waved a little purple notebook at me. "No. All good. Thanks so much." Then she spun her wheelchair around like a stunt driver doing a doughnut and zipped off toward the unit again. I headed out the door to my truck.

———

Judy Gordon's youngest daughter had gone off to Lewis and Clark in Oregon in the same outgoing flood that had taken Tyler and his friends and now she wanted a portrait painted of her dog. Transference much? Whatever her reasons, I was happy to get the commission.

Pet portraits were yet another piece of my income, as it were. They brought in a little more than my crocheting, but that isn't exactly setting a high bar. I'd seen Judy's dog and it was spectacularly ugly. A commission is a commission, though, and every penny I brought in made life a little easier for me and for Tyler.

My friends and I don't talk about money, but we're all extremely aware of it and aware of the differences in our various economic levels. Rayna was a stay-at-home mom and had been the entire time I'd known her. Her husband George made more than enough to cover their living expenses plus trips to cool places like Belize and Italy on the regular. I had no idea how much he really made except it was way more than I did. Sharon was a lawyer and her wife,

Mindy, was a lecturer at the University. Not rich, but definitely not hurting plus all those yummy benefits from the U. Tamika was a computer programmer with the state and her husband, Jamal, was a project manager for one of those huge construction companies that did giant projects. Again, not hurting.

I occasionally hurt. It was just me. One parent. One income. I'd been stretching the money from Travis's life insurance for close to fifteen years now as my back-up emergency fund, which I dipped into a little more often than I'd like. Most of my money was in my house. My big priority when I'd moved Tyler and me to Darby was to buy in the neighborhood with the best school. My house could pretty much fit twice into Tamika's and Sharon's houses and probably three times into Rayna's, but my kid got the same SAT prep and AP courses theirs did and that's what mattered most to me.

Rayna lived in an area that looked better than mine. Judy Gordon lived in an area that made Rayna's house look like a sharecropper's shack. You had to be buzzed in through wrought iron gates. Bougainvillea and lantana festooned the medians and saucer magnolia and almond trees blocked the view of the houses from the street along with the occasional soaring line of Italian Spruce.

I pulled into Judy's driveway. The house was a two-story Spanish-style stucco with a red tile roof and lots of archways and tile work. It was big enough that if I hadn't known better I would have wondered if it was a small hotel. I rang the bell and listened to it echo inside.

Judy answered the door wearing yoga pants and a drapey cotton shirt. Nice ones. Not Target ones. The kind that cost more than a couple weeks worth of groceries. She was an extremely thin woman with thick auburn hair she kept swept up on top of her head in one of those messy buns that take a lot of effort to create. She gestured for me to come in. "Sugar Pop's out in the sun room. Oh, do you mind taking your boots off?"

I kicked them off and put them on a rack clearly designed for visitors' shoes by the front door, glad I was wearing socks without holes in the toes. Some little anarchist seed in me wanted to keep them on and tap dance all the way to the sun room. I needed the money, however, and I was well aware of how good — and bad — word of mouth spread. I'd gotten this commission because of a portrait I'd done of Candice Tyler's cat Puck. Who knew where this one for Judy would lead? Unless, of course, I marked up her natural stone floors with my Payless ankle boots.

Sugar Pop – who looked like the love child of a dachshund and a dust mop – was sleeping on a pillow on a wicker love seat. She'd been shampooed and brushed and had a purple bow in her hair, but nothing could take away from the fact that she had a huge underbite and wiry hair that let patches of pink skin show through in places. Judy clearly loved her, though, and I wasn't there to judge Sugar Pop. I was there to paint her. "This is great. I'll set up my tripod." I unpacked my equipment, bending over the case with my camera. The afternoon light breaking through the windows came in at a good angle to bring out textures and definitions of everything without overshadowing anything. Not exactly the golden hour, but close enough.

"So anything new?" Judy asked. There was something funny in her tone.

"Oh, I'm still adjusting to Tyler being away at college." I played with the legs of the tripod until they were even. "You?"

"I hear you. I'm not quite sure what to do with myself

now that Madison is up in Oregon." She sat down on the wicker couch behind me.

"I started an art therapy job. That's been keeping me busy. That helps some." I smiled at her over my shoulder. We weren't so different.

"Oh, that's right. You work at Caring Hands," Judy said.

"Mmhmm. " I looked through the camera viewfinder. The angle wasn't quite what I'd wanted. I readjusted again.

"I meant you work at the same place that Brady Atkinson worked. You know, where that man died." The wicker creaked as Judy leaned forward.

I straightened and turned to look at her, my heart rate picking up a notch. "How did you know about that?"

"There was a news report on the radio about a suspicious death at the nursing home and then Eva Wentz posted a bunch of stuff online. It didn't take much to connect the dots." She crossed her legs and wrapped her hands around her knee.

Eva had wasted no time getting those photos up online and Judy Gordon had apparently wasted no time calling me. Now I wasn't sure if she really wanted a portrait of Sugar Pop or if she'd wanted me to get the DL on some gossip. She was only getting one of those things and it wasn't going to be dirt on my friends. "What about it?"

She had the good grace to look a little taken aback. "Nothing, really. Just curious."

I counted to ten. I'd probably be curious, too, if I wasn't in the middle of it. "It's a series of mistakes and misunderstandings. It will all be straightened out soon."

"But the man is dead, right? And they suspect Brady had something to do with it?" Her tone was breathless and her eyes were bright. Was she enjoying this?

I didn't care for that gleam in her eye. "Yes. Floyd is

dead. He was a sweet guy, a veteran of the Korean War, and a real gentleman." I couldn't keep the sharp edge out of my tone. He wasn't just some man. He was someone special. "And, of course, Brady didn't have anything to do with it. Don't be ridiculous."

Judy's perfectly maintained eyebrows arched up. "It's not like Brady hasn't been in trouble before."

"It's a long stretch from the things Brady has done to killing someone, Judy. My guess is that Madison hasn't always been perfect either. She just hasn't had the bad luck of getting caught." I knew that was mean. I couldn't help it, though. Poor Brady. I hated that even people who knew him could be thinking such things about him.

She put her hand on her chest. "Sorry. I didn't mean to offend you."

I shrugged and looked through the viewfinder again, but everything was blurry. I brushed the tears that had begun to form in my eyes away and went back to taking pictures of Judy's butt ugly dog.

SEVEN

I wasn't even fully awake on Tuesday morning when Tamika called me. "Freaking Eva posted an article about Floyd's death on Facebook."

"What? Why?" I pulled out my phone and brought up Facebook. Yep. On Eva's page there was a link to an article in the *Darby Express* about a suspicious death at Caring Hands. For her comment, Eva had written "I hope no one I know is involved."

"That's low." I took another gulp of coffee.

"What is her problem? Doesn't she have anything better to do?" Tamika fumed. "And you should see some of the comments. People can be so cruel."

"Did you call Sharon?" I asked, not sure what else to do to be helpful. Once again, I didn't have a whole to offer in the way of assistance.

"Of course. I wanted to call you and get all my ugly out before I called Rayna, though. She'll be upset enough already without me piling on."

"I'm not sure I'm the right person to calm you down." I told her about my conversation with Judy Gordon.

"At least you'll get a commission out of it," Tamika said.

"True. Judy Gordon will have to pay for her dirt. Too bad Eva won't."

"Amen."

Unlike Eva, I did have plenty to do and the sooner I finished the portrait of Sugar Pop, the sooner I would get to stop looking at her.

I tried combinations of the poses I'd caught in the photos to show off her best features. Not so easy when you weren't sure if there even were good features. There were her eyes, but that felt so cliché. Eyes are, well, eyes. Windows to the soul and all that, but still so overdone. Maybe her ears. They were cocked at an expressive angle in one of the photos that gave her an almost coquettish look. The angle downplayed her underbite as well and the purple bow covered a lot of the patchiness of her hair. I sketched a few variations of the angle and then one crazy outlier of her standing on her cushion with her paws on the arm of the chair looking like she was queen of the mountain. She wasn't so ugly. Once you really looked at her, you started to see her finer points. If I combined the queen of the mountain pose with the coquettish ear angle, I might actually have something. I started laying in the rough outlines of the portrait in charcoal. Then I looked up at the clock and realized I was about to be late for Caring Hands. I grabbed my purse and hightailed it out.

I made my mad dash into the basement for supplies, panting as I ran past Christy who I didn't think even noticed I was there or had gotten so used to be dashing in and out that she'd stopped reacting, then went to the employee lounge to put away my stuff and grab my jacket. I plowed into Detective Park as I came out. He grabbed my box of suncatcher supplies before they went crashing to the floor.

I shook my head. "What are you doing here?" Hadn't he just been here the day before? Was this like his new hang-out spot?

"Talking to me," Lillibeth said. I hadn't even seen her behind Park until she stepped out from behind him. She was that itty bitty.

"Oh." I took my box back from him. "Thanks"

Lillibeth pushed past me into the employee lounge and held the door open for Park. He nodded to me. "Nice to see you, Ms. Glaser."

I wasn't sure I shared the sentiment. As the door to the lounge swung closed behind them, I heard Lillibeth say, "I didn't like that Brady kid from the jump."

Grrr. I opened the door, stuck my head in, and said, "Brady did nothing wrong." Then let the door slam behind me. That had felt surprisingly good.

I hefted the box the rest of the way down the hallway and into the assisted living unit. Camila was up on a step stool tacking a poster up on the bulletin board as I walked into the assisted living area. I stopped to read the flyer. Caring Hands had scheduled a special meeting to inform family members of residents about identity theft and how to protect themselves from it.

I reached up to take the staple gun from Camila so she could have her hands free as she stepped back down. "Is this because of poor Tessie?"

"And Carmen and Betty and Miriam. They've all had people calling them claiming to be family members in trouble or people from the IRS or the bank or police offi-cers." Camila folded up the step stool and stored it back in the closet by the bulletin board.

I frowned. "That seems like a lot." Maybe Park should be taking statements about that instead of chasing after Brady.

She glanced over her shoulder at me as she walked back to the nurses' station. "It's really common among seniors. They're such good targets. They're too trusting. They don't always understand technology all that well and a lot of them have money."

"And they're a little confused?" Tessie had seemed so together one second and then so entirely off track the next.

"Not all of them. Irma is sharp as a tack." She straightened the big notebook that held daily orders on the desk.

True enough. "She is, but she's also kind of the exception."

Camila smoothed her hair back into the ponytail that contained it. "That's part of the reason we thought it would be a good idea to have an informational meeting for families and not only the residents. To give them some basics about how to protect their people, you know?"

"Sounds like a good idea. That number seems so high for one place."

She stopped and looked skyward. For a second, I thought she was going to sneeze. Then she intoned, "I pray, for word is out. And prayer comes round again. That I may seem, though I die old. A foolish, passionate man. Yeats."

Okayyyyy.

Down in the dining hall, I sorted through the suncatchers. A lot of people had made more than one so we'd have around twenty or so to sell. It wasn't going to be a big moneymaker, but it would be something. Let's face it, if I could figure out what would be a big moneymaker I probably wouldn't be teaching seniors to make suncatchers.

I got everything set up with the glass beads and plastic lids and the residents filed in and settled down to work.

Five minutes later, Javis McCarter called me over. "I'm done." Javis was only in his early 80s but had been in a wheelchair for a while. Like Irma, he seemed to shrink daily, his bushy white eyebrows taking up more and more of his face. His fingers were thick and gnarled from arthritis, but he still managed to do some fairly delicate work. I was always amazed at how people learned to adapt as their circumstances changed.

I looked at what he'd put together. There was no discernible pattern, but it didn't really matter. Once it was hung up in a window, the colors refracting through would be lovely. That was one of the good things about this particular craft. It helped the seniors work on their manual dexterity, picking up small pieces, and assembling things and pretty much anything they did was going to work.

"It's going to be lovely, Javis. May I?" I asked.

He nodded and I moved it over to another table to pour glue over it to let it dry. Yvette Lindsey came over to watch what I was doing. "Oh, that is nice. I like how you put that together, Javis. The colors really complement each other."

Javis sat up a little straighter in his wheelchair. "Thank you."

"Take a look at mine," Waylon Langston brayed from across the table. "Mine's much better." Waylon had recently gone from a manual wheelchair to an electric top-of-the-line model and the walls of Caring Hands had the scars to prove it. It was faster and bigger than Javis's manual or even Irma's Jazzy Pride. We had put a tray across the wheelchair arms so he could stay in it while he worked on his suncatcher because his chair was too big to pull all the way up to the table. He was already tall and with the extra height of the wheelchair, he towered over everything and everybody.

Javis sank down a bit in his dinky manual wheelchair.

"Waylon, this isn't a competition." I walked over to his side of the table across from Javis. "It's about expressing yourself and making something pretty to sell at the fair." Some people always seem to need to one up everyone else. Waylon was one of them. It wasn't a particularly endearing quality.

"Well, mine's prettier." He pushed it toward me. "See?"

"It's very nice, but so is Javis's." I glanced around to see who else might need some encouragement or help. Irma sat at another table facing this with one, but with nothing in front of her. "Don't you want to make a suncatcher, Irma?"

She gave me a look that answered that question pretty definitively.

"Would you like to make something else?" I asked, glancing around. I could probably cobble together supplies for a watercolor or some knitting.

She shook her head. "Don't worry about me. I'm down here for the company."

Now I gave her a look. This wasn't exactly the crowd that Irma hung with. Of course, it seemed like quite a bit of her crowd wasn't around anymore. Before I could say anything, though, Camila wheeled Gladys in.

Poor Gladys. She'd been here in Caring Hands longer than pretty much any other resident except Roland Chilvers who could barely get out of bed anymore. She'd been getting more and more confused as the months and years went on. I'd found some photos of her in the album the previous arts and crafts person had made. There'd been a time when she'd sat up straighter in her wheelchair and you couldn't see her pink scalp through her thinning white hair and her family had visited regularly. I didn't think I'd ever seen her with a visitor in the five months I'd worked at Caring Hands. Maybe they got tired. Maybe she stopped recognizing them. Maybe they'd moved away. Whatever the reason, it made me sad. It was like she was marking time here until she could leave and there was pretty much only one way residents left Caring Hands. I felt a little stab. Sometimes I felt kind of the same way, that I was just marking time.

"You can set Gladys up over there." I pointed to an open spot next to Irma. "I'll get her suncatcher out so she can finish it."

I rummaged through the half-finished ones and found the one I'd tagged with Gladys's name. My heart gave a little clutch as my hands brushed past Floyd's partially finished suncatcher. I wondered if I should put it in the box of giveaway items of Floyd's things his family had set out in the dining room. I set his suncatcher aside and brought Gladys's over to her.

Camila locked down Gladys's chair and said, "I'll be back in about a half an hour. It's Gladys's shower day. Isn't it, Gladys?" Camila patted her on the shoulder and left.

"What colors would you like to use to finish this up, Gladys?" I asked.

Gladys glanced around. "What've you got?"

"The usual. Blue, purple, red, green, yellow, orange." I looked at her piece that seemed largely made up of yellows and oranges. "Do you want to throw some cooler colors in there to give it some more depth?"

"Some what?" Her brow furrowed.

"Some blues or purples. They'll make the colors you already have there pop," I explained.

"If you say so." She clutched her baby doll to her chest.

I brought over a selection of beads in cooler colors and set them down in front of her. "Do you want me to hold your baby so you can use both hands to work on your suncatacher?"

Gladys clutched the doll closer and shook her head hard enough to send her glasses askew. "No. She's mine."

"Of course, she is. I just wanted to see if I could help with her." I looked more closely. The bandages were gone from her doll. "Your baby's all better. How'd that happen?" I asked.

She put one wrinkly finger up to her lips and said, "I can't tell you. It's a secret."

"That's okay. Let me know if I can help somehow."

"I have all the help I need." She dropped the doll into her lap and glared at me. I backed away.

A thought occurred to me. I went back to the box and got out Floyd's sun catcher and set it down in front of Irma.

She looked down at the half-finished project. "What's this?"

"Floyd's suncatcher. He didn't get to finish it. Would you be willing to? It would be a favor to me."

Irma sighed and tucked her purple notebook into the basket on the front of her Jazzy Pride after jotting something down in it and said, "Well, if it's a favor to you and it's for Floyd. I'll do it."

I put my hand over hers. "He was a nice man. I can't imagine why anyone would want to hurt him."

Irma looked up at me, one eye squinted shut. "There are all kinds of people in the world, Leah, and not all of them are nice."

After our session was done and I put my supplies away, I stopped into Irma's room to pluck those errant chin hairs. She rubbed at her chin when I was done. "I'm not sure if it's a blessing or a curse than I can't see them myself anymore." Then she patted my arm. "You're a good girl, Leah."

I patted her back. "Back atcha, Irma."

I decided to check on Javis. Waylon always seemed to be going after him. I could see how much it bothered him and that bothered me.

I could hear the low soothing rumble of Malachi's voice before I got to Javis's room. When I went in, Malachi was kneeling next to Javis's bed, peeling off a pain patch, the same kind that someone — absolutely 100% not Brady — had used to kill Floyd. After taking the patch off, Malachi folded it in half taking time to make sure the corners matched up perfectly so none of the inside of the patch was exposed then he looked up at me. He was wearing a pair of dark blue scrubs today that made the blue of his eyes even more striking than usual.

"Hi," I said from the doorway. "Okay if I come in?"

Malachi looked over to Javis who nodded. Then he said, "Sure. I'll be done here momentarily."

I left my box of supplies in the hallway and slipped in, leaning against the wall with my hands tucked behind me. "I wanted to see if you were okay, Javis."

Javis waved me away with the hand Malachi wasn't holding. "I'm fine."

I took a tentative step forward. "You sure? I thought your suncatcher was really lovely and so did a lot of other people."

He let his hand fall to the bed. "It's only a stupid craft project."

"No, it isn't," Malachi and I said in unison.

I looked over at Malachi and he bowed his head a bit and motioned for me to go on and stepped out of the room with the patch held carefully between two gloved fingers.

"What we're doing is a lot more than a stupid craft project. It's about self-expression and creativity and keeping your brain limber," I said. "Plus I really hope it makes you happy. Creating art should be joyous."

Javis grumbled. "It's not art. At least, not when I do it."

"I beg to differ," I said.

Malachi came back into the room without the old patch and with a new one still in its packaging. He put the new pain patch in another spot on Javis's arm and said, "You should give yourself more credit, Javis. I bet your suncatcher is beautiful."

We both said good-bye to Javis whose eyelids had already begun to droop as time for his afternoon nap neared and stepped out into the hallway.

"Where did you go with the used patch?" I picked up my suncatcher supplies and balanced them on my hip like a tired toddler.

He gestured to a red plastic Sharps container on the wall as we walked past it. The Sharps containers were where the staff threw out needles and stuff that could poke you. They were one or two on each spoke of the unit. "In there."

"They're not exactly sharp."

"But they are a hazard," Malachi said. "Putting them in the Sharps container is protocol."

"Why don't you just throw them out?" I asked as we walked down the hallway.

"To be safe." He stopped at the nursing desk and pulled out one of the big binders on the rolling cart. "There's still medication on there. We don't want someone to be accidentally exposed. There've been some really heartbreaking cases of kids touching one and being poisoned while visiting their grandparents."

I was all about keeping kids safe, but something didn't quite make sense to me. "Wait. If there's still medication on them, why are you taking them off?"

"Medications for chronic pain like Javis's work better if they stay at a consistent level in the bloodstream. We don't want to wait until there's no more medication going into Javis's bloodstream to start the new patch so we do it on a schedule. This way we know they're getting a steady dose." He made a note in the binder and put it back on the cart.

"That makes sense." We continued down the hallway.

"To you, it does. It's a battle around here to get everyone to do it. They have to walk away from the patient and walk back in. It's not always convenient. I've seen several of the nurses barely folding them in half and throwing the old patches into the garbage rather than taking them out to the Sharps container." He shook his head. "So what was up with Javis that you were worried about him?"

I sighed and kicked at the carpet with the toe of my boot. "Oh, Waylon was being a tiny little bit mean about a craft project."

Malachi made a disgusted noise in the back of his throat. "What kind of mean?"

"Oh, saying how his suncatcher was better than Javis's. Things like that." It sounded silly saying it out loud, but it hadn't felt silly when I'd seen Javis's shoulders slump.

"Waylon's a bully," Malachi said.

"I hadn't really thought of it that way." I hadn't labeled it. I'd just wanted it to stop, but Malachi was right. Waylon was bigger and stronger and more confident than Javis. It was no different than kids on the playground.

"Is there any other way to think of someone who picks on someone weaker than them? It makes me so mad." He clenched and unclenched his hands at his side. "I hate bullies."

I stopped, feeling like someone had really seen me for the first time in a while. Angry. That was exactly what seeing someone get picked on made me feel. "Yes. Exactly. Me, too. Waylon's not the only one," I said with feeling. "You should have heard what Lillibeth said to Brady when he tried to come back to work. She's a bully, too."

He snorted. "I did hear. So did everyone else probably. She wasn't exactly trying to keep her voice down."

I fell into step beside Malachi again. "I'm not quite sure what to do about it, though."

"You'll figure it out," he said. He rubbed a thumb along his chin. "I'll see if I can find some other ways to buoy Javis up a bit. Get him to stand up for himself. Call Waylon's bluff. It's the best way to get a bully to back down."

I smiled at him. "You're a very kind person, Malachi." Irma might be right about not everyone in the world being nice, but there were still a few out there.

He smiled back. "Takes one to know one."

———

After dinner, I went to work on my portrait of Sugar Pop. I set up at my easel with the sketches I'd made and my pastels and went to work. I couldn't stop thinking about how Malachi had disposed of that fentanyl patch and what he'd told me, though. Did a lot of people know that the patches still had medication on them? How easy would it be to find that out?

I washed my hands and grabbed my laptop and did a quick search.

It wasn't even a teensy little bit hard to find out. Even someone as bad at internet searches as I was could get all the information needed to know about used patches and how to extract the drug from it in about five clicks. I also found a series of articles describing how partially used patches had turned up in places and either poisoned someone accidentally or had someone overdose from using them. Malachi had disposed of Javis's patch exactly the way that was recommended, but he was right about not everyone generally following the protocol. Everyone meant well. Sometimes people were in a hurry, though. That's how all those accidents I'd read about had happened.

It wasn't a big of a jump to think that someone might dump a used patch in the garbage rather than carefully folding it in half and finding the nearest Sharps container or even get distracted and leave a used patch sitting on a bedside table or put something in a pocket, planning on discarding it properly later.

Who knew how many partially used patches could have been fished out of garbage cans or picked up from bedsides? The patches were small. It wouldn't be hard to slip them into something to smuggle them out. If you were worried about someone seeing you do that, toss the patch in the garbage and then be the person to empty the trash. Everyone pitched in on chores like that at Caring Hands. No one would think twice about it. I'd seen nearly everyone taking garbage out to the Dumpster.

A person could make a lot of money selling those used fentanyl patches. That was a pretty big temptation. What if Floyd had seen someone sneaking one of those patches out and had threatened to tell someone?

Sharon had pointed out that Brady was no longer a juvenile. If he got in trouble now, it wouldn't be in juvenile court. It would be big trouble. Would the trouble be big enough to kill someone to keep them quiet?

Then I shook my head. No. Absolutely no. Brady didn't do this.

Brady did a lot of hare-brained things, but not this. Not murder. I was sure of it. Wasn't I?

I shut my computer feeling a little sick.

EIGHT

Floyd's funeral was on Wednesday. His family held the service in the chapel at Caring Hands. I got out of my truck and took a moment to straighten my skirt. I'd kicked it up a notch from my usual jeans and boots for the occasion and had put on a black pencil skirt with a gray sweater and a pashmina over it. Clouds pressed down making the day unexpectedly overcast and gloomy. We usually celebrate rain in northern California. We don't get much of it. Watching it sink into the parched ground generally made me feel a sense of renewal. Today, it felt depressing. Appropriate for a funeral, I supposed. I walked to the front doors and they whooshed open. Then I stood there, not quite able to get myself to walk through them.

I hate funerals. I know nobody likes them. I really really hate them, though. I could have turned around and gone home. It wasn't like anyone would be taking attendance or even probably notice if I was there or not.

That wasn't quite true, though. I would be taking attendance. There was a reason we had these rituals. They made us slow down to take time to fully feel the impact of important milestones. Floyd was gone. We all needed to take a moment to grasp what that would mean and to say goodbye. I felt terrible that Brady wasn't here. I knew he'd wanted to be. After seeing how Lillibeth had reacted to him showing up for his regular shift on Monday, however, I was glad we'd listened to Sharon.

I steeled myself and stepped over the threshold as the doors started to whoosh back closed again. My breath started to come more quickly as I got to the doors of the chapel. A cold sweat broke out on my forehead as I pushed through the doors. The smell of the cut flowers nearly choked me.

Irma wheeled in beside me. "You all right, dear?"

I nodded, not really wanting to try to speak.

"Go sit down. You look shaky." She wheeled herself over to a spot in the back and pulled the little purple notebook out of her wheelchair pocket and started writing in it.

Christy was in the second row. Lillibeth and Camila were in the third row. I slipped into an empty seat in the row behind them. "Hi," I whispered.

They both turned, nodded at me, and then turned back toward the front. Lillibeth hadn't been as openly hostile to me since our showdown over Brady. I'd spent a lot of time trying to make her like me. Who knew that the solution was to be as mean to her as she was to everyone else?

I settled myself onto the hard seat and flipped through the small program I'd been handed on the way in. There was an oval photo of Floyd clearly from many decades earlier on the front. He was wearing something plaid and his head was thrown back like he was laughing. I traced the outline of his face with my finger. He'd been quite handsome back in the day. Dark hair and a firm jaw line and a twinkle in his eye all added up to quite the catch, in my opinion. Inside was the usual list of items. The opening prayer, the 21st Psalm, a poem, and the order things would happen in. Nothing fancy. Nothing weird. Thank goodness.

Gabriel from Happy Blossoms strolled down the aisle scanning like a periscope on a swivel until his eyes lighted on Christy. Then he was climbing over people's legs to get to the empty seat next to her. She barely acknowledged him as he sat down. Poor guy.

A pleasant citrus scent wafted over me and I looked up to find Malachi sliding into the seat next to mine. "Hey," he said quietly.

"Hi." I smiled at him.

Lillbeth and Camila turned around, did the nod thing, and turned back again although Lillibeth's shoulders looked like they'd climbed an inch or two closer to her ears.

"Are you okay?" he asked.

I shrugged. "As okay as I'm going to be at the moment."

He gave me a quizzical look, but let it drop.

Rayna thinks my reaction to funerals is all about me being retraumatized, that I'm reliving Travis's funeral at every funeral I attend. I could be. I don't really know. I don't remember much of his funeral. It's one of those things that I think my mind has mercifully blurred out for me. I remember making all the arrangements, ordering food, and making the program. I remember figuring out what Tyler and I would both wear. I remember driving to the funeral home. That's it, though. I know Travis's brother and one of his friends from college spoke and his sister read a poem, but I don't remember actually hearing any of it.

Pastor Faulkner walked in and everyone stood. He made the gesture for us all to sit. He started with "Dearly beloved" and I started to shake. Only a little. Just a bit of a tremble in my hand. I didn't think it was noticeable, but then Malachi put his hand over mine.

It was big and warm and a tiny bit rough. My heartrate slowed and I took a deep breath. I looked over at him to thank him. He gave me a quick smile and turned back toward the minister like it was no big deal.

Something inside me unfurled. A little cold rock in me melted a tiny bit. I turned back toward the minister, too, and let myself listen to people who cared about Floyd celebrate his life and I could really hear it for a change. The low buzz of my own past misery had been turned down a notch.

After the service, Malachi and I stood behind Lillibeth and Camila in the line to offer our condolences to Floyd's family. It was a whole Caring Hands contingent. Gabriel and Christy were ahead of them. Marty, looking particularly pale and pasty, from Let the Good Times Roll Wheelchair Sales and Service was behind us, his belly straining the buttons of his dress shirt. Maybe he didn't like funerals any more than I did. Next to him was Anna from the Can You Hear Me Now Hearing Aid Emporium. All I could see of her at the moment was her salt and pepper Afro as she bent over to read the program.

Brady was right. Everyone had loved Floyd. Even the people who delivered flowers to him or checked out his hearing aids to keep them working. How could someone have killed him? Why?

"He's in a better place," Camila said to Lillibeth with great certainty as if she could hear my thoughts.

My hand balled into a fist of its own accord. To my credit, I didn't take a swing at her.

There are a lot of things to hate about having your husband die. Like mountains of things. One of the things that seemed unnecessarily unfair were the incredibly stupid things people say. It's especially irritating when you can't pull their hair or scream in their faces because they're trying to help. I rolled my eyes. "How the hell does she know that?" I muttered under my breath.

"She could be right," Malachi whispered, giving me a little shoulder bump as we inched closer to Floyd's daughter and his grandchildren.

"Because of the COPD?" I asked.

Malachi nodded. "That's not an easy way to go."

"Poor Floyd," I said, imagining watching him struggle more and more to get a breath in.

"Maybe it would be better to float out on a cloud of Fentanyl than it would be to go out fighting for every breath." He sounded a little wistful.

I apparently wasn't the only one who wasn't sure about that better place thing, though.

"Life is life," Lillibeth said to Camila. "We don't know what's on the other side. We should preserve life whenever and wherever we can. Everyone I've ever brought back with CPR has been grateful for it."

"Have you brought back a lot of people?" I asked.

Lillibeth turned around, a look of surprise on her face as if she had forgotten we were behind her. "A few." She pressed her lips together and turned away from me.

"The righteous perish, and no one takes it to heart; the devout are taken away, and no one understands that the righteous are taken away to be spared from evil. Those who walk uprightly enter into peace; they find rest as they lie in death," Camila said with a definite nod. "Isaiah 57:1-2."

Hard to argue with that. I turned too Malachi. "What do you think?"

"That it's a moot point, right now." He gestured with a head nod to Floyd's casket at the front of the room. "Lillibeth is still a little angry about not being able to even try to bring him back, though. If I hadn't gotten there before her, I think she would have ignored the DNR entirely. She would have gotten there, too, if Adriana hadn't started taking off her clothes in the library. Lillibeth would have been the one to find him on her rounds instead of Brady finding him and me getting there before her after Brady pushed the call button."

I'd missed Adriana's latest striptease although I heard about it later. She'd gotten confused about what was her room and what wasn't. No harm. No foul. Still, no one wanted little old ladies wandering the halls in their unmentionables and Lillibeth had been the one to throw a blanket around her and get her back to her room.

"I guess it's good you got there first, then," I said.

He looked from me over to Lillibeth and Camila. "I guess it depends on who you ask."

We filed out of the chapel to make our way to the cemetery and I saw Detective Park standing in the back of the room in a corner. "Why on earth is he here?" I whispered to Malachi on our way to the parking lot.

"The detective?" Malachi held the door open for me.

The weather had worsened. The clouds were more menacing, making the air gray and damp and leaving a slight film of moisture on everything it touched. A gust of wind swirled around my ankles. I wrapped my pashmina tighter around me although the wind cut right through it. "I feel like he's here every time I turn around."

He stopped walking and gave me a funny look. "He's here because he's investigating."

"Now? What would be here to investigate?" I gestured to the crowd of Floyd's relatives and friends, most of them still touching crumpled tissues to tear-reddened eyes.

"Don't they say that criminals return to the scene of the crime?" He steered me toward my truck, his hand going from my elbow to the small of my back. It had the same settling effect that his hand over mine had had inside during the service. It radiated calm and strength and I felt my shoulders relax a notch.

Sharon really had been right. It was good that Brady wasn't here. No one could point to him and say he was returning to the scene of the crime.

I looked back over my shoulder to see Detective Park watching us as we walked to my car. I leaned into Malachi's strong arms rather than sticking my tongue out at Park. I am an adult after all.

———

I'd stopped cooking dinner after Tyler left. At first it felt like a lark. It freed up a lot of time. Popcorn and white wine seemed like a fine dinner to me. Even finer if I capped it off with a cookie or two or maybe some ice cream. I didn't have to spend a lot of time planning it or shopping for it or cooking it. I didn't have to think about what anyone else wanted to eat. Then I gained five pounds and figured out that spending the evening grazing ending up being a lot more calories than making an actual meal and eating it.

I still tried to keep it simple. One of the things about living in California's Central Valley was the amazing produce that was available. I'd gone back to Chicago to visit my mother one time after moving here and had been shocked at how awful all the fruits and vegetables in the grocery store looked. I was used to such an abundance at my fingertips. Shopping the farmer's market had become kind of a game for me. Pick up whatever was in season and figure out how to make a meal out of it.

Rayna, of course, always had shopped the farmer's market. Pretty much everything she fed her family was organic and fresh. She also usually had a list so she'd have whatever she needed for the meal plan she made every week on Sunday and carefully noted what she was cooking on which night on her calendar so she wouldn't forget, not that she ever would.

It was still overcast and cold. I'd changed back into jeans and boots and a sweater to meet Rayna. She had on an oversized sweater that had what looked like a mustard stain on the front. I didn't think I'd ever seen her with a stain on the front of her shirt. Food simply didn't dare to drop on her chest whereas the fronts of my shirts often looked like I was making a food-based Jackson Pollock reproduction. We hugged. I gave my chest a covert check after she turned around. The stain had looked dry and I'd suffer more than a mustard stain transfer for a friend like Rayna, but I didn't want to walk around with it either. We walked into the aisle between the white-topped tents piled with produce and flowers that now lined the street .

"How was the funeral?" she asked.

I picked up a bunch of asparagus. I could maybe grill it and put it on pasta. "Not as bad as I expected."

"Really? What changed? You're usually a mess after those." She picked up two bunches of asparagus and then put one back.

I told her about Malachi sitting next to me as I paid the young woman behind the table for the asparagus. I turned to walk away and then realized that Rayna wasn't beside me. I turned back around. She was standing by the table, mouth open, a gust of wind blowing her hair back.

"What?"

"You held hands with a man?" she asked, eyes open wide. "I think you should have led with that."

"We didn't hold hands. He put his hand on mine and it was . . . comforting." I felt a flush starting to creep up my neck, despite the chill in the air.

"This is the guy that was nice to Brady after Lillibeth was mean to him?" she asked finally walking away from the asparagus tent.

I nodded. No need to tell her the slightly snarky thing he'd said after Brady left. I wanted her to like him for some reason.

"At least someone was decent about the whole thing," she said as we walked on.

"Ignore Lillibeth. She's cranky with everyone," I said. I didn't add that it was possible that she was especially cranky with Brady because she didn't like me or anything about why Irma thought Lillibeth might not like me too much.

"She wasn't just cranky. She's made them stop letting Brady to come in to do his community service."

"I know. I'm so sorry." I guessed Brady hadn't told her about my role in the conversation with Dionne.

"They said something about the appearance of impropriety which was patently ridiculous. Now, of course, he has to find somewhere else to do his community service."

"I'll keep my eyes open."

She waved her hand. "Don't bother. No place is going to take him. Not with this hanging over his head."

"It's not like anyone else knows about it." Brady's name hadn't been mentioned in any of the news articles about Floyd's death, even if Eva had made it obvious to people who knew him.

She shook her head and looked away. "I wish. You should see some of the things that were posted on social media about Brady and some of the emails I've gotten." She quickened her step.

I trotted to catch up. "That bad?"

She bit her lip. "Hateful hateful things. Threatening things I'm not sure there's a social media platform where Eva hasn't said something mean that somehow casts suspicion on Brady." Rayna picked up her pace a bit and I trotted after her.

I sighed. It wasn't just people at Caring Hands and nosy people like Judy Gordon who were suspicious of Brady. A sinking feeling hit my gut. Even I had been suspicious. Hadn't I just been thinking about the possibility of Brady killing Floyd to cover up stealing fentanyl patches from Caring Hands the night before? If even I could have moments of suspicion, this would clearly follow Brady everywhere as long as he lived in Darby and maybe beyond. "Did you tell Sharon?" I asked.

"She said to stay off social media and ignore it." Rayna straightened her ponytail and tugged down her jacket and stalked off, leaving me to follow in her wake to the goat cheese booth. "It's not so easy when it's your kid."

Behind each stack of carefully wrapped cheese rounds was a photo of a goat in a little frame with their name. "Did those goats really give the milk for those specific cheese?" I asked.

If so, Wilma had produced the milk for the chèvre with dill, Eunice had produced the milk for the plain chèvre, and Lucinda the Saanen Goat had produced the milk for the chèvre with cranberries. I picked up the cranberry one. Lucinda was totally the cutest of the goats. She truly might be the GOAT of goats. That's how cute she was. There was something about her expression and the way her head was tilted. She looked like she was about to speak. It was a bit like the pose I'd chosen for Sugar Pop. It really got me.

"Absolutely. The goats are matched to their cheese," the young woman behind the table said.

Rayna shot me a look that plainly said she thought that was a load of BS. I bought it anyway. What harm could it do and Lucinda was really adorable. I tucked the cheese into the basket I carried. It'd be good in a salad alongside my asparagus and pasta.

We paused at a booth with samples of fresh strawberries. I tried one. It was early in the season and they weren't as sweet as they would be in a month. I started to walk on and the man behind the table said, "Hold on! Try this one." He held out another strawberry on a toothpick, his hand beneath it to keep it from falling. I shrugged and reached for it, our hands grazing as I took it from him. It was hard to tell how old he was. The wrinkles around his eyes could have come from age or from being out in the sun a lot. The hair at his temples was gray, but the rest of it was a dark blonde. He wore a light blue sweatshirt and jeans.

I popped the strawberry in my mouth. It was much sweeter. "What's the difference?"

He grinned. "Different field. It gets a bit more sun. What do you think?"

"Not bad." I picked up a pint. "How much?"

He stuck his hands in his jeans pockets and rocked back on his heels. "Two bucks."

The sign said four dollars. "What's wrong with them?"

"Nothing. Nothing. It made me happy to see you enjoy them."

I bought the strawberries and put them in my basket.

Rayna said, "I can't take you anywhere" as we walked away. I shrugged.

She picked up a bunch of broccoli at the next stand and then set it back down. "That's more than Brady and I can eat in a day or two."

"George won't eat it?"

"George isn't home. He went back out on the road."

My steps faltered with surprise. "How long is George gone for?" Maybe he'd be home soon. Maybe it was one last urgent trip.

"I don't know." Rayna set down the onion she was inspecting and moved on.

Now it was me that stopped walking, not sure what to say. Rayna motioned for me to keep going. "He had a presentation set up at a potential client's office and felt he had to go."

"Are you okay with that?"

"No, but there didn't seem much I could do about it. He cut the trip short by a day as a compromise. He'll be back early next week."

It didn't seem much like a compromise to me. I scrambled a bit to catch up. "Did you tell him you wanted him to stay?"

She shot me a look. "Of course I did, Leah. He said I was overreacting. That everything was going to be fine. That I was creating drama where there was none."

"You son was questioned in a murder investigation and someone tried to frame him by hiding a medication box in his locker!"

I got another look. "I'm aware of that, Leah. He pointed out that whoever tried to frame Brady did a poor job of it and that I should get over it and . . . ." Her words trailed off.

"And what?"

"And that maybe I should get a job or something so I didn't have to manufacture things for excitement." She didn't look at me as she said it.

Ouch. "You have a job," I said.

"Oh, yeah? What's that?" She laughed, but not in a way that sounded like she found anything funny.

"You know what it is. You keep your family together. You keep the house functioning and running smoothly." I was well aware of the many things that Rayna did that George probably never saw because I had to do all of them by myself. I saw Cynthia Norwood over by the strawberry stand. I waved to her and she started to wave back, but then lowered her hand and turned away. Weird.

Rayna waved my words away. "He's right, really. There's nothing we can do right now. We're in a holding pattern with what might happen to Brady, but not with the other parts of our lives. We'll still have the mortgage to pay and food to buy and now possibly legal help for Brady. We can't expect Sharon to do this pro bono if it goes forward. There's no point in him staying home to stew and worry. I'm doing enough of that for both of us and he can be home in a few hours if I need anything."

All of that was true and logical, but somehow didn't make a difference to my heart. Maybe all the love and support I'd seen in that hug he'd given her in my entryway didn't run all that deep. "Well, I'm right here if you need anything."

She reached out and took my hand. "I know and I appreciate it. Now distract me with stories about this new man-friend of yours with the special calming hands."

NINE

THE SALAD with Lucinda's goat cheese had been amazing. While I was eating it, it occurred to me that it would be fun to have a photo of each of our senior artists by their work when people came through the Spring Fling. I knew it made me want to buy more chèvre than I should have because Lucinda the Saanen Goat looked so darn pretty. Maybe someone would buy suncatchers because they liked the look of Yvette. She'd made four of them. Definitely more than one could expect her family to buy. And she was a cutie.

I spent Thursday finishing my portrait of Sugar Pop, putting in the last touches of highlights and deepening some of the shadows to make sure the eye was drawn to the coquettish cock of her head as she stood on her pillow, tiny front feet on the arm of the wicker chair. Credit goes to Lucinda again for really crystallizing for me what I was trying to get to in Sugar Pop's portrait.

Tamika phoned me at about ten-thirty.

"We might have a problem."

My heart sank. "Another one?" I thought this all was supposed to get easier.

"I don't know where one ends and another begins anymore." She sighed.

"Lay it on me." I set down my pastels to give her my full attention.

"Brady is supposed to be staying off social media, right?"

"Mmhmm. What's he posting?" She wouldn't have brought it up if he hadn't been.

"There's been some not so pleasant talk about him online. I think he might have created a fake profile and is posting some defense from that." I could hear the tap of her keyboard.

"How big a problem is it?"

She sighed again, bigger this time. "I'm not sure. It's why I'm calling you. If it is him – and that's still an if – he's mainly sticking up for himself. Even if the cops figured out it was him posting, I don't think there's anything here they could use against him."

So far, Brady had been uncharacteristically compliant. Maybe it would be better to let him have this one small outlet so he didn't totally explode. "Let's keep an eye on it. If it looks like it's going to be a problem, we can jump on it."

"Okay. That was my first thought, too. I didn't want to upset Rayna any more than we already have." There was more keyboard clicking. "He hasn't posted anything new since last night."

"I'm worried about Rayna. I'm not sure what else to do for her, though."

"I hear you. She wasn't wearing make-up on Saturday. I think it's the first time I've ever seen her without at least mascara and lip gloss."

I hesitated, but then said, "There was a stain on her shirt today at the farmer's market."

"On Rayna's shirt? This is getting bad, Leah."

"The sooner we clear Brady's name, the better off she'll be. She'll be able to put this all behind her." I put my pastels back in their box.

"We better get cracking, then."

———

On Friday, I got to Caring Hands a few minutes early to see if I could get a photos of people to put next to their artwork. Detective Park stood at the front desk talking to Christy when I came in. I waved and while she did look up briefly from inspecting her fingernails, she didn't wave back. Neither did he. As I went past, I thought I heard Christy say, "he just looked like a hooligan to me."

She didn't say Brady's name, but I had a feeling that was who they were talking about. I took a deep breath and opened the door to the basement. For a moment, I stood and looked down the dark stairs into the murkiness. I flicked on the light, but it was in the center of the downstairs area and cast almost no light onto the steps. Park and Christy had stopped talking and were both staring at me.

Fine. It was fine. I stepped down, holding tight to the banister and feeling it wobble a tiny bit. Cautiously, I went the rest of the way down. I hauled up the quilt and then went back down for the suncatchers. Then I made another trip for the clay pots. By the time I went down for the watercolors, I was practically skipping down the steps. What had I been so afraid of? They were fine. The wobble in the banister had clearly been my imagination.

Upstairs, I loaded my boxes onto a cart to take them

down to the multi-purpose room. Christy wasn't at the front desk, but Detective Park was standing in the lobby making notes. I opened my mouth to say something and he held up one hand to stop me. "I know," he said. "Brady is innocent."

"As long as we've got that straight," I said. As I went down the hall, I saw Lillibeth as she came through with a garbage can to empty into the Dumpster outside the back entrance. I stopped to watch her go, to see if maybe she would go through the trash, but Marty and Anna were walking out together and held the door to the unit open for me and I couldn't figure out how to loiter and watch Lillibeth without being weird. Plus, we needed to shut the door. Gladys scooted by, her babydoll once again covered with bandages, and no one wanted her to make a break for it. I turned to walk alongside her. "Did your baby get hurt again?" I asked.

She clutched the doll closer to her chest. "She's fine. In a day or two, she'll be like new." Then she darted off.

I went through all the crafts and made a list of everyone who'd done something for the fair, grabbed my digital camera and trotted off to take their photos.

I stopped in Tessie's room first and took a series of photos of her, then let her pick which one she'd want to represent her. She sighed. "All those wrinkles. Where did they come from?" She put her hand up to her cheek.

"Experience?" I suggested.

"That doesn't explain those chin hairs," she said peering more closely at the photo.

I pulled my handy tweezers out of my pocket. "Would you like some help with those?"

In reply, she leaned back her head to give me access to her chin. After I was done, I took another photo and didn't focus it quite as sharply. I showed it to her.

"Much better," she said. "Thank you."

"Not a problem. What are you up to for the rest of the afternoon?" I said as I gathered up my things.

"Staring at the walls, I suppose." She sounded disgusted.

Without Brady, no one seemed to be circulating the library cart or putting videos on the television by the nurses' station. "Do you want me to see if there are any good books in the lending library? Or a movie you could watch?"

She shook her head, tight little curls never moving an inch. "I want to play solitaire."

That seemed like an easy fix. "I'm sure there's a deck of cards around here somewhere. I'll go look."

"Don't bother." She held up her hands so I could see how much arthritis had buckled them. "I used to play on my phone and now they've taken it away."

She sounded so sad. There had to be a way to let her play solitaire without her being swindled. "Let me look into it. I'll see if there's anything we can do." I was sure there were handheld electronic solitaire games. Maybe I could find one and bring it to her. They couldn't be terribly expensive.

Bernard, Miriam, and Carmen were in their rooms and I snapped quick photos of them all. Yvette, however, was not in her room. Gabriel from Happy Blossoms was standing by her bedside table. He jumped as I walked in.

"Hi, Gabriel. What are you up to?" I asked.

"Checking to see if Yvette's flowers needed any water or anything." He shifted from foot to foot and then gestured at a bouquet that stood on her bookcase.

"That's a thing floral delivery people do?" No one had ever checked up on my floral deliveries. Of course, it had been a good long time since anyone had sent me flowers.

Maybe it was a thing now. There were lots of things that didn't used to be things that were things now that I didn't know about. Tyler generally managed not to roll his eyes as he explained them to me, but not always.

Gabriel shrugged and straightened the ball cap with the Happy Blossom logo he wore. "I don't know about other floral delivery people, but I do. The flowers make the people here so happy. I like to make 'em last as long as I can."

How nice. No wonder he was always around. It was extra service like that that made people recommend a small business. Maybe I was wrong about his crush on Christy. "That's really sweet."

"I thought I might have left some plant food here when I delivered the bouquet." He pointed at the bedside table next to him and did the foot shift thing again.

"Oh," I said. It hadn't occurred to me that he wasn't standing next to the flowers he was supposedly checking until that moment and that I'd seen that kind of shifting from foot to foot a few times before in my life. It had meant that Tyler either had to pee or there was something he was trying to keep me from seeing. Since Gabriel was a grown man, I assumed he could handle his own potty needs. What could he be hiding?

"What are you doing here?" he asked as if he was wondering the same thing about me.

"Hoping to snap a quick photo of Yvette for our display at the Spring Fling."

"She's at lunch." He took a step away from the bedside table with its "World's Best Grandma" mug.

I didn't want to leave the room until Gabriel did. Something about the way he kept shifting from foot to foot made me want to keep mine firmly planted on the ground. "She should be back any minute then. I'll wait."

"Well, okay then." Gabriel hitched up his trousers and headed out of the room. I heard him say, "Excuse me, Irma," as he walked out. I peeked out in time to see the back of her Jazzy Pride scooting around the corner.

———

It took a while, but I managed to get photos of everyone who had worked on crafts for the Spring Fling with their faces clean and their hair brushed. Shortly after, I shepherded my Clay Club through making miniature fruit replicas to make into refrigerator magnets. My next stop after Caring Hands was going to be back to Judy Gordon. I'd finished Sugar Pop's portrait and wanted to deliver it. I'd put the painting in my locker rather than leave it in my car. The odds of anyone breaking into my car and stealing it were vanishingly small, but I'd put enough hours into it that I felt uneasy leaving it out there exposed. I pulled it out as Camila and Malachi walked in together, their shift getting ready to end.

"What's that?" Camila asked as she took off the cardigan she wore over her scrubs to put it in her locker, draping it over the stack of books. Turns out Camila was the one with the poetry books in the locker I'd broken into to show Detective Park how worthless the locks were. Go figure.

"A painting of a friend's dog." I explained.

Camila turned, eyes lit up. "I love dogs. Can I see?"

I hesitated for a second and then shrugged. I didn't always like to show my work to random people. They could be surprisingly unkind from time to time and there was nothing like a nasty comment made in what the person always said was jest to take the wind completely out of my sails. I felt pretty good about the Sugar Pop portrait. I didn't want anyone to pee on my parade, but Camila seemed genuinely interested. "Sure. Why not?"

I put the portfolio down on the table, untied it, and opened it up. Then I unwrapped the painting and set it on the table.

Malachi laughed. It rumbled in his chest and set off some butterflies in my stomach. "The painting is beautiful, but that dog is hideous."

Camila gave a gasp and clasped her hands together under her chin, like a little angel in a Renaissance painting. "Blessings on thee, dog of mine, pretty collars make thee fine, sugared milk make fat thee! Pleasures wag on in thy tail —Hands of gentle motion fail nevermore, to pat thee!"

"Is that from the Bible?" Malachi asked.

Camila snorted and shook her head. "No. Elizabeth Barrett Browning. She wrote it to her dog Flush." She turned toward me. "You painted this, Leah?"

Malachi shifted to take a closer look at it. "It's really great. I feel like I know this dog from looking at your painting."

I flipped my hair back over my shoulder. "Thanks."

"It really is lovely," Camila said. "Who is it for again?"

"A woman I know. I do them on commission," I explained, wrapping the painting back up. And a few free-bies for friends. I was pretty certain all of my friends had a painting of a beloved pet who was either not with us anymore or simply wasn't quite as spritely. I'd done one for myself of Mr. Fluffbottom curled up in a basket in the sunlight. It was a nice way to remember them.

Malachi said. "People hire you to do these? That's pretty cool."

He sounded so proud of me. My shoulders straighten a bit.

"Do you think you could do one of my Jackie K?" Camila pulled out her phone and showed me a photo of a truly adorable Yorkshire Terrier.

"I absolutely could. Jackie K would be way easier to do a cute portrait of than Sugar Pop here." I pointed at the painting.

"Let's do it!" She clapped her hands. "What's the first step?"

"I'd like to see Jackie K in the flesh, or the fur, I guess. Maybe take some photos. Get to know him a little bit. A good portrait captures more than what a dog looks like." At least, I tried to capture more than what the dog looked like. A lot of it was in the way they interacted with people and that was hard to capture in a simple snapshot. There was also something about head tilts and paw placement that could be very ephemeral. It was best to spend at least a little time with my subjects.

"Could you come next Tuesday? Maybe around 4 p.m.?" Camila bounced on her toes.

Four o'clock the light could still be pretty harsh. "Could we make it a little later? That way we can get some good light. Maybe around six o'clock?"

"Absolutely." She practically skipped away.

"I think you might have a new best friend," Malachi said, pulling his leather jacket out of his locker, leaving a big duffel bag inside.

"You can never have too many of those." I wrapped the painting back up and put the portfolio back together.

"I wouldn't know."

A melancholy note in his voice made me look up. "You

don't have a BFF?" I asked. I knew I was lucky to have three, but the idea of not having any hadn't occurred to me.

He shook his head. "I guess I learned to keep myself to myself as I was growing up. Foster care will do that to a kid."

My eyes grew wide and a bit wet. "You were a foster kid?"

He nodded. "My father died when I was fourteen. Multiple sclerosis. My mom kind of checked out on me after that. There weren't any relatives to take me and it's not like anyone wants to adopt a fifteen-year-old." He shrugged. "It was only a few years."

I wanted to hug him so much that my arms twitched. "I'm so sorry. I didn't know."

"It's not exactly something you put on your resume and it was a long time ago." He shrugged into his jacket. "What about you? Where's your family?"

I fiddled with the string around the painting. "Back in Chicago. We're not . . . close."

"No? Why?" He sat down on the edge of the table.

"My dad took off when my sister and I were pretty little. My mom did her best, but . . . Well, her best wasn't always all that great." My sister and I were, in the most positive light, nuisances for my mom. In all fairness, she was pretty young. Only in her mid-twenties. And she definitely hadn't signed up to do the whole raising kids thing by herself. She wanted to go out and to have fun and little kids got in the way of that. When Travis died and I realized I was going to be a single mother not all that much older than she had been, I vowed to do it differently than my own mother did. Tyler would be my priority and would know that nothing was more important or interesting to me than him. I shrugged. I'm not sure if my mother understood it was an implied criticism of her or not, but she definitely found my choices questionable at best and it served to put an even bigger distance between us. "It's complicated."

"It always is." He straightened up, patted me on the shoulder and said, "See you around, Leah."

I watched him go, my heart beating a little faster than it should for someone who was standing still.

———

I pulled up to Judy Gordon's palatial estate and rang the bell. I was about to push the button again when the door opened. I supposed it took a while to get to the door from wherever she was in there. She looked like one of those 'Stars: They're Just Like Us' spreads of actresses in hundred-dollar sweatpants. Expensively, intentionally and artfully casual. "Oh, good, Leah. Come on in. I'm looking forward to seeing the finished product."

I winced. I didn't really like thinking of my artwork as a product, but I supposed that was what it was in this case. A product. Something I manufactured to order. A widget. "Great," I said, kicking off my shoes without being asked and putting them next to a pair of chunky-heeled shoes with bows that had me drooling with envy.

She led me back to the sunroom again where Sugar Pop still held court from atop her special pillow.

"So do they know who killed that friend of yours yet?" she asked, glancing over her shoulder.

"No." It seemed best to meet that directly.

"Oh. So it could still be anyone."

I knew exactly who she meant by anyone. I gritted by teeth and kept my mouth shut. I lay the wrapped portrait down and carefully unwrapped it.

It looked nice. I'd chosen to put Sugar Pop in bright

sunlight, blowing out part of her hair where it was particularly patchy. I'd deepened the purple color of her bow to bring out the warm hues of her coat and put a sparkle in her eyes that made the way they crossed a little less noticeable.

"Oh," Judy said, chewing on a thumbnail.

I looked from her to the portrait. "Oh?"

"Yes. Well, I thought it would be bigger."

"This is the size we agreed on, Judy. I'm sure I still have the emails where we discussed it." I was really sure I did and that I'd double-checked the dimensions we'd decided on before I started the final painting.

She waved her hand in the air. "Oh, I'm sure you're right. I just had it pictured as bigger in my head."

There wasn't a whole lot I could do about that now. I casually laid my invoice on the table next to the portrait.

Judy sucked her teeth. "That's quite a bit."

It was probably less than she'd spent on the pair of shoes I'd seen in the rack by the front door. "It's what we agreed on plus the framing costs, which we also discussed beforehand." My face flushed. Did she think I was overcharging her?

Judy tapped an index finger against her lower lip. "You have to admit it's a lot for something so small."

In my head I counted up the hours I'd spent taking the preliminary photos, doing the sketches, doing the actual portrait, and getting it framed. I was basically asking for about ten dollars an hour. That wasn't even minimum wage.

I sighed. "Fine, Judy. What do you think it's worth?"

Judy named a number that was about half of what we'd agreed on.

"That's not what you said in your emails when you asked me to take on this project." Heat rose up in my face.

She chewed on the side of her thumb. "I know. But that

was when I'd pictured it as bigger. I'm not sure I really want something this small." She took a step away from the table.

I considered my options. I could walk. I could pick up Sugar Pop's portrait, tuck it under my arm, and leave Judy with nothing. But then I'd be paid zero dollars per hour and I'd be stuck with a portrait of Judy Gordon's butt ugly dog. I closed my eyes and counted to ten. Then to twenty. Then thirty. Then I said, "Okay then."

Judy clapped her hands together. "I knew we'd come to an agreement."

Had we? Is that what we'd done? I was pretty sure I'd knuckled under. That wasn't the same thing, was it?

Judy wrote me a check that I damn sure was going to deposit on my way home, then walked me back to the front door. "It really is a lovely portrait, Leah. It's just kind of small. But, you know, I know a lot of people. I'll be sure to show it to everyone. It'll be great exposure for you."

I left feeling like I'd like to expose a few things to Judy.

I didn't, of course. I put my boots back on, got in my truck, and drove away. I was halfway home when my phone pinged. I glanced over to see what it was. My security system had sent an alert. The back door of my house had been opened.

＃ TEN

THE BACK DOOR. The one where someone would be out of view from the street and could spend a few minutes figuring out how to get in.

Maybe I'd forgotten to lock it. Maybe it had blown open.

Except I knew I hadn't. I knew I'd latched it and locked it.

Someone had opened the back door of my house. What should I do? My alarm system was what they call self-monitored. I got a message, but it didn't summon the cops or the fire department or emergency vehicles. I hadn't wanted to add the monthly fees for that to my already tight budget. I started to see the pointlessness of having it at all as I dithered over how to proceed while someone might be ransacking my house.

Calling the police seemed premature. What if I got home and it was truly the wind or a cat or a glitch in the system. How stupid would I feel? And if word got around to Detective Park about the hysterical woman who called the police when a stray cat bumped against her door and triggered her alarm system? How would I ever get him to take me seriously about Brady being innocent.

But what if I wasn't wrong? What if someone had broken into the house and was still there? I could already see the newspaper articles about the stupid woman whose alarm had gone off and had then waltzed into her house alone anyway. It would be like the scene in a horror movie where the heroine goes into the basement with the entire audience screaming at her to get out of the house. Why have an alarm system in the first place if you weren't going to be alarmed when it went off?

I was spinning in circles. I did what I usually did when I got myself in a twist. I called Rayna.

"The alarm went off at my house. Someone opened the back door," I said in a rush as soon as she answered.

"Where are you?"

"Driving home from Judy Gordon's."

"I'll meet you at your house in five minutes, right? Don't go in without me."

"Don't you either!" I didn't want Rayna to be the person in the newspaper article who had gone into the house she shouldn't have, either, and she had a key to my house, just like I had a key to hers. And to Tamika's and to Sharon's.

"I wouldn't dream of it," she said.

Rayna and Brady got to my house at almost the same moment I did. We met on the sidewalk. I gave her a questioning look. "He was desperate to get out of the house," she whispee red.

I could understand that. Brady had basically been on house arrest for a week. The three of us looked at the house. All the lights were on. The wind gusted, making me shiver. Rayna reached down and took my hand and Brady moved to stand between us and the house as if his thin frame would be some kind of barrier.

"I'm not sure I've heard of anyone breaking into a house and turning on all the lights," Rayna said. "Aren't you supposed to be stealthy during a B&E?"

"Lights on in a house aren't suspicious. A flashlight beam playing around is," Brady said, sounding authoritative.

Rayna and I exchanged a worried glance. He must have noticed our silence because he turned to look at us then held up his hands in front of himself. "I've been watching a lot of true crime shows while I'm stuck at home. I'm not speaking from experience."

Good to know. We all turned back to look at the house. "What do your crime shows tell you about situations like these?"

"That you should call the police." Yet he took a step toward the house.

A shape passed in front of one of the windows. I grabbed Rayna's arm and she clutched me back. "Whoever it is, is still there," she whispered.

Then the door opened. "Mom, are you going to stand out on the sidewalk or come in?"

———

"I thought you were a burglar!" I smacked Tyler's arm once we got inside. "I almost called the police."

"I'm glad you called my mom instead," Brady said. "Better only one of us is involved with the cops."

Everyone froze.

"Oh, come on," Brady said. "That was a little bit funny, wasn't it?"

"NO," Rayna and I said in unison.

"I wanted it to be a surprise," Tyler said, looping an arm around my shoulders. "I thought it would be fun. I forgot about the security system."

"Fun as a heart attack," I muttered, and then relenting, put my arm around his waist and squeezed. "It's good to see you."

He'd grown since he left for school. He'd been taller than me since the tenth grade, but now I tucked under his arm. I gazed up at him. He needed a haircut and his clothes needed a wash, but he looked wonderful to me. He was only a few years younger than his dad had been when I'd met him and I could see so much of Travis in him that it hurt sometimes. The shape of his eyes and the cowlick on the back of his head were all directly from his father. There was more, though. There was something about how he held himself, something about the way he paused before making a decision, something about how he approached the world that had to be genetic. I squeezed him tight. "Really really good to see you."

He squeezed me back. "That's more like it." Then he turned to Brady. "Wanna play some video games?"

"Dude, I can so beat your ass in League of Legends. I have had wayyyyy too much practice."

The boys headed to Tyler's room and Rayna and I went into my kitchen. "Distract me," she said. "What's new?"

I pulled mugs out of the cupboard. "Judy Gordon ended up paying me about half of what she agreed for that portrait of Sugar Pop."

"What?" Rayna asked, clearly offended. "She stiffed you after making you look at her ugly dog for hours on end?"

"She said it would give me good exposure."

"That really burns my toast." Rayna almost never swore. She seemed to always have a ready supply of things like burn my toast, and oh, shoot, and shut the front door, and cheese and rice.

It wasn't how I would have put it, but I knew what she meant. "My toast feels burned, too, but I didn't feel like I had much choice. It was either take what she was offering or get paid nothing for looking at her ugly dog for hours on end."

"It sets a bad precedent. You shouldn't let people do that to you," Rayna said. "You're worth more. Maybe you should have gone with the nothing and taken the portrait with you."

I looked out the kitchen window toward the street as I filled the kettle for tea. A light went on in a car parked across the street, a few feet down from where Rayna had parked her Rav4. No one got out, though. I peered closer. It was some kind of four-door sedan. Maybe gray. It was hard to tell in the dark. The silhouette inside the car looked familiar.

"Is that Detective Park?" I asked.

Rayna came over to stand next to me. "I'm not sure. Is that a Chevy? I've been seeing a Chevy with tinted windows I didn't recognize parked in our neighborhood lately. There was one parked next to my car when Brady and I went grocery shopping, too. I hadn't realized it was such a popular car."

The light in the car went out and whoever was in it, pulled away from the curb and drove away.

———

Saturday morning, Rayna suggested we walk to Espresso Yourself rather than drive. My jeans weren't getting any looser so it seemed like a good enough idea.

I left a note for Tyler who was still asleep and walked over to her house through the park, skirting the edge of the swimming pool and the climbing wall. I trailed my hand through a hedge of rosemary, enjoying the herby smell it released into the cool morning air.

Rayna looked like she hadn't slept. Or maybe hadn't taken off her mascara the night before. Come to think of it, it didn't look like her hair had been brushed either. It had kind of a rat's nest in back the way Tyler's used to when he insisted on combing his own hair and would only comb what he saw in the mirror. I waved to Eva as I went by, but didn't stop to chat. She seemed to always be out working on her yard whenever we walked by. She must trim the hedges with a nail scissor. Rayna very pointedly did not wave, but did wave at her neighbor Monique who was out in her front yard playing with her little boy Jack. Playing might not be the right word. Chasing might be a little more accurate. Monique grabbed him by the strap on the back of his overalls right as he started to climb the trellis she'd set up for a climbing rose. He squirmed at first, then stopped and planted a big wet baby kiss on her nose. She laughed and hugged him close.

My heart did a wee clutch. Those days were gone for me. No more baby kisses. No more climbing into my lap. No more little sticky hands clutching mine. The boys were basically men now. Men with problems much larger than a potential stick from a rose thorn.

"You might not want to antagonize Eva," I said quietly as we walked on.

"Why not? She's done everything but actually broadcast

Brady's photo on a Wanted poster, right?" Rayna picked up her pace a little. "Why doesn't she have to consider not antagonizing me?"

It was a good question and one I didn't have an answer to.

"I mean," she went on, jabbing at the button for the cross walk like she might shove it all the way through the utility pole. "Why is it always the nice people who have to suck it up? Why is it always the person who hasn't done anything wrong that needs to smooth things over or to apologize or to rise above? Why do we always have to suffer the pain of going high when they suffer nothing for going low?"

"I'm not sure," I mumbled.

"Why doesn't Judy Gordon who, frankly, probably spends more on underwear than you spend on food and shelter, feel bad about stiffing you out of what is pocket change for her but makes a difference in whether or not you can cover your mortgage?" The light turned and she struck off across the street, glaring at someone in an SUV whose front end had come a little too close to the line. "Why do you have to accept less than what you agreed on and why are you the one expected to keep things calm and peaceful?"

It took me a few steps to come up with something to say. "Because we care about what's right? Because we want to be good people? Because we have consciences?"

"Why don't they?" Bitterness tinged her words. Then she repeated the same question, but just sounded sad. "Why don't they?"

We finished our walk to Espresso Yourself in silence. We stepped into the coffeeshop and Rayna and I waved to Tamika and Sharon and ordered our coffees. Or tried to. Rayna gave her order, paid, and went to sit with Tamika and

Sharon. The cashier's eyes were already on the guy behind me when I got up the register. "Non-fat sugar-free mocha," I said.

"Huh?" She looked at me as if I'd appeared out of nowhere.

I repeated my order.

"Oh, right. Large mocha," she said.

"Non-fat. Sugar-free," I repeated.

"Of course," she said. I handed her my money and she gave me the change, but was clearly already focused on the dreamboat behind me. I left her to it and went over to sit with everyone else. I didn't need her attention. I needed my coffee.

"Leah let Judy Gordon stiff on her Sugar Pop portrait," Rayna announced to the group as we sat.

"No, Leah," Tamika said.

Sharon groaned and shook her head and said, "Astonishing. Just astonishing."

I shrunk down a bit in my chair. "She didn't stiff me. She just didn't pay what we agreed to."

Tamika cocked her head to one side. "Isn't that kind of the definition of stiffing you?"

"Why would Judy want a portrait of that butt ugly dog, anyway? She's not even one of those so-ugly-it's-cute puppies," Sharon said.

"That's kind of Judy's call, isn't it? And if she wants to pay me to paint Sugar Pop so she can remember her in her prime . . ." My words trailed off.

There was a second of silence. I don't think any of us had escaped having a pet die. Even the ones we were relieved were gone – Tamika and Jamal's geriatric cat hadn't used the litter box reliably for two years before he went – were mourned and missed.

Finally, Sharon spoke again. "That reminds me. Could you make me one of those dog toys you make? The ones from old T-shirts?"

The soft T-shirts I use make the toys particularly good for old dogs, which Beau most certainly was at this point. "Of course. I probably have a few stashed away."

"Thanks. I need something to distract Beau. He lies in the doorway of Max's room half the day, like he's making sure he won't miss it if Max comes home."

"Oh. That's sweet." And sad. I could imagine their aging Labrador sprawled on the floor waiting for his boy to come back.

"Yeah. I know. I'll pay you for it."

I wasn't that hard up for money. "Nope. It's a gift from me to Beau."

Rayna shook her head. "Well, you shouldn't let that portrait be a gift from you to Judy. She should pay you what you're worth. You wouldn't let anyone do that to Tyler. You wouldn't let them do it to Brady or Max or Jayden, either. How come you can stand up for other people, but never stand up for yourself?"

"I stand up for myself."

Sharon snorted.

"Coffee for Rhiannon," the barista sang out and Rayna got up to retrieve her drink.

"Still going for the low profile?" Tamika asked, when she sat back down.

"For what good it does with Eva posting about me and my family every chance she gets." Rayna flung herself back into her chair.

I was happy for the change in subject. I didn't want to talk about Judy or the Sugar Pop portrait. Rayna was right (not unusual). I wasn't sure why I was the one who had to feel bad about it, but I did.

"We thought we saw Detective Park outside my house last night when Rayna and Brady came over. She thought she might have seen the same car at her house and at the grocery store. What's up with that?" I asked. I glanced over my shoulder as if Park might be there behind me and instead saw the guy who'd been behind me in line was picking up his coffee and thanking the barista. "I heard him interviewing Lillibeth about Brady at Caring Hands earlier this week and I think he was talking to Christy, the receptionist, about him, too. Shouldn't he be looking for actual evidence instead of just hounding Brady?"

Rayna took a sip of her coffee and must have realized I didn't have anything. "You ordered a coffee, right?"

I nodded and gave another furtive glance at the cashier who was inspecting her split ends.

"Oh, for Pete's sake, Leah." Rayna got up and marched over to the counter. She said something and pointed at me and the young woman looked up. I waved. She looked at me as if she had never seen me before. Rayna leaned in and the girl scurried off. Rayna stalked back over and plopped herself down.

"Thanks," I said.

She waved my thanks away. "That actually felt pretty good." She sat up a little straighter in her chair.

"It wouldn't be surprising if the police were keeping track of Brady's movements and taking statements. He is still a person of interest as far as they're concerned," Sharon said, going back to the earlier topic.

"Are there any other persons of interest?" Tamika asked.

Sharon shook her head. "Not that they're sharing with me."

It didn't seem like Detective Park was asking questions about anyone else. "Then we should give them some," I said, leaning forward.

"Maybe they're stuck. There doesn't seem to be a reason for anyone to kill Floyd. I know they've checked his financials and done some basic background checks," Sharon said.

"Well, someone had a reason. Not only to kill Floyd, but also to try to frame Brady for it," Tamika said as she took a small bottle of lotion from her bag and smoothed it on her hands.

That chilled me. Whoever would have done that would have had to have an awful lot of knowledge about the people at Caring Hands and how things worked around there. That meant that it was highly likely that it was someone I knew, at least in passing. I shuddered. I'd been around a murderer, one willing to throw suspicion on a kid who already had plenty of trouble. What else might someone like that be willing to do? It didn't bear thinking about.

Sharon had pulled her legs up crisscross applesauce and started to stroke the end of her braid. "Rather than trying to figure out who would want to get rid of Floyd, maybe we should think about who has it in for Brady? Or at least dislikes him enough to try to put the blame on him?"

"Lillibeth," Rayna and I said in unison.

"Do we know why she has it in for Brady?" Sharon sat forward.

"I don't think she likes any of the kids who come through doing community service and Irma said it might be partly because of his association with me." I felt the color coming up in my cheeks.

"Why would that make a difference?" Tamika asked.

I got even pinker.

"Girl, do you have dirt that you are not sharing?" She poked me with the toe of her Skechers.

"I don't know if it's dirt. It's just . . . Irma thinks Malachi, the physician's assistant, might be a little interested in me and that Lillibeth is interested in him so . . ." I wasn't sure how to finish that sentence.

"Wait. A man? Are you interested back in him?" Tamika and Sharon both sat up straighter.

"She held hands with him." Rayna waggled her eyebrows.

"We didn't hold hands," I protested. "He put his hand over mine during the funeral service. It was a compassion thing, not a romantic thing." But then there'd been that hand at the small of my back as we'd walked to our cars. That had felt like more than compassion. And that moment of connection in the employee lounge. And that moment when we'd talked about bullies and how much we hated them.

"Do you want it to be a romantic thing?" Tamika asked, rubbing her hands together.

Did I? He was handsome. He was kind. He was smart and employed. I was single and Tyler wasn't at home anymore. He didn't need me the same way he had back when he was a little kid. "I don't know. It's been so long since I've gone down that road. I'm not sure I recognize the signs anymore."

"Well, tell us about them."

"My heart beats a little too fast when he's around. I get a funny feeling in my stomach when he laughs and I keep flipping my hair when I talk to him." I put my face in my hands. I knew what that sounded like.

Tamika clapped her hands together. "Love! Leah is in love!"

"Probably more like lust," Sharon said. "Seriously, it's been a long time since she's gotten some."

"She isn't the only one," Rayna said. Before I could ask her to elaborate, she pushed on. "Okay. So Lillibeth might not like Leah, but why on earth would she murder Floyd?"

"What do we know about her?" Tamika asked.

I knew she used to be an emergency room nurse and that she liked turkey sandwiches with coleslaw for lunch and that her hair was always perfect. "Not much."

"Allow me," Tamika said and starting tapping away at her smart phone. It was only a few seconds before she said, "Hmmm."

"What?"

"I'll text you all the links." She hit a few more buttons and all our phones pinged at once. I opened the first link. It was from a Bay area newspaper.

The headline read "Hero Nurse Saves Toddler at Shopping Mall." A photo of Lillibeth, hair dripping wet, but with a huge smile on her face accompanied the article. A two-year-old had been playing by the fountain at the Del Monte Mall when he slipped into the water. The father had turned away for only a moment, but that moment was more than enough. Lillibeth saw the child floating face down in water as she came down the escalator. She pulled the baby out of the fountain and performed CPR. According to the article, a paramedic at the scene said, "It's difficult to do CPR on someone so small without hurting them. Ocampo did an amazing job with both her quick thinking and her gentle touch."

The next article read "Passing Nurse Saves Electrocution Victim." Fifty-eight-year-old Cristina Cross had fallen onto the BART tracks and the electrified third rail next to them after becoming dizzy and disoriented due to complications from diabetes. Lillibeth had been waiting for the same train. She'd jumped down and despite receiving a shock herself was able to move Cross off the rail and start CPR while other people alerted the stationmaster to stop the train and turn off the electricity to the track. "I owe her my life," Cross had said about Lillibeth. "I owe her everything."

She'd also done CPR on a seventy-eight-year-old man who'd had a heart attack while on a recumbent bike at the gym. Lillibeth had been on an elliptical on the other side of the gym and had seen slump over. The man's wife told the reporter that Lillibeth should be given a special medal for what she'd done.

"Wow. That's a lot of opportunities to do CPR on people," Sharon said, looking up from her phone.

Tamika pointed at her. "And those are just the ones that come up on a quick internet search."

"She mentioned doing CPR on people at Floyd's funeral and about how grateful they always were." I tore the sleeve off my coffee cup and folded it in half and then in half again. "And Malachi said she was mad that he hadn't allowed her to do CPR on Floyd." I paused. "And Harvey Cornish."

"Interesting." Sharon jotted down some notes in her phone.

"She worked in an Emergency Department before she came to Caring Hands. That's a big change," I said. Stuff happens fast in emergency rooms. Everything is at a high level of intensity. Nothing was at a high level of intensity at Caring Hands. Everything moved pretty slowly.

"So she's taken a job considerably less exciting than her old one. She misses that excitement. She's gotten a lot of attention and praise for performing CPR on people and they won't let her do CPR at the new job," Sharon mused.

"She could try to create situations that were more exciting. Opportunities to perform CPR. That kind of thing," Tamika said, leaning forward and lowering her voice.

"Why does everyone think we all want excitement?" Rayna asked, clearly thinking about her conversation with George. I cast a sympathetic glance her way and she gave me a resigned shrug.

"How? How would she create excitement?" Sharon asked, also leaning forward and getting quieter.

I chewed on that for a moment. "Floyd died from an overdose of fentanyl. Not a heart attack. Maybe she's using drugs to create these situations and Malachi stopped her from finishing what she started with both Harvey and Floyd."

"It takes more than CPR to bring someone back from a fentanyl overdose," Rayna said.

She had a point. "It takes naloxone or something like that," I said.

"How hard would it be for a nurse to get hold of that?" Sharon asked.

"Not hard." Tamika chimed in. "They're practically begging medical professionals to carry it around with them at all times." She held up her phone again so we could see a headline about naloxone on the screen. She could seriously Google anything faster than anyone else. If there was ever an Olympic Googling team, Tamika would be the star player.

"What about getting the fentanyl in the first place, though? How would she get that? It's pretty well-regulated,"

Sharon asked. "I would think there'd be a fuss if any had gone missing at Caring Hands."

"It might take her a while to get enough to almost kill someone, but I think I know how she might get it at Caring Hands without anyone noticing." I explained about watching Malachi dispose of Javis's patch and how he'd said some of the nurses threw them away instead of disposing of them properly.

"Wait." Sharon held up her hand. "The only reason anyone knew that Floyd had been killed rather than slipping away during his morning nap was because Lillibeth made a fuss. Why would she call attention to it?"

I sat with that one for a while then said, "Malachi said something about it really being Lillibeth who should have found Floyd or, at the very least, the one who should have been called when Brady found Floyd, that it had been a fluke that Malachi had gotten there before Lillibeth."

Sharon made a rolling motion with her hand. "Explain, please."

"Brady was stocking the library cart, but Adriana started taking off her clothes in the library and Lillibeth had had to go convince her to keep her pants on. Brady left while Lillibeth was still getting Adriana back to her room and went to Floyd's room. If Lillibeth hadn't had to help Adriana, she would have gotten to Floyd before Brady did as she made her rounds. Lillibeth should have been the one to find Floyd."

"So?" Tamika said.

Now I rubbed my hands together. "Work with me here. What if Lillibeth intended on getting there and resuscitating Floyd for the thrill and the excitement and the accolades, but then Brady got there and called for help and Malachi got there first. Maybe she was worried Malachi would notice something that could get her in trouble like the injection site. Maybe she decided to preemptively cast suspicion on someone else before it could be cast on her."

"And Brady stumbled right into it." Rayna dropped her head.

If that was the case, yes he had. Like he always seemed to do somehow. I reached over and took her hand and gave it a squeeze. She squeezed back.

"That's pretty diabolical," Tamika said.

"More diabolical than killing people so you can resuscitate them?" Sharon asked.

"No. Not more diabolical than that. That's pretty much peak diabolical." Tamika offered Sharon her bottle of lotion as if it was a prize for making a good point.

"So what do we do with this information? It's a big jump from someone getting attention for doing CPR to killing people for the jolt of bringing them back," Sharon said.

"We need something more," Rayna said. "We need some kind of proof."

"I'll keep an eye out to see if anything seems suspicious," I volunteered.

"No," Sharon said. "Do not keep an eye on Lillibeth or show the police how to break into lockers or, well, anything else. Keep your nose out of it. Let them do their job."

"Well, that's the problem. Are they doing their job? Are they looking for who actually killed Floyd or are they looking for ways to pin it on Brady?" I asked. "Or maybe they think if they leave it alone for long enough it will go away and that Floyd was an old man who was already close to the end and no one really cares. Except . . ."

"Except what?" Sharon asked.

Rayna said, "Except it will never go away for Brady. We

all know it was someone else, but unless we figure out who that someone else is, Brady will always be under a cloud of suspicion. If not officially, then behind his back and that will be just as harmful. He'll never be able to put this behind him."

"So if it is Lillibeth, how are we going to prove it?" Tamika asked.

I had no idea. Not even a scintilla of one.

———

I could hear Brady and Tyler before I even opened the door. Their voices were deeper now, but the cadences were still the same. If I shut my eyes, maybe it would take me back to those days when they were two sweet little ten-year-olds and our biggest problems were being on time for school and outgrowing soccer cleats faster than I could buy them rather than who was a suspect in a murder investigation.

I poked my head into Tyler's room where the noise was coming from. They sat side by side on bean bag chairs on the floor, each clutching a controller, swaying as if by moving their bodies they could get the cars they were controlling on the screen to move faster or take the turns better. The floor was covered with empty glasses and dishes with a splayed-open paperback copy of John Le Carre's *Tinker, Tailor, Soldier, Spy* on top of it. all I picked it up. "Who's reading this?" I asked.

Brady raised one hand from his controller, but didn't take his eyes of the screen. "I'd started reading it to Floyd. I thought it was going to be lame, but it was actually kind of cool. I wanted to finish it. I asked Malachi and he said it was okay for me to take it home to read it as long as I brought it back. It's all about these old-timey spies from before there were cell phones or email or anything. They had to really live by their wits. Floyd loved that stuff."

"And now you do, too?" I asked.

Brady blushed and shrugged. "Yeah. No. I guess so. Floyd made it hella fun. He used to talk about where he'd put a dead drop and stuff like that. He made it kind of come alive."

"What's a dead drop?"

"One person would hide something in a predetermined place, a public place, but like in a corner or something where no one would think to look. Then they'd send a signal to the other person to look there. That way they could exchange stuff without ever meeting up," Brady said.

I smiled and ruffled his hair. He was too old for hair ruffling, but I couldn't help myself. Brady and Floyd had truly become friends, sharing interests and books. He had a good heart, that kid.

I left them to their game and went to the kitchen. I felt like baking something. Not because I felt stressed, but because I felt happy. It was good to have my boy home, to hear his voice in the other room, even to smell his stinky sneakers in the hallway. My cell phone rang with a number I didn't recognize as I pulled out mixing bowls and flour and sugar and cocoa. I let it go to voicemail and started creaming butter and sugar. I'd just popped the brownies in the oven when Tyler and Brady came into the kitchen filling the room with their enormous feet and boisterous energy.

"We're going to play basketball," Tyler announced.

I glanced out the window. It was highly California out. Sunny and warm. "Put on sunscreen and maybe take some water."

"Mommmmmm," Tyler said.

I held up my hands. "Sorry. I know you're grown-up.

You decide on whether to have water and sunscreen all by yourself. You're not too grown-up for brownies, are you? Maybe I should have checked before I made them."

"I hope I'm never too old for brownies." He filled up two water bottles, grabbed the sunscreen, and kissed my cheek and then they were gone.

I pulled out my phone to set the timer for the brownies and saw that I had a voicemail. It must have been from that call I ignored. I pressed play.

"Hello, Leah. My name is Sandra Roebuck. I'm a friend of Judy Gordon's and I just got back from her house. That portrait you did of Sugar Pop is brilliant. Brilliant! Would you be available to paint a portrait of our bunny? Call or text me at this number and let me know!"

Maybe Judy had been right. Maybe giving her the portrait of Sugar Pop at a discount would end up working out for me. If I got a few commissions that paid full price, it would more than make up for the discount I'd given her. Maybe I didn't need to get angry and stand up to her after all. Keeping the peace might pay off, although that look of satisfaction on Rayna's face when she struck terror into the barista's heart seemed appealing, too. I didn't want to call back right away, though. No need to look desperate.

I went to Tyler's room to pick up some of the detritus the boys had left. The spy book still sat on top of the heap. I picked it up to set it aside and a piece of paper fluttered out. It was only a folded piece of note paper that Brady must have been using as a bookmark, but it made me pause. I hadn't seen the piece of paper until I picked the book up and I wouldn't have unless I had. It would be easy to slip a folded-up Fentanyl patch or two or three into a book and walk out with it with no one thinking twice about it the way no one thought twice about seeing Lillibeth take the trash out.

What if Floyd had thought twice, though? What if with their interest in spy stories and dead drops, Floyd had realized what Brady was doing and confronted him?

I looked around. The boys wouldn't be back for at least a half an hour. I turned the book upside down, fanned out the pages, and gave it a good shake, feeling horrible that I had even thought to check. Nothing fell out, of course. Even if Brady had been using books to smuggle out patches, he wouldn't have been dopey enough to leave them in there and carry them around. No. What I really discovered by doing that was that even I wouldn't totally believe that Brady had nothing to do with Floyd's death until we found out who had really done it.

ELEVEN

MONDAY MORNING, I dropped Tyler at the Amtrak station for the trip back to Santa Barbara with a bag stuffed full of sandwiches and cookies.

"Mom, I'm only going to be on the train for a few hours and they have a dining car." He looked at the bag doubtfully. We stood side by side on the platform. Bees buzzed around the flowering rosemary that spilled over the edge of the planters dotted around.

"A dining car with overpriced junk food." I shook the bag at him.

"Mommmmmmmm," he said.

"Don't argue. Just take the food." I shoved it into his arms, then the train came and with a kiss on my cheek, he was gone, disappearing into the sliding door.

I stood on the platform and watched the train pull out, feeling that odd pang of bittersweet sadness that stabbed me each time he went. This had been what I wanted for him, what I'd worked toward for him. I was so happy for him.

I just wished I didn't feel so damn sad for myself.

At least this time I didn't feel like I wasn't sure what to

do with myself. I had to get to work. For myself and for Brady.

I make a quick call to Sandra Roebuck about her bunny.

"Thank you for calling me back. I just loved that painting you did of Sugar Pop. So cute!"

"Thank you. I'm glad you liked it. You were interested in me painting a rabbit?" I asked.

"Yes. Our bunny Cinna."

Cute. Cinna Bunny. I hoped the rabbit was as cute as its name. "What size portrait were you interested in?"

"The same as Judy's portrait of Sugar Pop."

Hmmm. Someone seemed a little too anxious to do things like Judy did. I told her my usual price for that size portrait.

There was a pause. "Oh," she said. "Judy said she paid quite a bit less for hers."

So much for Judy's discount paying off for me. "What were you hoping to pay?"

She named the exact same price as Judy. Once again I did the mental calculations. I'd still make some money after buying the canvas and paints. It was only my time and what was I doing with it anyway these days. We made an appointment for me to meet Cinna and I went to Caring Hands.

———

The street in front of Caring Hands is lined with oleander bushes. In the past few days they had burst out with pink and white flowers. The air had changed, too. The slight bite of winter chill was gone. I stood by my truck and waited a second, trying to center myself in the moment the way our yoga teacher was always trying to get us to. I inhaled a deep breath of the perfumed air and headed inside.

There's a clipboard that hangs in the employee lounge at Caring Hands with everyone's schedule. I took a quick glance at it when I got it in. Lillibeth wasn't on it for the day. As I put my purse and jacket into my locker, I eyed hers. I could easily bump it open and take a peek inside. No one else was in the break room.

I opened the door to the hallway and looked up and down. No one was coming or going. Everything was quiet. I shut the door and gave Lillibeth's locker the hip check, shoulder shove, and yank combo and it popped open to reveal . . .

Nothing. Well, not nothing, but nothing interesting.

I wasn't sure what it was I expected to find. Maybe newspaper clippings about her heroic efforts all tacked up with red string between them. Maybe a list of people with Harvey and Floyd at the top of it. Maybe a photo of Brady with exes over his eyes.

If I'd thought about it I should have expected to find exactly what I did find. It was like a collection of all the things my friends and I kept in our purses. Some ibuprofen, some lip gloss, a comb, some tissues, a couple of protein bars, and a bottle of lotion, except Lillibeth's were all generics or store brands. It was like she had to be all of us rolled into one and she had to do it on a budget. I eased the door shut, clicking it closed as Malachi breezed in. I jumped away from the locker, startled. My heart pounding. Had he seen me closing the locker door? Or had it been all the way shut when he came in?

"Hi, Leah." A frown creased his brow. "Are you okay?"

"Sure," I said, too quickly. "Absolutely fantastic. You?"

He looked back and forth between me and Lillibeth's locker, his eyes narrowing. "You sure?"

I nodded — again too fast — feeling like a bobblehead. "Totally sure. Totally fine."

He sat down in one of the plastic chairs and leaned back. "Uh huh. Sure you are. What's really going on?"

We barely knew each other and he could already read me so well. I sighed and sat down across from him. "How long have you worked with Lillibeth?"

His brow creased. "Ocampo? She started here about the same time I did a little over six months ago, but we didn't really start working together until I switched to days."

"When was that?" I asked.

"Maybe three weeks ago." He crossed his arms over his chest.

That wasn't a lot of time, but he had such a good grasp of character and could read people so well. Maybe he would have noticed if there was something off about her. "What's she like?"

"What do you mean?" He moved back a bit from me.

"I mean, what's she like to work with?" I pressed.

He loosened his arms. "I think you know the answer to that as well as I do. She's got a bit of a hair trigger, but her heart's in the right place."

"Is it? Are you sure about that?" I leaned forward.

"What is it that you're really asking me about, Leah?" he asked.

"I was thinking about what you said at Floyd's funeral about Lillibeth. About how she would have resuscitated Floyd if she'd gotten there before you." I ran the side of my thumbnail along the edge of the table, not quite wanting to meet his eyes.

Malachi leaned forward toward me. "Lillibeth wouldn't

be the first nurse to be fast with CPR. Usually that's considered to be a good thing. Just not here."

"Has she resuscitated anyone else here?" I asked.

He looked up at the ceiling as he thought. "Yeah. I think so. There was Connor Hammad. He was a short-timer, here to recover from a hip replacement."

I picked at the peeling veneer of the table. "Did he have a DNR?"

"No. I don't think so. If he had, there would have been some trouble. Plus he wasn't a candidate for one. He didn't have any other health problems besides the bum hip." He pushed back in his chair and stretched his legs out in front of him, crossing them at the ankle.

"If the only problem was his hip, why did he have a heart attack?" That seemed strange. Unless someone was so desperate to do CPR they made sure they would have a chance to do it.

"It happens, especially during that first month after surgery," Malachi said. "They're not sure why. Hip replacements and knee replacements both raise the chance of having a heart attack. Hips are worse than knees, but only by a little."

So no one would be suspicious if someone who had had a hip replacement had a heart attack, the way Malachi didn't seem the least bit suspicious right now. "And Lillibeth was the one to find him and to resuscitate him?"

"Yes."

"Has anybody else been resuscitated since you've been here?" I asked.

He looked up toward the ceiling again, then shook his head slowly. "Not that I can think of. It's not that common around here."

"Hmmm." The only person to have been given CPR in

the past few months had been given it by Lillibeth. She tried to give it to two other people, but Malachi stopped her. I looked out the window at the courtyard, at the empty tables where no one seemed to sit anymore since Floyd was gone and Brady wasn't allowed back in, at the bird of paradise plants bobbing in the breeze like they were dancing for an audience that forgot to show up.

"What are you thinking, Leah?" Malachi asked.

I shook my head. "I don't know."

"Well, let me know when you do know." He stood up and brushed off his hands on his scrubs.

I glanced up at the clock and jumped up. I was going to be late. "Talk to you later?"

"I'm counting on it." He smiled and damned if I didn't flip my hair. I walked down the hall to Watercolor Society with a little bounce in my step.

Watercolor Society was somewhat smaller than my general crafting group, the clay club and the yarn circle. Not everyone had the manual dexterity to wield a brush or the patience to work in watercolor. Arthritis. Parkinson's. Essential tremors. They could all cause shaking that made it really hard to control where your paint went. Watercolor Club ended up being a pretty select set of residents. It was nice to have a small group, though. I felt more like I was actually helping people express themselves rather than just trying to keep anyone from hurting themselves.

Our goal was to do sets of small watercolors that I would turn into greeting cards to be sold at the Spring Fling. I set up the still life we'd work from that day. A half-peeled orange, some daisies, a silver teapot, and an egg. Darlene Robson, Marlene Eyles, Bryan Mason, Hannah Sutton, and Mohammed Cartlidge filed in and I set each one up with a small travel watercolor kit and some extra brushes.

"It looks a little sparse, doesn't it?" Hannah said.

She wasn't wrong. I wasn't sure what to do about it, though.

"We could add some more flowers," Mohammed suggested. "Flowers are always nice."

"Betty usually gets flowers from her kids at the start of the month. They should still be fresh." Marlene sat down and added some water to the dry cakes of color in her tray.

"I'll go look." Who else had I seen with flowers? Tessie had had a nice bouquet in her room awhile back. They'd be a little wilted, but that would just make them more interesting to paint. Maybe she'd be ready to part with a few of them. Miriam had some kind of plant by her front door and I'd seen Gabriel coming out of Betty's room not too long ago so she probably had flowers, too. My steps faltered a little. Tessie, Miriam, Betty. Wasn't that the same list of people Camila had told me had been scammed? How big a coincidence was it that the list of people who had been scammed was the same as the list that had flowers regularly in their rooms? It felt like a pretty damn big coincidence to me.

And hadn't there been flowers in Floyd's room when he died?

Gabriel from Happy Blossoms was here all the time. All. The. Time. I'd thought it was because he was trying to woo Christy, but perhaps that was what he wanted us to think. Maybe mooning around after our overly-highlighted receptionist was a cover. Maybe he wanted to be here to glean information about the residents so he could trick them later. He'd acted so strangely when I found him in Yvette's room. I'd thought he was hiding something at the time because of how he shifted from foot to foot like a little boy caught doing something wrong. Maybe I'd caught him in the middle of lifting some important piece of ID or an account number. Maybe he'd tried that on Floyd and Floyd had figured it out and Gabriel killed him to keep him quiet.

My heart raced. I could check the register at the front for people Gabriel delivered flowers to and compare it to Camila's list of people who had been scammed.

It would still be a lot of "what ifs" and "maybes" and "could haves," but it felt like the start of something I could give to Detective Park to get him off Brady's back and on to someone else's.

———

It took all my patience to stay in the moment in Watercolor Society. I did it, but I knew I was distracted. I wanted desperately to check the ledger at the front desk to see if there was anything behind my suspicions.

Everyone who wasn't an employee was supposed to sign in and out when they come in and out of Caring Hands. The sign-in sheet was at the front desk where Christy sits. Almost no one does it, but Gabriel didn't miss many opportunities to talk to Christy. It was a good bet that he'd make sure to spend as much time at the desk as he could by actually filling in the visitor's sign-in sheets completely.

Watercolor, however, is not for the impatient. You couldn't layer paint on top of paint. Well, you could, but you wouldn't probably like the muddy mess that would be produced. It was good to let things dry between applications. I kept a few blowdryers around, but even they took time. And you definitely couldn't pile paintings up at the end of the session without doing some damage. It felt like it took forever, but I couldn't bear to mess up the sweet scene that Darlene had painted of the tulip as it bowed over and lost a few petals. It nearly made me weep. The way

Mohammed had painted the reflection of the orange in the silver teapot added both dimension and a sense of poignancy to his painting. They'd make such lovely cards. I had to treat them carefully.

So after I finally got everyone's paintings dry and stacked, I made my way to the front desk.

"Hey, Christy, could I look at the visitor sign-ins?" I asked.

"Why?" She twirled one lock of highly highlighted hair around her index finger.

"I wanted to check something." My tone was nonchalant. At least, I hoped it was.

"What thing?" She stopped twirling.

I needed to think fast. I didn't want to tell her it was to catch a thief and a scammer until I thought it might really be about catching a thief and a scammer. "I was going to check who hadn't gotten many visitors lately so I could send their families an invitation to the Spring Fling."

"We send everyone's families invitations to the Spring Fling." Twirling resumed. "It's one of our biggest fundraisers."

"Well, this would be a special invitation. A personal one." I considered twirling a lock of my own hair, but decided to give her back her own flat stare and nothing more. We stood there for a moment and finally she huffed.

"Fine. But you can't take it anywhere. You have to look here." She shoved the register half-way across the desk at me.

I slid it the rest of the way across without taking my eyes off hers until she finally backed away. I flipped the register open and began scanning. I'd been right about Gabriel taking the extra few minutes to fill out the register completely. Anna from Can You Hear Me now and Reuben from Let the Good Times Roll both always signed in and out, but didn't always list who they were going to visit. Gabriel did, though. I ran my finger down the page, looking for the names Camila had mentioned in her list of people who had had been the victims of a scam.

Each one of them had had at least one flower delivery in the last six months. They weren't the only people Gabriel had delivered flowers to. There were at least a dozen others. Two of that dozen? Harvey Cornish and Floyd Winstead.

What if Floyd had caught Gabriel stealing Harvey's identity or doing something else shady and then Gabriel killed him so he couldn't expose him? Gabriel was in and out of here all the time. I'd seen him taking garbage out to the Dumpster when he was switching out bouquets. He could easily sneak out a few Fentanyl patches that someone had thrown out instead of flushing. No one would notice him looking through the garbage if he was taking it out.

I jotted down the names on a slip of paper, thanked Christy, and went back to the unit.

"Hey, Camila, can you tell me again which of the residents have had issues with scams?" I asked.

She held up a finger for me to wait while she finished writing something in one of the resident's big binders. "What now?"

"The residents who've had their identities stolen or been scammed somehow. Do you have their names?"

She leaned back in her rolling office chair and regarded me levelly. "Why?"

Great. Why did everyone want to know why? "I, uh, thought maybe I'd make them each some kind of special craft. You know, to cheer them up."

"How would that help in anyway?" She crossed her arms over her midsection.

"It would cheer me up to get a little gift, to know someone was thinking about me." Sadly, that was actually not a lie.

She shook her head. "You're weird, but okay. She slid a folder out from underneath the desk blotter and read out the names. Betty, Tessie, Carmen, and Hannah. Check, check, check, and check.

I rubbed my jaw. Not all of them were on the list of Gabriel's deliveries, but three of them were. That was enough to arouse suspicion.

"Thanks," I said to Camila and headed down the hall.

"So what do you think you'll make them?" She called after me.

"Hmm?" Make who what?

"The craft. To cheer them up. What will it be?" She made a rolling motion with her hand.

Oh, dear Lord. I was going to have to get better at this lying thing. "It's a surprise."

I stepped outside into the courtyard and called Sharon. Sunshine glinted off the tables and a hummingbird buzzed by the feeder someone had hung over one of the planters. Sharon's voicemail message played in my ear. I left a message asking her to call me right away and then texted her for good measure. But now what? It felt too important to sit on.

I pulled Detective Park's card out of my wallet. Surely, this was non-squishy information. I called him.

"Yes, Ms. Glaser," he said, sounding weary. "Are you calling to tell me that Brady didn't do it?"

"No. I'm calling to tell you that I think I've found a reason someone else might have done it or at least done something." Maybe it had been a mistake to call him. Maybe I should have let Sharon handle it or figured out who was going to do the presentation on identity theft. It didn't feel like he was taking me seriously.

"Oh, really?" He sounded more interested. "I can meet you at your house in fifteen minutes."

I hadn't much liked having him in my house. "No. Meet me at Caring Hands. I'll wait for you in the lobby."

I went back inside and started down the hall toward the lobby. Irma scooted around the corner in her Jazzy Pride. "You're still here?" she asked. "I thought you'd be gone for the day."

"Normally I would be. Something . . . came up." I looked down at Irma as she rolled next to me. She was so astute. Maybe she could back me up on the connections I was seeing. "Have you noticed anything odd about Gabriel?"

We glided past the library. The cart stood empty and unattended. Brady really had done a nice job of picking books for the residents. It was a shame that he wasn't here to do it. A shame for him and a shame for Caring Hands both. And shame on me for thinking he might have used his library cart duties to smuggle Fentanyl patches out. She squinted one eye up at me. "The flower delivery kid?"

"That's the one."

"Besides the fact that he has the hots for the reception-ist?" she asked.

I snorted. So I wasn't the only one who'd noticed that either. "Besides that, although that might end up being helpful."

"Helpful for what?" she asked, as we rounded the corner past the gift shop.

I hesitated. It was conjecture, but I really thought some-thing odd was going on with Gabriel. "There seems to be a certain amount of crossover between people who get flower deliveries and people who've been the victims of scams."

She hit the brakes on her Jazzy so hard it squealed. "Is that so?"

I shrugged. "At a cursory glance, yes."

"What are you going to do about it?" she asked, pulling her notebook out of the pocket on the front of her scooter and jotting something down.

"I'm going to meet Detective Park in the lobby in a few minutes. I think he'll want to hear." There didn't seem any reason to lie to her.

She lifted her chin. "I might have information, too."

For a second, we stared at each other. Then I asked, "Irma, do you want to come with me?"

A grin spread over her face. "I do. Give me a minute to powder my nose."

The lobby was a nice little space that didn't get a lot of use. There were two love seats and a couple of arm chairs arranged around a gas fireplace. It was one of the places where Gabriel delivered fresh flowers every week so it was always cheerful. Based on the look on Detective Park's face when Irma and I rolled in, he definitely hadn't expected both of us. Park recovered quickly, though, jumping up to move one chair out of the way so Irma could pull up next to the couch and hold a chair out for me. Pretty manners, if nothing else. They went with the suit.

"How are you, Ms. Warren? Did you also have something to tell me?" he asked.

"Maybe," she said, straightening her blouse.

"So what was it that you wanted to tell me, Ms. Glaser?" Park leaned back in his arm chair.

I explained what I'd noticed about Gabriel's deliveries

and the people who'd been scammed. "I'm concerned because I saw him in Yvette's room a few days ago."

His brow creased. "Was he delivering flowers?"

"That's the thing. He wasn't. He said he was checking up on the bouquet he'd delivered before to make sure it was staying fresh." I looked over at Irma who was scribbling in her notebook. "Yvette wasn't in her room and he wasn't really standing all that close to the bouquet."

Park nodded. "A little weird."

"That's what I thought! Plus he was doing this thing shifting back and forth that Tyler used to do when he was trying to get away with something. Anyway I checked the visitor log and almost all of the people who have been scammed had a flower delivery in the preceding weeks." I sat back in my chair, feeling a bit triumphant.

Park tapped his foot and stared at the gas fire in the fireplace. "Did everyone who had a delivery get their identity stolen?" he finally asked.

I shook my head. "No. But maybe he hasn't gotten around to them yet or he's trying to keep the connection from being too obvious."

Irma pointed her pen at Park. "She's got a point, you know. There are lots of service people we let waltz in and out of our rooms without thinking about it. We all let them in and out and tell them all kinds of things. The kind of personal things someone could use to scam us later. Our grandchildren's names and where they live and when people's birthdays are and the names of their pets."

Park rubbed the back of his neck. "Who else have you spoken to about this?"

I shook my head. "You two are the first."

"Good. Let's keep it that way. I'd appreciate it if you

wouldn't mention this to anyone else." He pulled out his own notebook and wrote something in it.

"No one?" Surely he didn't mean Sharon or Rayna.

"No one." He shut his notebook.

Maybe he didn't fully understand what this could mean.

"There's one more thing, though."

"What's that?" Park asked.

"Harvey Cornish was one of the people Gabriel delivered flowers to and there were flowers in Floyd's room when he died. What if Floyd caught Gabriel stealing Harvey's identity and Gabriel killed Floyd to keep him quiet? Gabriel was here the morning Floyd died." I wiggled my toes in my boots as if that would let me get the words out faster.

Park's eyebrows went up. "He was?"

I nodded. "Absolutely. I almost ran into him as I was coming in."

Park shook his head. "It's a big jump from stealing a few hundred dollars from someone to murder and we don't even know he's guilty of the stealing . . ."

"The first murder could have been an accident," Irma suggested, interrupting him.

"What do you mean?" Park asked.

She shrugged one shoulder, winced, and then rubbed at it. "Maybe it was Harvey who caught Gabriel and Gabriel killed Harvey. Perhaps Harvey saw Gabriel in the act and said something. People don't like to be confronted. They lash out if they feel cornered. Sometimes lashing out is a bit more powerful than they expect, especially if someone is a bit fragile." She gestured down to her own body as a case in point. "Maybe Gabriel wanted Harvey to stop talking and ended up smothering him. Then suddenly it isn't a few credit card numbers. It's murder and it seems worth it to murder someone else to keep that quiet. So if Floyd suspected Gabriel and Gabriel figured that out . . ."

Park and I stared at her.

"What? When you've been around as long as I have you've seen a lot of stuff. Human nature isn't always pretty." She straightened up in her scooter with a self-righteous wiggle.

"It makes more sense than it being Brady," I said. "Brady had no reason to hurt Floyd. None. And according to Brady, Floyd had suspicions about Harvey's death. He was convinced that there was something off about it."

"It seems to me you should be looking into what happened to Harvey, too," Irma said to Park with a significant eyebrow quirk.

He spoke carefully. "I will consider that." Park stood, signaling the end of our meeting.

"You do that. Now I need to go. It's time for pudding." Irma fired up her Jazzy Pride and promptly backed into the wall behind her. She threw it into gear and Park shoved his chair out of the way as she made a swooping turn to get out of the lobby and head back to the unit.

I stood and followed after her.

"Leah," Park said, motioning for me to stop.

He took a step closer to me and said, in a soft voice, "Be careful. Irma's right about one thing. Crime causes chain reactions. Someone does one thing wrong, then does something more wrong to cover it up, and it keeps escalating."

"What are you getting at?" I asked.

He took my elbow. His grip was gentle, but firm. "I mean let me take care of this from here. Stop investigating."

"I'm not investigating," I protested. "I'm noticing. It's not my fault that I notice things."

"As long as all you're doing is noticing and you're letting

me know what it is you notice. And please don't mention this to your friends. Let me figure out what's happening here first before you tell them your theory. I don't want anything to compromise this investigation." He let go of my elbow and gave me a small salute, then turned toward the doors.

Not mention it to my friends? I wasn't sure there was anything I hadn't mentioned to my friends in the last decade. Certainly not something as important as this.

Irma and I made our way back to the unit. "What was that last little tête-á-tête about?" Irma asked.

"He asked me to let him take it from here. He said you were right about crimes setting off chain reactions." I entered the code and held the door to the unit open for her.

She sailed through. "Smart young man," she said.

"Not all that young," I said. "He's easily my age."

Irma snorted. "Like I said. Young."

It was all relative, I supposed. We rolled up to the nurses' station. "There you are." Kendrick Tisdall, one of the evening shift nurses, stepped out from behind the curved counter. She was a white woman in her mid-twenties with hair that could not possibly have become that color red naturally and a full-sleeve tattoo on her right arm and some more ink snaking up out of her scrubs around her neck. "I was wondering where you got off to."

Irma waved one hand in the air. "Consulting with the local constabulary."

"The what?" A wrinkle formed on Kendrick's brow, then she shrugged. "Whatever. Is it time to get you ready for dinner?

Irma pointed imperiously toward her room and said, "Lead on, MacDuff." Then she started up her Jazzy Pride, rammed into the side of the nurses' station, backed up and tried again, this time only winging it slightly, and drove toward her room with Kendrick trailing behind her, shaking her head and laughing.

I went back to my car and called Rayna. "Could you ask Brady something for me?"

"Sure. What?"

"I want to know if he ever had any run-ins with Gabriel."

She was back in a few minutes. "He asked who Gabriel was so I don't think so. Why?"

"A theory I'm working on." Or that I'd managed to get Detective Park to work on instead of following Brady around. It felt terrible not to tell her every detail about it, but I definitely didn't want to do anything to keep Park from investigating Gabriel or anybody who wasn't Brady.

TWELVE

On Wednesday, we had our final suncatcher craft session before the Spring Fling. It was hard to believe it had been two whole weeks since Floyd's death. Irma had done a lovely job of finishing his suncatcher for him. I'd put both their photos next to it when I put it out in the booth.

I was feeling pretty happy as I got set up for my suncatcher group, but then Tessie walked in looking even happier than I felt. "You look pleased," I said.

She pulled a phone out of her pocket and wiggled it in the air. "I got my phone back! I can play solitaire again!"

I felt a little wave of guilt. I'd forgotten to look for one of those handheld solitaire games for her. "Good for you! How'd you manage that?" I set more boxes of glass beads out onto the table.

A funny look crossed her face. "I'm not really sure. I guess I argued long enough that my daughter gave it back. It seems fair. I did give her back her record player back when she was fourteen and broke curfew, after all. "

"Turn about and all that?" I found a frame and beads for Tessie to work on.

"Apparently."

"And the phone has solitaire on it?"

She laughed. "Two different kinds."

"You're a wild woman!" I smiled.

Tessie wasn't the only one with a new phone. Betty and Miriam had new phones, too. There must have been a sale.

"No new phone for you, Irma?" I asked, when she came in.

"No. Still have my old one. It'll do," she said, although I couldn't help noticing how she was watching the other people with their new phones. We all want new toys, after all.

I counted up the suncatchers we had for sale at the end of the afternoon. Fifty-two! I'd bought the beads at the dollar store and the adhesive in bulk. We could charge five dollars a piece for them and still turn a profit. I felt quite accomplished. I happened to be having a good hair day, too. I wondered where Malachi was.

When the class was over and everyone had walked and rolled out, I balanced the box of finished suncatchers on my hip to put in storage until Sunday's Spring Fling. There was a bounce in my step as I walked down the hall. I heard Malachi's voice in Roland Chilver's room. Bingo. I poked my head – with its good hair – in to say hello.

Malachi spooned some applesauce into Roland's mouth. Roland made a face. "It's so bitter."

"I know. I'm sorry. It'd take a heck of a lot of applesauce to completely hide the flavor of the crushed-up pill, but at least this way it's easy to swallow this way, right?" Malachi crumpled up the little paper container the applesauce and been in and tossed it into the garbage. "Oh, hi, Leah."

"Hi, Malachi. How are you, Roland? Will you be coming to the Spring Fling on Sunday?" Roland didn't come to many of my classes. I'd been told he had been losing mobility for years, but now his hands had stopped working well, too. They'd begun to curl in on themselves and he wore braces to keep his fingernails from digging into his own palms. Even my simplest crafts like the suncatcher one required some hand mobility.

"Of course. I've been to every one of the last five," Roland said.

That was impressive. Not to be too morbid, but not a lot of people lasted five years in this area of Caring Hands. It might not be the absolute last stop on the way out, but it wasn't far removed.

"That's great." I turned to leave, but spotted Roland's checkbook sitting out on his dresser. "Roland, you probably shouldn't leave this out. Can I put it away for you?" He probably shouldn't have it here at all. He'd be better off if her family kept it for him and brought it in when he needed it, especially with all the scams going on in this place.

"No. Leave it there," he said.

"Are you sure? It really would be safer if . . ." I opened a drawer of the dresser to slide it in.

"Leave it," he barked.

I froze. "Sorry."

Malachi gestured with his head for me to follow him out. "Talk to you later, Roland. Have a good nap."

In the hall, I said, "I don't think I've ever heard him raise his voice like that." I put my hand to my chest

Malachi patted me on the shoulder. "You never know what's going to set them off. Plus, he's so helpless. He can't get up to move things around where he wants them. It's got to be frustrating." He walked toward the nurses' station and I walked with him.

We'd reached the nurses' station and I paused to rest the box on the desk.

He made a note in the big binder that held Roland's chart and said, "Can I help you with those?"

They weren't really that heavy, but having some company as I went down those basement stairs wouldn't be all bad. "Do you mind?"

"Not at all." He took the box from me and we walked out of the unit.

I opened the door to the basement for him and reached around to flick on the light. "I hate those stairs," I said.

"Really?" He stepped down confidently.

"I always think something's going to come out from underneath them and grab my ankles." I shuddered as I followed him down the steps.

"What kind of something?"

"I don't know. Ghosts. Ax murderers. Zombies. Ghosts of Zombie Ax Murderers. The usual."

He laughed. "Yes. Of course. The usual." He plunked the box down on the table in my storage area. "I'll escort you back up to safety."

Safety. It was a good thing and Roland's checkbook definitely wasn't safe with Gabriel still wandering around. Where was Detective Park when you needed him? He should be protecting all these people's checkbooks and phones, especially after what I'd told him. "You'll be sure to call Roland's family? That checkbook shouldn't be out like that. Anybody could grab it or even tear out a check or two while he was sleeping."

Malachi nodded. "I know. I'll talk to his family about it. I don't want him added to the list of people who've had things stolen or been scammed."

"Exactly. Although it doesn't seem like he's going to be

grateful about it." I shook my head. "Irma's right. I should listen to Detective Park and stop digging around."

He stopped on the stair above me and turned around. "Irma said that? About what? When?"

"Earlier this week. I, uh, was talking to Detective Park and Irma happened to join us." I paused, too, to keep from running into him. With him on the steps above me, I had to crane my neck back to look him in the eyes. I grabbed the railing to keep me steady. Was that wobble back?

"What were you telling the detective?" The usual good humor was gone from Malachi's voice.

Damn it. This lying thing was harder than people made it look. I stepped down one stair so we weren't so close and I could keep my balance. "Just some things I noticed."

He paused and looked at me, brow furrowed for a moment, then said, "Irma's right and so is the detective, Leah. You really should stay out of this. It's great you let him know whatever it is you noticed, but let the police take care of it. This is serious."

I thought about Brady trying to begin his life as an adult with the cloud of suspicion always over him. "So am I, Malachi. So am I."

———

It was time to head over to Camila's and meet Jackie K. She lived in a neighborhood a lot like mine. The houses were a little older, a little smaller, a little darker, but they were loved. Lawns were tended and walls were painted. Sidewalks were swept and trash cans were tucked discreetly behind privacy fences.

I parked along the curb a few houses down from the house and walked along the cracked sidewalk to her house where I beheld the first honest to God Bathtub Virgin Mary I had ever seen in the flesh, or in the porcelain I guess. If someone hadn't actually upended an old bathtub, burying part of it in the ground, and placing a statue of the Virgin Mary inside it, it sure looked as if they had. Catty corner to her was a statue of Jesus as a shepherd with a little lamb. I climbed the steps to the porch and nearly stepped backward off of it when I saw the Santa Muerte sculpture grinning at me with her scythe from the corner.

I pushed the bell and the first few measures of *Amazing Grace* rang out. Camila answered right away with Jackie K, who was even cuter in the flesh than he was on camera, in her arms. "Leah, come in!"

I followed Camila inside and froze. I had never seen quite so many crosses in one place ever and Travis and I toured Italy on our honeymoon and went into a lot of churches. There were nearly as many candles as there were crosses, those long columnar ones with saints on the front. There was also a series of photos ranged along the living room wall. Two dogs, one cat, an elderly couple.

"This is . . . nice," I said, not sure of what else to say.

Camila smiled. "This is Aileen and Ted." She touched the photos of the dogs.

They were both Yorkshire Terriers like Jackie. "They're very cute."

"Yes. They were. Aileen crossed the rainbow bridge five years ago and Ted went a little before that. I like to imagine them up there together playing in the clouds, out of pain. Aileen had horrible hip problems and Ted had liver issues. I was sad when I had to make the decision to put them down, but I knew I'd released them from pain and that they were in a better place."

Like she thought Floyd was. I sensed a theme.

"This is Lizzie," she said pointing at the photo of the cat. "She crossed the bridge not too long after Ted. She'd developed kidney disease and was wasting away. Poor sweet thing."

Then she pointed to the elderly couple. "And those are my parents. Daddy passed into the kingdom of God when I was twenty-two and Momma followed him a year later, almost to the day." She turned to me and smiled a big beaming smile. "I think they might be with Aileen and Ted and Lizzie, all together waiting for me in heaven."

She looked so happy. Like there was no doubt at all in her mind that there was a heaven and that her family and pets would be there when she got there. I wished I had that kind of faith, that I felt so sure that Travis would be waiting for me somewhere or that there even was a somewhere to wait.

"So where is Jackie's favorite place in the house?" I asked. The more comfortable a pet was, the more likely I was to get a good portrait shot.

She gestured for me to follow. "Right this way."

I followed her out to a sunny back porch. It was small, but beautifully tended with pots of scarlet bougainvillea and lavender and daisies. She set Jackie down on a glider.

Jackie – or Jackie K as Camila called him – was definitely going to be an easier subject for a great pet portrait than Sugar Pop. Not only was he way cuter, he had way more personality. It was like he knew we were doing a photo shoot, cocking his head and crossing his paws and turning this way and that as if he was making sure I got his good side. I almost yelled out "work with me!" a few times.

When I'd snapped about a bazillion shots, I straightened up and rubbed my lower back. I thumbed through what I had and couldn't help smiling. This was going to be fun. He had so much character. "I should have some prelim-inary sketches for you next week at the latest," I told Camila.

"Oh, goody! I can't wait. I wish I had known to do this when Aileen and Ted were still young and in their prime. They got so sad as they got older. It really hurt to watch them age. It would have been nice to have portraits of them before that." Camila clasped her hands at her chest, looking a little like one of the saints on one of her candles.

"We all slow down sometime," I said, rubbing at my back again.

She nodded emphatically. "Oh, yes. Death comes for us all. Even though it's sad for those of us here, I don't think we should be afraid of it. It's our gateway into the next world, after all."

I wasn't so sure about that. "No need to rush going through it, though, right?"

She crouched down next to Jackie and scratched beneath his chin. "I suppose not. I wish it was easier for us to walk through that gate. Too often it's marked with pain and fear. We see it all the time at Caring Hands, don't we? Sometimes there's so much suffering I'm not sure I can bear it."

That was true. So true it made me catch my breath a little. I'd been there when a couple of our residents came to the end of their journeys. I'd watched their families going in and out of their rooms, hollow-eyed and pale, and heard some of what went on inside the rooms as everyone tried to make people as comfortable as they possibly could be. I'd been there for Travis's last days, too. Even though he had very little pain — brain tumors are like that — it had been awful to sit by as he lost the ability to walk and talk and take care of himself in any way. I shut my eyes hard and took a few deep breaths. This wasn't the moment to go down that road. "There's not a lot we can do about that, though."

Camila buried her face in Jackie's fur. "I'm not so sure about that, Leah."

I got a weird chill. Her voice had gone flat, almost robotic. "What do you mean?"

She stood, gave Jackie a pat, and opened the door to see me through the house. "There are options. People don't always take them, but they exist." We reached the front door and she gave me a big smile as she opened it and ushered me through. "See you at work!" She shut the door and I was left alone on her porch with Santa Muerte.

THIRTEEN

It's NEVER good news when you pull up to the retirement center and an ambulance is parked in front. It's especially not good news when the lights aren't on and there are no sirens. That means something bad happened and dealing with the aftermath isn't urgent.

I pulled into a parking place and watched as a gurney with the sheet pulled all the way up was wheeled by two paramedics. Whoever was under the sheet barely made a bump. It was someone small. The breeze picked up and leaves swirled around my feet. I shivered.

I slung my messenger bag over my shoulder and walked in, not stopping at the employee lounge to leave my stuff. A clump of nurses and aides stood by the nurses' station. "Who?" I asked.

Everyone knew what I meant. Lillibeth turned and said, "Irma."

I took a step back, feeling like I'd been physically shoved. "Ohhhh. Poor thing."

Camila crossed herself. "She's in a better place now." It's quite possible that Irma was in a better place. Our present plane of existence wasn't really doing her many favors these days. Most days, she was in pain. Her limbs had ceased doing what she wanted them to do. But nobody really knows for sure and I resented the people who seemed to think they did. When Travis died, every time someone said that to me I wanted to scream. How could there be a better place than with Tyler and me?

Lillibeth must have felt much the same because she gave Camila a bit of a side-eye. "We don't know what place anyone is in. She still enjoyed her family and her food."

"And her gin," I added.

"And her gin." Lillibeth nodded. "It really is a shame."

"What happened?" I asked.

Lillibeth shrugged. "She lay down for her morning nap and didn't get up for lunch. These things happen."

True enough. Although that's what they'd said about Harvey Cornish, too. He didn't wake up. It's what they would have said about Floyd if Lillibeth hadn't gotten upset and suspicious. "Can I do anything to help?" I asked.

Gladys scooted past, a new babydoll – or at least one that had been repaired sufficiently not to need bandages – in her lap.

Lillibeth looked around as call bells up and down the hall started to go off. It was nearly lunch time and people were getting impatient. "Her granddaughter is down there. Maybe bring her some boxes to help her pack stuff up." She hesitated. "There's a waiting list for the bed."

I caught her drift. It seemed terrible to rush a grieving family out of the facility, but the truth was that Caring Hands was one of the nicer places in the area and there were always people hoping to move in.

"Of course." I stowed my messenger bag in my locker then went to the supply closet and found a couple of boxes that had previously held adult diapers and insulin syringes. Caring Hands went through those things like Kool-Aid through a knocked-over sippy cup. I carried them to Irma's room.

A young woman sat on Irma's bed turning a photo over and over in her hands. She had that beautiful creamy skin that we all take for granted in our twenties. Hers was olive and her dark hair was straight and black and fell halfway down her back. She turned toward me when I walked in and I could see the tears standing in her large brown eyes.

"Hi," I said from the doorway.

She let the photo drop into her lap. "Can I help you?"

I shook my head and brought the boxes into the room. "I'm Leah. I'm hoping I can help you. The nurses thought you might need some boxes and some help packing Irma's things."

"I'm Jessica, her granddaughter." She stood.

I nodded. "Are you the photographer or the lawyer?"

She smiled. "The photographer. The lawyer gets in tomorrow."

"She was so proud of you both." It wasn't like I had to tell her. Irma's walls were filled with photos of her grandchildren at graduations and weddings and family vacations. They were what she wanted to look at. "She talked about you all the time."

Jessica turned in a circle. "I don't even know where to start."

"How about I start with her clothes? Maybe you want to pack her photographs?" I gestured to the one in her hands and to the other framed photos ranged around the room. It didn't really matter where she started. Having a specific task was always helpful, though.

She nodded and took a box.

I opened the first of Irma's drawers. Chances were her family would take everything directly to Goodwill once they got a good look at them, but it didn't hurt for them to be neatly folded in case they wanted to look through it all for something. She didn't have much. Four pairs of elastic-waisted polyester pants. One blue, one black, one tan, one green. There were around eight short-sleeved shirts and an equal number of long-sleeved ones. There was a sweatshirt with a photo of all her grandchildren on the front, three cardigans, and one winter jacket I hadn't seen her wear before. It looked new.

Then it was time for the more personal drawers. The underwear. "Should I throw these out?" I gestured to the open drawer.

Jessica put her hand to her mouth. "I - I'm not sure."

It had been hellishly hard to throw out anything of Travis's. It seemed like a betrayal not to save every shred of everything of his, but at a certain point, it did get ridiculous to tote around boxers and t-shirts that would never be worn again. I'd kept a couple pairs that I wore as pajamas and chucked the rest, but it hadn't been easy. I gestured to the other boxes. "I think those will have the things you really want to keep."

"Okay," she said, a look of gratitude on her face.

I dug my hands in to the drawer, planning to grab them all out in a clump and hit something hard. I pulled it out. It was a jewelry box. I opened it. Irma's pearls. Good thing I hadn't tossed the whole drawer. I needed to be more careful as I went through her things. "Except these. I'm sure you'll want these."

Jessica took the long slim box and held it to her chest.

Then it occurred to me that the one thing I hadn't found was her purple notebook. I went over to her Jazzy

Pride and looked in the side pocket. Nothing. I checked in the bedside table and her bathroom cabinet and under her mattress. Nothing, nothing, nothing.

That notebook had been her constant companion lately. Where was it now?

"Are you looking for something in particular?" Jessica asked.

"A notebook. Your grandmother had been keeping it."

She nodded and smiled. "Yeah. She thought she was Miss Marple."

"Miss Marple?" A chill ran through me.

"Yeah. Like in those Agatha Christie stories? The old lady who solves mysteries?" Jessica folded one of the boxes shut.

"Have you seen it?" I asked.

She turned in a circle. "No. Not yet. I'm sure it's here somewhere."

I would have been, too, originally, but not anymore. Thinking about Irma's notebook, however, made me remember the box of Floyd's odds and ends that his family didn't want that they'd left for any residents who might need them still sat in the dining hall. It hadn't occurred to me to look through it for anything that might have to do with Brady.

It was still sitting in the corner. I peeked inside. There were a few sweaters, some books, some stationery. I sighed. He'd led such a long an interesting life, but it all came down to his. A few things in a box on a table in the back of a room. A pad of paper in the box caught my eye. I pulled it out. Was this the pad of paper the note with Brady's name had been written on? Maybe I could figure out if anything else had been on that piece of paper.

I held it up to the light at an angle to see if there were

any indentations in the paper. There were, but I couldn't figure out what, if anything, they meant. I tucked the pad in my back pocket and went down to the basement to where my supplies were. I shook my head as I opened the door to the basement. Why on earth had I been so frightened by those stairs? They were just stairs. Sometimes my imagination was a bit overactive.

I skipped down the steps to my corner and found a box of charcoals. Gently, I ran one of them horizontally over the pad, just like the directions I'd read for the leaf rubbings I was thinking about doing for our new set of crafts after the Spring Fling. The places that were indented by Floyd's pen stayed white while the surface of the paper turned gray.

The top of the page did indeed say "Brady." Lower on the page read the message "the cafeteria always serves spaghetti on Tuesday." Weird. That was wrong. Wednesday was spaghetti day. Everyone knew that. Why would Floyd want Brady to know that anyway?

I flipped the page over and did my charcoal rub trick again. The same message showed up, but a little fainter. I sighed. There was no guarantee that the spaghetti message had even been on the same page as Brady's name. One more bright idea that came to nothing.

Rayna wasn't quite ready when I got to her house on Saturday morning. Brady let me in and I walked into the kitchen behind him, leaning on the breakfast bar then immediately lifting my arm. Mindboggling. There was something sticky on Rayna's kitchen counter. I scooted over to the sink and got a dishcloth to wipe the counter down navigating around a stack of dirty bowls in the sink. I didn't think I'd ever seen dirty dishes in Rayna's sink. Had she been ill?

"How's it going?" I asked Brady.

He shrugged.

"That good?" I laughed, wringing out the rag and hanging it back over the faucet.

"Staying at home all the time is hella boring." He rubbed his face.

Poor kid. "I bet. What are you doing to keep busy?"

He sighed. "I signed up for some online classes. They're boring, but they're less boring than doing nothing."

It couldn't be easy. We had to find a way for Brady to get back to his normal life. "I bet. We'll get this cleared up, though. Then you'll be able to do whatever you want to do again."

He turned to me his face suddenly more serious than I think I'd ever seen it. "I've been trying to figure what that it is, what it is I want to do, I mean."

That was more philosophical than I'd heard Brady be since the boys had had to pick a philosopher to study during a unit on ancient Greece in sixth grade and he couldn't decide between Heraclitus and Plutarch.

He looked down at the counter, dragging a finger through some crumbs. "I really liked working at Caring Hands. I liked Floyd and Irma and Tessie and Mohammed and Howard. Gladys freaks me out still, but I could get used to that. Maybe I can do something that would let me work with old people. Not anything, you know, medical, but something like helpful, you know?"

I did know. "Brady, that's fantastic." I hugged him.

He squirmed. "Don't get all excited. I haven't actually done anything yet," he pointed out.

I let him go. "That's not true. You've done plenty. You

made some really great connections with people and figured out that it's something you want more of."

Rayna came down and we walked out the door. The second we stepped out Rayna's house, though, Eva popped out of hers. I could see that she had her phone in her hand, angled as if she was trying to take a picture without anyone noticing. She was like some kind of evil gossipy jack-in-the-box. I shook my head and kept walking. What kind of person got satisfaction from publicizing someone else's unhappiness or misfortune? What kind of world did we live in when there were no repercussions for that, but there were for people doing their best under trying circumstances?

Rayna shook her head "What is wrong with that woman?"

I didn't have an answer. "I wish I knew."

Rayna stopped. "I'm going to find out." She turned and walked back to Eva's house, not waiting for me to follow. "For Pete's sake, Eva. What are you going to post about me and my family now?"

Eva stepped back. "What do you mean?"

Rayna took another step toward her. "You know what I mean. All your nasty little insinuations. Do you have any idea what havoc you've wreaked on my kid's life? What has Brady ever done to you? What have I ever done to you?"

Eva straightened, pulling her shoulders down and holding her head high. "It's a free country. I can say what I want."

She threw her hands in the air. "Of course you can. By why would you? Don't you have anything better to do?"

For some reason, that last question seemed to take the wind out of Eva's sails. She slumped back down. "No."

Rayna took a step back. "No what?"

Eva opened her mouth like she was about to say something, then shut it and turned around and went back into her house.

Rayna stood still for a moment and then walked back over to me. "What just happened?" I asked.

"I'm not sure," she said.. "Come on. Let's go."

"What has gotten into you?" I asked as we walked on.

"I'm not sure, but that felt really good." She shook her head. "Like really really good. Way better than yelling at that barista."

Monique and her son, Jack, were outside as well.

"Where are you two off to?" Monique asked. Jack buzzed around her legs on his Big Wheel making zoom zoom noises. Cassidy, the young woman who rented the granny flat over Monique's garage, positioned herself between Jack and the rose bush so he couldn't crash into it.

"Meeting some friends for coffee," Rayna said.

"Grown-up friends?" Monique asked. "Jack! Not in the street. Stay on the driveway."

I nodded.

She turned back toward us then quickly away. "Inside? Jack! Don't chase that cat."

I nodded again.

"And you'll just talk?" She sighed.

I kept nodding.

She sighed. "That sounds heavenly."

Rayna patted her on the back. "It won't be long and you'll be meeting friends for coffee, too."

"I sure hope so!"

We walked on. We were at the corner when we heard a crashing noise followed by a child's wails.

"I don't miss that phase," Rayna said.

I sighed. "I kind of do."

She snorted. "No, you don't. You just think you do. You glamorize it."

"I don't ever remember feeling glamorous." I had felt needed and like I had a purpose and like I had a reason to exist, but not glamorous.

She gave me a look. "You know what I mean."

I did. I wasn't sure if she knew what I meant, though.

"I'm so sorry about Irma." Tamika wrapped her arms around me as soon as we walked into Espresso Yourself. For a moment, I let myself relax into her warm and comforting hug.

"I know you were fond of her," she said, rubbing circles on my back.

I nodded, not quite trusting myself to speak yet.

"Do they know what happened?" Sharon asked from her place on the couch.

"She didn't wake up from her morning nap." I'd known she wasn't well. Of course she wasn't well. But there had been such a vitality to her still, such a sharpness. It seemed like it should take more than a nap to snuff her out.

"There'll be an autopsy, right?" Rayna said.

I shook my head. "Probably not. She wasn't well. She was under a doctor's care. Doctor Timms will sign her death certificate."

"Without really knowing what happened?" Sharon looked up at me.

"She was old. People expect old people to die," I said. "Some people think it's a good thing. Camila is big into people going to a better place when they die and for their deaths to be quiet and peaceful like that. You should see her house!" I shuddered.

"Why were you in her house and what was wrong with it?" Tamika asked.

"I'm doing a portrait of Jackie K, her Yorkie. I'm telling you it was the creepiest house I think I've ever been in and that includes the Haunted House that Katie Burns made for the Cub Scout Halloween celebration when the kids were in fourth grade."

Now it was Rayna who shuddered. "What was she thinking? That thing was terrifying. It was supposed to be for ten-year-olds."

"I don't care if they were twenty-year-olds. Who chases people with an axe for fun?" Tamika asked.

The clear answer was Katie Burns. She maybe had some anger issues or perhaps some homicidal fantasies to work out. Her kid was kind of a brat.

"What was so creepy about Camila's house?" Sharon asked, always one for getting the facts.

I described the crosses and the candles and the photos and the portraits and the little shrines everywhere and the Santa Muerte on her porch. "And the way she talked about the dogs and the cat and her parents." I shook my head. "It didn't feel quite right."

"What was the name of the dog again?" Tamika asked.

"Jackie K. Why?" I turned toward her.

She asked another question instead of answering mine. "And some of the others?"

"Lizzy B. Aileen. Ted."

Tamika tapped her index finger against her lower lip.

"What?" Sharon asked.

"Hush," she said. "I'm thinking."

"What's going on with the hunky Physician's Assistant?" Sharon asked.

Before I could answer, Tamika said, "Oh, uh uh," and set her phone down.

"What?" I asked.

"Those dog names? Those are all names of serial killers," Tamika said.

I stared at her. "Wait. What? No. Which serial killers?"

"Aileen Wournos. Ted Bundy. Lizzie Borden."

Oh, my God. Lizzie B. It had never occurred to me that could stand for Lizzie Borden and her axe. "How did you figure that out?"

"I'm not sure. Something about the list of names you were saying triggered something. I started searching and then it was pretty obvious." Tamika chewed on one fingernail.

They couldn't be. Who would do that? "What about Jack?"

"You said it was Jackie K, right?" Tamika cocked her head.

I nodded.

Tamika picked up her phone and turned it around so I could see the image on it. Jack Kevorkian. Dr. Death. Champion of assisted suicide for the terminally ill.

FOURTEEN

I WAS glad to have the distraction of getting all the last-minute details ready for the Spring Fling Fair. Irma's death had hit me hard. I'd miss her bright smile and quick wit. I'd even miss how careful you had to be when she was driving her Jazzy Pride nearby. I hadn't realized how much I'd looked forward to seeing her until I faced the prospect of not running into her – occasionally literally – in the hallways.

I kept waiting for something to happen to Gabriel. Surely Park would be able to gather enough to arrest him. Once he did that, maybe he would be able to tie him to Floyd's murder and Brady's name would be fully cleared.

I had four booths to set up and tend that Sunday. The suncatcher booth, the clay club booth, the booth for the yarn club and one for the watercolor club. My fingers were crossed that it would go well. It would be part of proving that it was worth what they paid me to come in each afternoon and do arts and crafts.

I'd taken photos of all my clients and laid them out next to whatever craft it was they'd made. Georgina and Miriam and Carmen and Javis and Yvette and Waylon. I faltered when I hit Irma's sun catcher and the photo I'd taken of her, sitting up as straight as she could, chin tilted up, and a little twinkle in her eye. I ran my finger along the side of her face in the photo and held the sun catcher up to the light. The colored beams danced on the table, wavering a bit, but still making a colorful and sweet pattern. Gently I put Irma's photo and her suncatcher back in the box. Maybe I'd call her family and see if they wanted it. It might be a nice last memento. If they didn't want it, I might keep it for myself.

Grudgingly, I had to admit that Christy had done an amazing job turning the dining room into a festive space. Green and blue tulle swags twined around each other decorated the walls and windows. Streamers swooped down from the ceiling. Tables were covered with flowered tablecloths and mini-lights. The corners held sprays of flowers. It was maybe a little reminiscent of an Under the Sea Prom Night, but it still worked.

The Fling had drawn a good crowd. A lot of residents' families were there, of course, but there were also staff and staff's family, people from the local churches and temples who knew residents, service people like Anna and Marty. And, of course, Gabriel.

I kept my eye on him as he strolled through looking at the crafts and people's photos. It was a great opportunity to meet family members and learn their names and what they sounded like and how they behaved. How many more people would he be able to scam with information he picked up today? I had an urge to snatch everything he touched away from him, but I didn't want him to know we were onto him. How long was it going to take for Park to do something about him?

Tessie's family came through and admired the hat and

scarf she'd knitted. "Mom, these are beautiful," her daughter said.

Tessie smiled. "Thank you."

"I'm going to get them for Andre."

It continued like that. It really was sweet to see the families being so impressed with what their relatives could still do and how proud the clients felt when their families admired their work.

At least, it was sweet until Waylon Langston's family showed up.

"See. I made that one." He pointed at the suncatcher that was next to Javis's photo.

Javis bristled. "You did not. That one's mine. I made it, you old coot."

Waylon rotated his wheelchair to face Javis. "What did you say?"

"I said it's mine, you deaf geezer." Javis made sure to enunciate deaf geezer very carefully.

"I'm not deaf and you're wrong." Waylon pounded his fist on the arm of his wheelchair.

Javis leaned back in his chair and very coolly said, "It's sitting right in front of my photo. It's mine."

"Well, then, Miss Artsy Fartsy over there screwed up. She put the wrong one in front of your photo." Waylon pointed a finger at me.

I did not much appreciate being called Miss Artsy Fartsy and I really didn't appreciate Waylon saying I'd screwed up in front of all the families and staff and administrators. "I'm pretty sure this suncatcher is Javis's, Waylon. Yours is over here in front of your picture." I pointed the way, trying to redirect his attention, but Waylon was having none of it. He grabbed the one in front of Javis's photo.

"Put my suncatcher down, you nasty thief!" Javis backed his manual wheelchair up to get some momentum going and rammed his wheelchair into Waylon's, managing also to bang into Pastor Matthams who yelled, "Hey! Watch it!" Waylon, on the other hand, didn't budge. The electric wheelchair outweighed the manual one by a lot.

"It's not yours! You're the thief!" Waylon turned on his electric wheelchair and drove it forward. Luckily, the speed had been turned down all the way to the little turtle insignia so the bump was fairly minor.

"You want me to watch it? I'll give you something to watch." Javis backed his wheelchair up again and rammed it into Waylon again. And again nothing much happened.

"Javis! Waylon! Stop that." I came around the table to separate them.

But Waylon had had enough. "It's mine" He backed up his electric wheelchair, cranked it all the way to full rabbit to get maximum speed and jolted it forward into Javis as I came up behind him. Javis's wheelchair went shooting back with the full weight of the chair, plus Pastor Matthams who'd gotten caught in the middle, and Waylon's electric chair all giving it momentum. The next thing I knew I was flat on my back on the floor staring straight up at Malachi's face, trying to get air back into my lungs.

"You okay?" he asked.

I didn't want to answer. I was afraid I would cry. I'd worked so many hours to make the arts and crafts booths go well and two old men who behaved like toddlers had knocked the air out of me. Literally.

Next Camila's face and then Lillibeth's face joined Malachi's. "Did she hit her head?" Lillibeth asked.

"I can't tell." Camila held a finger up before my eyes

and moved it left and right. "Her eyes are following my finger, but she's not talking."

"I'm fine," I said.

"That's good. I don't think Javis's wheelchair is." Camila straightened and she and Lillibeth went to untangle the wheelchair collision.

Malachi knelt down next to me and did a quick set of squeezes up and down my legs and arms. "I don't think anything's broken."

"You're doing better than these chairs," Camila called over. "What a mess."

"Let me take a look," Marty said. "I've got my tool kit in the car."

It was nice of him. It had been nice of him to show up at all, but then to offer to work on Sunday afternoon, too, seemed above and beyond the call of duty.

"Do you think you injured anything?" Malachi asked.

"Only my spirit," I said. I put my hands over my face. I would not cry. Would not. Would not. Would not.

Malachi gently peeled my hands away from my eyes and held my hands in his. I felt that same spreading warmth and calm that I'd felt when he'd put his hand over mine at Floyd's funeral. "Spirits are hard to mend. Give me a bum ankle any day," he said. He gave my hands a squeeze and let them go.

I rubbed my hip where I'd fell on it. "That's going to hurt at yoga tonight." I sighed and looked around at the undersides of the tables and chairs. There were a few wads of gum stuck to under one of the tables. I wondered which aide had put them there. It definitely wasn't any of the residents. Chewing gum and old teeth did not mix. Some kind of pamphlet had been taped to the underside of one of the chairs, too.

"You do yoga?" Malachi asked.

"Every Sunday night at seven at the Here and Now Yoga studio downtown with my friend Sharon," I said, trying to see what the pamphlet said.

"This is partly my fault." Malachi stood and reached his hand down to help me up. "It's possible I gave Javis too much of a pep talk about standing up to Waylon."

I laughed and sat up to take his hand, then stopped. "Hold on a second." I scooted over to the chair on my bottom and pulled the pamphlet off. It was a users' manual. Smart place to keep it, really. If the chair broke, one of the first places you'd look would be underneath it and presto voilà there would be the user's manual and the warranty information. I stuck it back on.

"What is it?" Malachi asked as I took his hand and let him help pull me up.

Something about sitting on the floor looking up and finding something important started to niggle at the back of my brain. Tyler went through a phase of hiding my car keys when he was three. At first, it would take me hours to find them. Then I noticed a pattern. If I got down on the floor so I was looking at the world from his vantage point of the height of a three-year-old, it suddenly became easy to find what he'd hidden.

"Is Irma's Jazzy Pride still here?" I asked.

"I think so. The place the family was donating it to hasn't come to pick it up yet," he said.

I dusted off my jeans. "Do you know where it is?"

"Sure." He turned and gestured with a head nod for me to follow him back to a storage closet. There among the clean sheets and towels stood Irma's trusty steed. I hit the button, fingers crossed it still held a charge. It was only half juiced, but I didn't think I'd need to run it for long.

"Okay then." I sat down and rode it out of the supply closet.

Malachi trotted next to me. You could get some good speed going in one of these things if you set that dial to full rabbit. No wonder Waylon sent us all flying like that. "Where are you going?"

"Back to the unit."

Malachi hit the code and opened the door for me. I drove Irma's Jazzy Pride along the perimeter of the unit. I shrank down in the seat so I would be more at the same eye level she would have looked at the world from.

At first, it was a bit disappointing. I found some dust, more gum, and some Pokemon stickers that I'm guessing someone's grandkid had stuck on the walls.

"Do you want to tell me what you're doing so I can help?" Malachi asked.

I thought about it for a second. "No. I'll be embarrassed if I'm wrong."

And then I wasn't wrong. Tucked up under the railing that ran along the hallway near Irma's room was something purple. I stopped, reached up and plucked Irma's purple notebook out . No wonder no one had seen it. She'd hidden it at what was her eye level, shrunken down in her Jazzy Pride. It was like when Tyler used to hide my car keys. I just had to look at the world as she would to find it. "Irma's notebook."

He stood back and gave me a round of applause. "Well done."

I gave a mock bow. Or as much as a bow I could in a Jazzy Pride.

"You seem pretty pleased. Was there a reason you wanted it?" He leaned against the wall.

Now my brow creased. "I'm not sure. I thought it was weird that it was gone. Her granddaughter said Irma thought she was Miss Marple. Then she died and the notebook disappeared. It made me curious." And suspicious. Could she have seen something or heard something that would help clear Brady? Had she figured out what Gabriel was doing? Or was it going to be like Floyd's notepad and garner me nothing more than an erroneous menu listing.

Malachi held out his hand. "Do you want me to give it to the family?"

"Thanks. I'll do it. I wanted to talk to them anyway. I really loved Irma." Damn it. Those stupid tears threatened again. I wheeled the Jazzy Pride around and drove it back to the storage area and took a few moments to compose myself.

I tucked Irma's notebook into the back of my jeans, under my white jacket, and went back to help clean up everything that had been flung about by the fling.

I had just enough time after the Spring Fling and before yoga to go to Sandra Roebuck's house to take a look at her bunny. I shoved Irma's notebook into my purse and toted my camera and some drawing supplies to my car and took off without saying good-bye to anyone.

Sandra's house wasn't quite as nice as Judy Gordon's, but close. She had on a pair of yoga pants and a draped shirt when she opened the door, her hair piled on top of her head in a messy bun. Everything looked like Judy's, just not quite as expensive. "Hi, Leah, come in." Then she paused and pointed to a shoe rack. "Would you mind taking off your shoes? We're trying to have a shoe-free house."

A strong sense of déjà vu washed over me, but then there was Cinna who was truly as adorable as her name. She was a floppy-eared thing with light brown and white markings and a little triangle nose that made my fingers tingle they wanted to sketch her so much. She was no Sugar Pop and I meant that in the best way. "Oh, she's wonderful," I said, crouching down next to her.

"Thank you. She was so great with the kids when they were young. I think she misses them." Like Sharon's dog Beau, waiting night after night in front of Max's door. "Maybe I should do portraits of them for her." I laughed.

Sandra didn't. She looked like she was actually considering it.

I stood up. "I have another commission ahead of yours so it might take a few weeks." Another commission from someone who might actually pay me.

"Great. Do you think you can have it done in time for Easter? I'd love to show it off." She paused. "You know, you might get a whole lot more clients from that."

Clients who weren't willing to pay me what I was worth? What my work was worth? I wasn't sure that was much of a deal. I rubbed at the bruise on my butt I'd gotten from my close encounter with Javis's wheelchair. Some money was better than no money, though. I said okay and then left to meet Sharon. I didn't really feel like it, but I'd skipped the week before because Tyler had been home and I really didn't have an excuse to skip it again.

We'd started doing yoga ostensibly to get some exercise, but I'd also wanted to get some of that serenity and centering people always talked about when they talked about yoga. I did feel more centered at the end of a class, but also a little empty, a little more in tune with the nothingness you were supposed to achieve then was entirely comfortable. I felt like nothing more often than I liked already. I would have rather felt like something.

Sharon looked in dire need of quiet and centering as she strode down the sidewalk where I waited for her. Her dark hair was escaping from her braid and part of her shirt had come untucked. She thrust her yoga mat at me and said, "Gotta change. I'll be out in five. Save me a spot."

I grabbed her mat from her and went into the studio proper. I staked out two spots in the middle on the right side and glanced at my watch. Sharon was definitely taking her time. The class was already into our second sun salutation when she tiptoed out of the changing room and joined us.

"The police asked Brady to come in for another interview," she whispered.

I frowned as I circled my right arm overhead to move into Warrior Two. "Why?" I said to the back of Sharon's head.

"I'm not sure," Sharon said, sinking lower into her lunge. "They said they had more questions. I don't like it."

We dropped our right arms and moved into Exalted Warrior. If only I felt as powerful as the poses we were doing. We circled back into plank, lowered ourselves halfway to the ground into Chataranga Dandasana, and swooped up to downward dog. My ponytail brushed my mat as I turned to Sharon and said, "Maybe it's a good sign. Maybe they want to know what he saw that morning rather than what he did."

We shifted into a side plank and extended our legs to move into fallen triangle or Patita Tārāsana. I groaned.

"I hope so," Sharon choked out.

I looked up to see the instructor glaring at us and shut up for the rest of the class although I couldn't stop thinking about Brady being interrogated again when he'd done nothing wrong. When we got out to the lobby area to get our shoes, Sharon turned away to check her phone and made a funny noise in the back of her throat. I pulled my phone out, too, to turn the ringer back on. There were three alerts on my phone from my security system. I must have gasped, because Sharon turned back around.

"What is it?"

"A window broke at the house and the back door was opened." I held out the phone so she could see the alerts. "The first one is from forty-five minutes ago."

"You still don't have the alarm system being monitored by anyone?" She put her hands on her hips.

I shook my head.

"Astonishing." Sharon shoved her arms into her jacket and grabbed my hand. "What are we waiting for? Let's go."

I pulled up to my house a few minutes behind Sharon. She drives crazy fast. There was no way I could have taken the curve at Yew Lane the way she had. She had practically been on two wheels.

She marched up to the front door and turned around to wait for me to open it.

I hung back, my heart beating faster than it had during the accelerated sun salutations we'd just done. "Maybe we shouldn't go in. What if whoever broke the glass is still inside?"

"Do you want to call the police?" She cocked her head to one side.

What if was like the last time and there was a perfectly good explanation? I unlocked the front door and we stepped inside.

"Well, someone's definitely been in here or you've really let your housekeeping skills slip since Tyler went to school," Sharon said.

All the cushions on the couch had been thrown onto the ground and ripped open. Foam bits were everywhere. Books were strewn all over the floor. Kitchen cabinets had been dumped out.

The worst was in my bedroom, though. The drawers from my dresser had been pulled out and dumped. The mattress on my bed was askew. My panties and bras spanned over the top of everything like a very intimate rainbow. "What now?" I asked.

"Now you definitely call the police and report it." Sharon's phone pinged and she glanced at her watch.

"I can take it from here if you need to go." Whoever had done this was clearly gone. They weren't lurking in a closet waiting for everyone to leave. I hoped.

"No. I'm not going until I see this dealt with appropriately." She crossed her arms over her chest and stuck her phone in her pocket. "Mindy can wait two seconds for once."

That didn't sound good. I called the police non-emergency line. "I'd like to report a break-in."

The woman on the other end made one of those "mmm mmmm mmm" noises. "Do you know approximately when it happened?"

I looked at my phone to see what time the first text alert had come in. "Seven-thirteen."

"It's only a little after eight, ma'am. Are you inside the house?"

"Yes."

"Are you sure you're safe?"

"Yes," I said, feeling the exact opposite.

"Is anything missing?"

"I don't know. I haven't really looked yet. I didn't think I should touch anything in case there were clues or something."

"Clues?" She sounded confused.

"Yes. You know. Fingerprints or DNA or something."

The woman made a funny little noise. "For these kinds of things, we don't generally do a lot of investigation. People mainly need us to make a report for insurance reasons."

"So no fingerprinting or anything like that?" I asked.

"Not generally. Not unless there was something of great value taken," she said. "Has there been something of great value taken?

I looked down. I didn't actually own anything of great value for someone to steal. Maybe my computer or my camera. I went to the room I use as an office and studio where they were both sitting, some of the few things to remain undisturbed, then came back in. "My computer and camera are still here."

"What about jewelry?" she asked. "Want to check on that?"

My engagement ring and wedding ring and Travis's wedding ring were all in my safety deposit box at the bank. "I don't have a lot of jewelry that's worth much."

She paused and I could hear some keys clicking. "We'll send someone over to make a report in a bit."

I hung up and picked up the throw pillow I'd made from Travis's shirt. It had been cut open and thrown on the floor. Granted, it was old and worn and probably should have been replaced, but I'd still liked to rest my cheek against it when I felt sad or lonely. It was a piece of him I could keep around. Now it was ruined. Sliced through in a way I didn't think I could repair.

Sharon came over and put her hand on my back, not

saying anything, but letting me know everything I needed to know in that one touch.

"Do you have insurance to make a report to?" Sharon finally asked.

I nodded. Insurance wasn't going to be able to replace the pillow, though. I set what was left of it down on the coffee table and picked up some other torn and ripped cushions.

There was a knock at the front door. Sharon indicated with a head nod that she'd answer it. She came back a few seconds later with two uniformed police officers, one short and one tall, one LatinX and one white, both women. "Mind if we take a look around before we ask any questions?" the taller one asked.

"Be my guest." I gestured for them to go in.

They'd been gone for about five minutes when there was another knock at the door and I opened it to find Detective Park. He had on jeans and a Henley under a hoodie. It was a far cry from the nice suits I was used to seeing him in, but definitely didn't look any worse.

"What are you doing here?" I asked.

"You called the police, didn't you? Well, I'm police." He smiled, then turned to the uniformed cops as they returned to the living room. "Anything to report?"

The shorter cop said, "Everything's been searched, but a lot of the damage is in the bedroom. Very focused and personal." We followed her into the room. She gestured to the contents of my lingerie drawer spread on top of everything like embarrassing frosting on a pathetic cake. Thank goodness I'd gotten rid of all my granny panties.

Park turned in a slow circle "Someone was looking for something."

"But what?" I turned around in a circle myself as if the

something would reveal itself then realized I was once again heading into interpretive dance territory. I glanced over at Sharon who seemed not to have noticed as she stood with her hands on her hips, disapproval rolling off her in waves. I wasn't sure if it was for the police or for my underwear or for my twirling.

Park rubbed the back of his neck. "I was going to ask you that myself. What do you have that someone might want?"

I tried really hard to come up with something of value that I owned, something that someone else would want enough to try to steal it, something that anyone would want at all. I looked around my room at the bed board I'd bought at a second-hand store and painted, at the drapes I'd made myself from fabric in the clearance bin, at the rug I'd latch hooked while sitting on the sidelines of a soccer game. I couldn't come up with a single thing that anyone besides me would want. "Nothing that I can think of."

Park nodded a few times and then asked, "You left here at what time?"

"Earlier today. I was at the Spring Fling at Caring Hands, then I had an appointment with a portrait customer, then I had yoga class." I walked back to the living room. It felt too weird to have that many people in my bedroom. It's not some place I'm use to sharing.

In the living room, Park leaned against one of the armchairs. "And what time is your yoga class?"

"Seven." I put a cushion back on the couch

"Every Sunday?"

I nodded.

"And the first ping came at around seven-ten?"

I nodded again.

Park glanced over at the taller uniformed cop and gave

her a look. She blushed and then pulled out her notepad and scribbled something down. "That's pretty convenient. It's like they knew your schedule. They knew you'd be gone by a little before seven and that you wouldn't be back for over an hour. They waited until it was past the time you'd be back if you'd forgotten something and took their time searching here knowing that you wouldn't be looking at your phone during yoga."

"How would someone know that?" Why would someone want to know that? I barely wanted to know it.

"By watching you." He said it simply with no drama.

"Are you saying someone's stalking me?" A shiver ran up my spine and my voice went up a bit, too.

"I'd say someone has been watching. I'm not sure it's risen to the level of stalking yet, but I think it would be wise for you to keep your eyes open for the next few days. Take a few extra seconds to look at your surroundings when you're out. See if you notice anything or anyone that doesn't seem quite right." Park pulled a card case from his pocket, pulled out a card, and scribbled something on the back of it. "This has my contact info at the station and my personal info as well. I want you to call me if there's anything — and I mean anything — that seems out of place." He motioned to the other cops and they all walked back to the front door.

"Thanks," I said. "I appreciate the help."

I shut the door after them and turned to Sharon who looked very much like she was trying not to laugh. "What?"

"I appreciate the help?" She slapped her thigh.

"What's wrong with that?" I asked, not sure I got the joke.

"It depends on what it is you think he's trying to help with." She grinned.

"What are you suggesting?

She pulled her braid over her shoulder. "Nothing. I'm sure Detective Park shows up for all the local B&Es."

That hadn't occurred to me.

"Have you felt like anyone has been following you? Have you gotten that weird being watched feeling?" she asked.

I shook my head. "No. Unless you count Detective Park being there every time I turn around."

"I don't count that. It's annoying, but it's his job." She tugged at her braid. "You are kind of oblivious, though."

"I am not! I notice lots of things that other people don't," I protested.

"True. But then you don't notice things that everyone else does." She gave me a hug. "I've gotta get home. Mindy's going nuts. Are you okay?"

Was I? Not really, but there wasn't anything anyone else could do about it. "I'm fine. Right now, I just want to clean this mess up and go to bed."

"Call someone about that back window first, okay?"

I nodded and saw her out. I went back to my bedroom and started gathering up my underwear and putting it back in its drawer. It occurred to me that I should text Tyler. I couldn't imagine this making it onto anyone's gossip radar, but you never knew. I didn't want him to worry. I suspected that last trip home had been all about making sure I was okay. I reached into my purse to pull my phone out and my hand hit something hard and square. I pulled it out. Irma's notebook. I hadn't had a chance to really look at it yet. I'd been busy meeting Cinna Bunny and going to yoga. The front cover had a spray of lilacs on the front and the phrase "Choose Happy." That had to be a gift. That was way too sweet for Irma. I opened it.

The first page had two dates with a list of names

beneath each. The names I recognized instantly. They were staff at Caring Hands. Lillibeth, Camila, Malachi, Kendrick, Christy, Dionne, and I were on the list among others under one date. Lillibeth, Camila, Christy, Dionne, and I were on the second one, too. I recognized one of the dates, too. It was the day Floyd had died. I had a suspicion about the other and did a quick Internet search.

Bingo. The second date was the day Harvey Cornish died. Were those the people who were on duty at Caring Hands on those dates?

I flipped the page. The next few pages read almost like a log of comings and goings and events around Caring Hands. I saw notations about Detective Park searching Brady's locker and dates and times about the comings and goings of Gabriel as well as Anna and Marty.

Then on the final page was a list of seven names with dates next to the names. The first name on the list was Harvey Cornish. I recognized two other names. They were both Caring Hands residents that had died in the months before Harvey did. I did a quick internet search on my phone for the rest of the names. The first item that came up for each of them was an obituary.

They were all dead. All but one of the people on the list had been a Caring Hands resident. All but one had died in the last six months. That person was dead, too, but it was closer to a year ago and not at Caring Hands. She'd lived in the Bay Area.

The room swayed around me. Why did Irma have a list of dead people in her special notebook? And why these specific dead people? They weren't the only ones who had died at Caring Hands while I'd been working there. About a month ago during lunch, Effie Shelinger had been eating chocolate pudding one second. The next she was flatlining on the floor. It was if someone had snapped their fingers and she was gone. I'd had to sit with my head between my knees for about ten minutes before the room stopped spinning around me when it happened although there were worse ways to go than with a mouthful of chocolate. Effie wasn't on Irma's list. I checked twice. Neither were two other people I knew had died in the same time period, their families crowding the hallway around their room as they came to say their good-byes.

So what was the connection? And where to look for it. I slipped the notebook back into my purse and went to brush my teeth and get ready for bed. Patient files would undoubtedly be the best place to start looking for a common thread between them, besides just being dead. Caring Hands had a big old three-ring binder full of paper for each patient. Most of the time, those binders lived on a cart that sat behind the nurses' station. At least, for current residents. I happened to know where they stored the three-ring binders that detailed the medical records of residents who had died.

In the basement. Right next to where I stored most of my art supplies.

I looked around my mess of a bedroom. Maybe it wasn't so much that I had something someone wanted. Maybe I had something they didn't want me to have. A subtle difference, for sure, but still a difference. Maybe someone didn't want anyone to see what was in Irma's notebook.

But who? Who even knew I had the notebook? Who had been there when I'd found it? The fair had been crowded. Most of the staff had been there for one reason or another. Clients. Families. Friends. Anyone could have seen me find it and put it in my purse. Lillibeth had. Gabriel certainly had. They'd all been there when I'd told Malachi about going to yoga tonight, too. It would have been easy for any one of them to look up the studio's class schedule online and to figure out exactly when I'd be gone and likely to have my phone off.

They all also knew my work schedule and way too many other things about me and my life.

I called the window repair people and told them it was an emergency.

FIFTEEN

Whoever had tossed my house hadn't smashed my coffeemaker. For that, I was exceedingly grateful. It didn't make the mess I had to clean up any better, but at least I had the energy to tackle it.

I started small, picking up the silverware and dish towels that were strewn around. At least, they weren't broken. I'd lost quite a few plates and mugs, including one that had a photo of Tyler on it from when he was seven. I still had the photo, though. That could be recreated. The dishes were all secondhand anyway and very few of them matched. I'd start collecting them again. It might even be fun, going to estate sales and garage sales and thrift shops to put it all together.

There wasn't much in the dining room. I righted the chairs and put cushions back on the chairs. My living room couch, on the other hand, looked to be a lost cause. I stacked up the cut-open cushions. I'd take them to the trash later. I was about to put the Travis pillow on top of the pile, but at the last second took what was left of the cover off it and put it in my bedside table.

My bedroom took some time, but with the exception of a few pillows things were still largely intact. By the time I was done with all that, it was nearly time to get to work. I wanted to get in early and do a little poking around before I had to start my class.

I swore the basement steps had gotten darker and colder despite it being a sunny day. I flicked on the light. Stark shadows from the balustrade slats ran diagonally across the steps. The smell of damp concrete rose up like a creepy perfume. Somehow, it didn't matter. Whatever power the stairs held over me was gone.

The records for inactive residents — a polite way of saying dead patients — were kept in a storage space close to the area I'd been given to store my art supplies. It had a chain-link door and a handle with a key, but it was never locked. It was almost never even closed. I guess they felt the lock on the door to the basement was sufficient security.

Each patient had a large binder, which was good, because the records were long. Even the people who only stayed a short time generated a lot of paper. The binders were lined up on metal bookshelves that ran around the three walls of the storage space. I took Irma's notebook out of the back pocket of my jeans where I'd stowed it, hidden under the blazer I was wearing, and looked up the first name and found the associated binder. I pulled it out and set it on the metal table in the center of the space. It didn't take long to find what I was looking for. The records were arranged going backwards chronologically so the most recent pages were at the front of the book.

Xavier Pinner was found dead when they'd come to wake him up for breakfast. Nobody actually wrote "it's a blessing" in the medical record, but everything else they wrote pointed to that. Xavier had fallen in the shower and hit his head hard enough to cause a brain bleed. He went from being fairly functional to being close to a vegetable in pretty short order.

Josephine Bent was found non-responsive in her bed. Again, she was someone whose health had taken a rapid decline. Several bouts of pneumonia had exacerbated the symptoms of her congestive heart failure.

Howard Carlisle had a stroke. A week later he was dead in his bed.

Evie Bradley had fallen and broken a hip. She'd gone from living in one of the independent living cottages to needing twenty-four-hour care. Then she'd apparently had a heart attack. At least, that seemed to be what they were guessing happened. Malachi had said it was surprisingly common. Dr. Timms had signed off on the death certificate without an autopsy.

All of them had died quickly and quietly after their health had taken a significant downturn. All of them had died in their sleep and been found by someone on day shift who had come to wake them up for breakfast. I jotted down the names and phone numbers of their next of kin in Irma's notebook.

"What are you doing in there?"

I squealed and whirled around. Malachi. I pressed my hand to my heart. "You scared me."

"Sorry." He didn't look sorry. He looked worried, then he seemed to take in more of our surroundings and frowned. "Leah, those records are confidential. You could get the facility in a lot of trouble looking through them."

He picked up Evie's binder, shut it, and after checking the name on the edge, re-shelved it. The edge of the binder made a click as it connected with the back of the shelving unit. He dusted his hands off and turned back to me.

"I think Caring Hands might have more to worry about than a HIPAA breach." I said, but re-shelved Howard's binder as well. I'd learned what I could already.

"What does that mean?" He put his hand on mine, stopping me from picking up the next binder. I stilled. The calm he seemed to exude from his pores finding its way to my heart.

"I think these people's deaths might be connected." I gestured to the binders.

"Um. Not to be rude, but duh?" He let go of my hand and gestured around at the shelves. "These are all people who have died at Caring Hands."

"But these people," I said, pointing to Josephine's binder and Xavier's binder. "They're all people who had taken sudden turns for the worse." I shifted back on my heels already hearing how ridiculous I sounded.

"Again, so? People often take turns for the worse before they die and people here at Caring Hands are generally here because they've already taken that turn or seem about to." His face stayed soft even though his words sounded harsh. He picked up Josephine's binder and re-shelved it. B and C are pretty close in the alphabet and he stood close enough for me to inhale the citrus and linen smell that followed him around. "I hate to say it, but plenty of people die here. It's expected. How come you're looking at these specific ones then? And not some of the others?" Malachi asked, looking around at the rows of binders that surrounded us.

"Their names were on a list in Irma's notebook." I thought about what I'd read in the files so far. "That's what started it. But it's not just that now. All of them died in pretty much the same way. Peacefully. In their sleep. With no one else around."

Malachi leaned back against the locker wall and crossed his arms over his chest. I wondered if he knew the way that pose plumped up his biceps in his short-sleeved scrubs. "Doesn't sound like a bad way to go to me. They've come to the end of their journeys. They've done their work, lived their lives. A lot of them are waiting for it to be over."

Something about that resonated with me, something I'd been thinking for a while, something that kept me up at night. I turned and leaned my back against the shelves. "Sometimes I feel the same way," I whispered. It wasn't anything I'd said out loud to anyone. I didn't know why I was telling Malachi now. Something about the intimacy of the small space surrounded by all these books full of the lives of people who weren't here anymore loosened my lips and the way his presence seemed to always leave me feeling calmer and more centered. It made me feel safe and brave enough to look at what I was really thinking and feeling.

He dropped his hand to his side and went very still. "What do you mean?"

I shrugged. "I feel like I've accomplished what I'm supposed to accomplish. After Travis — my husband — died, I knew I had to keep it together for our son. I had to keep Tyler healthy and get him to school and feed him. It was my focus. Everything else was secondary."

"You're a mom. Of course, that's your job." He relaxed a bit against the metal table.

It was a job that I'd dedicated the last eighteen (nineteen if you count pregnancy!) years to, but what was I supposed to do now? "Tyler is almost launched. I mean, I know he's still kind of a kid, but he's in college and heading in the right direction. He doesn't need me in the same ways anymore and over the next few years he'll need me less and less. My job is basically done. I feel a little useless, like these people probably did." I gestured at the binders again.

Down in the basement, sound was muffled. In the silence that followed what I'd said, I could hear the hum of machinery that kept Caring Hands running and the sound of Malachi next to me breathing, but nothing else.

The sound of the door creaking open interrupted us. Then it slammed shut and footsteps clicked on the stairs. Malachi's eyes got big. "We can't get caught in here," he whispered. "We'll both get in trouble."

He grabbed my hand and led me toward the old hydrotherapy room. I pulled back. "Not there," I whispered. I might not be scared of the stairs anymore, but the hydrotherapy room was another matter all together.

"Why not?" He looked back over his shoulder.

I wasn't sure how to describe how I felt about that, either. "It's spooky."

He pulled me closer to him and whispered in my ear, "I won't let anything happen to you." All the hair on my arms stood up.

Then we were inside the hydrotherapy room. Malachi pulled the door almost closed. I turned and pressed my eye against the crack to see who might be coming down the steps. Malachi pressed in behind me, his chest broad and warm and solid against my back. I could feel the steady thump thump thump of his heart.

"It's Lillibeth," he whispered, breath warm on my ear. "Maybe she won't notice anything."

I hoped not. Xavier's binder was still out on the table.

Lillibeth rounded the corner from the stairs, marching with purpose and determination as always. Then her steps faltered as she went past the room with the binders. She stopped and backed up and went in. We couldn't see her, but I heard the same little snick of the edge of the binder hitting the back of the metal shelves that I'd heard when Malachi reshelved Josephine's binder.

Then she was walking to the stacks of equipment. She picked up a walker and hefted it over her shoulder. I slumped in relief when she was out of sight on the stairs.

I turned to face Malachi and suddenly we were altogether too close. His chest pressed to my chest. His lips inches from my lips. The basement went from cold and clammy to blazing hot in about ten seconds. "Maybe we'll get lucky and she won't think anything of it," I said.

"Maybe we'll get lucky indeed." Malachi's pupils had dilated to the point his eyes looked black. "And for the record, I don't think you're useless at all."

And then he kissed me.

———

To say I was a little distracted during Yarn Circle was an understatement. I miscounted stitches and had to pull out four rows of the baby blanket I was working on and Tessie had to ask me for another skein of yarn three times before I heard her. "What's gotten into you?" she asked as we packed up.

I wasn't going to tell her I'd been playing tonsil hockey with Malachi in the basement and had gotten myself into a state because of it. "Oh, there was a break in at my house last night. It's a mess and I guess I'm distracted trying to figure out how I'm going to replace everything that was broken." I wasn't entirely lying. Buying a new couch wasn't really in the budget for the month. Maybe I could string the old cushions along for a while with duct tape and patches.

"Oh, you poor dear!" she said. "First you end up going

ass over teakettle in front of God and everybody at the Spring Fling and then someone ransacked your house? No wonder you can't keep purls straight from your knits." She patted my arm.

It was nice of her to cut me the slack. It was more than what people did for her on occasion. One little slip up with a scam artist and they'd taken away her phone. I put my hand over hers for a second and thanked her. I hoped that a little of the calm and warmth that Malachi had seeped into me would be passed onto her.

When I took the yarn back down to the basement, the door to the inactive patient files was closed. I gave the knob a quick turn. Someone had locked it. I wouldn't be getting any more information from there. Had Lillibeth figured out that I'd been in there? I hoped not. I especially hoped not if Malachi was right and we could get into trouble for it.

———

A pick-up truck half-full of furniture and three cars stood in front of my house when I pulled up at a little after five. George and Jamal were carrying the remnants of my old couch onto the driveway. Sharon and Tamika walked out behind them a stack of ripped-up cushions.

I parked on the street and got out of my truck and looked at my friends and their partners. "What's going on?"

Rayna came out of the front door with a particularly mangled cushion and tossed it with its ruined counterparts. "Sharon told us what happened to your furniture. We decided to clear it away and give you something to sit on while you figure out what you want to do next."

I went in. A sectional sofa stood where my old sectional had stood. It wasn't brand new and it wasn't a color I would pick, but it would definitely do. A few throw cushions in bright colors and an afghan thrown over the back of it and it would probably look like nothing had changed. Except the Travis pillow, of course. There was no replacing that.

"Where did this come from?" I asked.

"My mom's storage space." Tamika looped an arm over my shoulder. "Really, you're doing her a favor. Without that thing, we can downsize it and save her some money each month."

I leaned into her, not quite able to speak right away. "Thanks," I finally whispered.

She gave me a squeeze. "It's nothing."

Rayna came back in carrying a bag of potato chips and that onion dip you make with sour cream and onion soup. "I brought snacks." I wasn't sure what I was more shocked by, the fact that her hair wasn't pulled into its usual smooth low ponytail or that she'd brought such an unhealthy treat. The closest thing to potato chips that Rayna had ever brought before were homemade kale chips and, trust me, those were not potato chips.

Mindy and Sharon followed her in carrying a low coffee table. "This was in our garage. I thought it would go with the couch," Mindy said.

"It does," I stepped out of the way so she could set it down. Rayna promptly set the chips and dip on it.

Jamal poked his head in. "Hey, Leah. If you'll let us use your truck, George and I will take your old couch out to the dump while you guys get settled in here."

I tossed him the keys without hesitation. "Thank you."

Mindy brushed her hands together. "I need to get going, too. I've got a lecture to prepare. See you later?" She gave Sharon a kiss and then headed to the door. "Don't be too late, okay?"

I cracked open a bottle of wine and got out some glasses.

"How did Brady do at the police station?" I tucked myself into my corner with my own glass of wine, grateful to have a spot that felt so like mine already.

"At least this time they didn't bring him in in handcuffs so Eva didn't have anything specifically related to Brady to post about. She vague-booked something about wanting to feel safe in her own neighborhood," Rayna rolled her eyes and crammed a handful of potato chips into her mouth and washed them down with a pretty substantial gulp of wine.

"It only got three likes and one person asked her what the hell she meant," Tamika said.

Sometimes I actually felt a little sorry for Eva. What must it be like to have a mind that worked that way? "What kind of questions did the police ask?"

"It was your Detective Park again," Sharon said. "He asked a lot of questions about other people Brady saw around the facility, but not only on the day Floyd died. Kind of more generally who he saw around the place. I wasn't sure what to make of it either."

I considered protesting that he wasn't 'my' Detective Park, but I was feeling too much good will with all the furniture. "Maybe they're looking at other people as suspects." Maybe Detective Park was finally investigating Gabriel. I was dying to tell them about it.

"I hope so." Sharon pulled her legs up. "So what's with the potato chips? We never have potato chips."

"Well, we should have potato chips more often," Rayna said. "And ice cream. And cookies. God damn it."

I'm not saying we never had those things, but it wasn't usually Rayna who brought them or suggested them and it was definitely not Rayna who damned them. Sharon and I must have been staring at her.

"What?" she asked. "Why shouldn't we do whatever we want? Everyone else does. And where has doing everything right gotten me? A husband who thinks I'm hysterical. One kid who barely speaks to me and one who the police are questioning about a murder. I don't know how much time I have left, but I'm going to spend it eating potato chips and onion dip if I want to." She scooped up a big blob of dip on a chip and crammed it into her mouth, chewing noisily while staring at us.

Sharon, Tamika, and I all took chips, dipped them, and ate them while keeping our eyes on her. It felt like we were partaking in some kind of initiation ceremony or ritual, but much tastier than dipping parsley in salt water at Passover.

Rituals reminded me of funerals, which brought me back to Caring Hands. "Hey, is there a way to find out who died at Caring Hands in the last six months?" I asked Tamika.

"What? Why would you need to know that?" Sharon asked.

I explained about the names in Irma's notebook. "I know it's not all the people who died at Caring Hands because I can think of three more that aren't on the list. I don't know how to figure out how many more there might be or why they didn't make Irma's list."

Tamika crunched thoughtfully on another chip. "We could probably start by looking in the obituaries in the newspaper. That would give us a starting point."

That sounded like a plan. "How long would that take?"

"Do you need them tonight?" she asked.

"I think tomorrow would work."

"I'll have it to you by ten, but what is it that you think you'll find out?" Tamika asked.

I hit the end of my crochet row and turned it. I really

wanted another potato chip. "I'm going to see if there's a connection between the people on Irma's list."

"You already know there's a connection. They all died at Caring Hands," Sharon pointed out.

She sounded an awful lot like Malachi.

SIXTEEN

Tamika had the list of names to me by nine the next morning while I was still sitting at my kitchen counter drinking coffee. In the last six months eleven people had died at Caring Hands. Five of them, including Effie, weren't on Irma's list.

Why that set of names? Why only six plus our outlier? What was special about them that wasn't special about the other five people who had died at Caring Hands in the past year? Not one of them was on Camila's list of people who had been scammed. Those people were all still alive. "I wish I could call them and ask them questions, but I'm not sure what excuse I could use."

I could hear Tamika drumming her fingers. "What if you said you were doing some kind of special memorial book or something? Something you'd want a little background info for?"

"That's brilliant! I could call all of them."

"Except Phoebe Giles' family," Tamika pointed out.

"Yes. Except Phoebe's." I pulled my legs up beneath me. "Did you find out anything about her?"

"She died nine months ago at a nursing home in the Bay area."

"Which home?" I poured myself another cup. I was going to need my energy.

I heard her keyboard clicking. "Loving Arms in Fremont."

Hadn't one of the people Lillibeth resuscitated been near Fremont? "Have you seen any more posts from Brady online?"

"No. They stopped and whoever it was deleted the profile."

Interesting. I wondered if there was any connection between the classes Brady signed up for and his getting rid of the fake profile. After we hung up, I got out a pen and a pad of paper. I stared at the list of names, unsure where to start. I decided to start at the top. Boring, I know, but better than staring at the names trying to figure out which might be most important all night

I called Josephine Bent's daughter.

"I'm doing a special In Memoriam project honoring the people at Caring Hands who have passed away in the last year and your mother's name came up." I doodled a cat in the margin of the notebook.

"An In what?"

"In Memoriam. It will have a photo of your mother and some information about her and her life. You know, so people remember her." I gave the cat a top hat.

"Oh, that would be nice. It would be nice to remember her how she used to be instead of how she was at the end."

"I take it that was hard." I stopped doodling.

"Awful. Thank goodness we didn't have to live with it for long. When the doctor told us she could last for months in that state, we all felt terrible."

My heart gave a little stutter step. "But it didn't last for months?"

"Oh, no, she died in her sleep two weeks after she had the big stroke. Truly, it was a blessing."

We talked a bit more about Josephine and how she liked to write poetry and garden and how no one could make the chocolate frosting she used to make quite as well as she had and then we hung up.

I took a deep breath and dialed Howard Carlisle's emergency contact number.

"May I speak to Marisa Carlisle?" I asked when a woman answered.

"You got her, but if you're selling something I'm about to blow a real loud whistle into the phone."

"No! Not selling anything. I'm with Caring Hands," I said quickly.

She harrumphed. "Caring Hands? What on earth could you be calling me for now? Dad died four months ago."

"I know. That's kind of why I'm calling. I'm doing an In Memoriam project. You know, something to keep those who have passed here in mind." It actually wasn't such a bad idea.

"You're calling the families of everybody who died at Caring Hands? That's gonna be an awful long list. Pretty much everyone who checks in there checks out feet first, if you know what I mean?" She laughed until it turned into a coughing fit.

I did know. I'd said much the same thing myself. Not quite as gleefully, but the sentiment was the same. "It won't be big. Maybe a page or so on each one. What can you tell me about your Dad?"

Marisa drew in a long breath. "Let's see. Dad was born in Kansas in 1932, but my grandparents moved the family out to Oregon when Dad was a kid. He grew up in Port-land. Played basketball for U of O and then went into the Army."

"So he was a veteran," I said.

"Sure was. Damn proud of his service, too. He was in Korea. Learned all about engines over there and came back to work at Higgins Engine Company in Woodland. Met my mom. Married her. Had me and my brother Ken."

"Sounds like a nice life."

"He certainly thought so. He liked playing golf and crib-bage and pretty much did that until the morning that he didn't wake up."

"He died in his sleep?"

"Yep. They came in to get him up for breakfast and he was gone." Marisa paused for a moment. "It was so like him. No muss. No fuss. Didn't like a lot of drama. I think he was worried there would be a lot of drama after getting that cancer diagnosis. It sounded like it was one of those things that might drag on. Put that in your In Memory thing, okay? The no drama thing. He'd like that."

"I will. Thank you."

"So is this related to that other thing that the old guy was doing?"

That set me back on my heels for a moment. "What other thing and which old guy?" Maybe she was confused.

"Someone called here asking about how Dad died not too long ago. He said he was from Caring Hands, too." Her tone softened. "Not that I mind having a chance to talk about Dad. I miss him. But you all ought to pool your resources so you don't double up like this. Waste of time."

"Good idea. Do you remember the name of the person who phoned?" I asked.

"Hold on. I think I scratched it down here some place."

Papers rustled on the other end of the phone line. Something thumped and a dog barked. "Here it is. Name was Floyd."

"Floyd Winstead?" My heart sped up. How did Floyd know to call Marisa Carlisle?

"Maybe. Didn't write down the last name. Just Floyd and his phone number. Said to call if I thought of anything else I'd like to tell him."

"And he said it was for the In Memoriam project?"

"Hmmmm." She clucked her tongue a couple times. "Come to think of it, no. Didn't say anything about an In Memoriam thingie. Just said he wanted some background info on Dad. Told him pretty much the same thing I told you."

Floyd had called asking for information? That little warning bell in my head was getting a bit louder. "Thank you."

"Nah," she said. "Thank you. Let me know when this In Memoriam thing is ready to go. I'd like to see it."

We hung up and I sat for a moment, pondering. Floyd had asked questions about Howard Carlisle. Irma had had Howard's name on a list in her little purple book. And now Floyd and Irma were both dead. I shivered.

I called the contact information for the first name on the list of people who had died in the last six months, but wasn't on Irma's list. Wilma Metzler's emergency contact was her daughter, Patricia, who answered on the second ring. I went through my song and dance about the In Memoriam project again.

"What do you want to know about Mom?" she asked, sounding confused.

"Oh, anything you'd like to tell me about." I was definitely in needle in the haystack territory.

"Well, she didn't move out here to California from Michigan until she was in her 70s. I was here and my brother is in Oregon. Michigan was too far away."

"And too cold, too, I bet."

She laughed. "That, too." She paused. "She was a great mom. I know everybody says stuff like that after someone dies, but she really was. She was the mom who always helped out on field trips and baked cookies and cheered for us. I don't think she missed a single one of my field hockey games back when I was in high school and she went to pretty much every soccer game my kids played after she moved here."

"That sounds nice." I thought about my mom back in Chicago. I'd mostly been relieved when she didn't show up for things. I didn't know if Tyler missed having a grandma or grandpa to cheer for him on the soccer sidelines or to bake cookies for him or to teach him how to play chess or the other things I'd seen grandparents do for my friends' kids. I did my best to cheer and bake and teach enough for an entire battalion of grandparents.

"It was nice. Really nice. For her and for us. I try to remember that, that we had all that good time." There was a little crack in Patricia's voice. A little one, but still. I felt like a heel for dragging her through her grief again.

There was a sharp uptake of breath and then she said, "Is that the kind of stuff you need?"

"That's great," I said, trying to figure out how to ask if there was anything odd about how Wilma had died. "I take it she passed suddenly?"

"Well, suddenly for someone over ninety, yes. It was pneumonia. She'd been getting a little confused. They think she aspirated some food. It was downhill really fast from there."

"So it was surprising," I said.

"Well, not so surprising that we didn't all make it there. My brother, our kids, me, my husband, we were all there with her as she took those last breaths. The last thing she heard was us telling her we loved her and would miss her."

I swallowed hard, but my voice still cracked a bit as I asked, "Has anyone else from Caring Hands contacted you since your mother passed?" Had Floyd called all these people or just the ones that were on Irma's list?

"We got a nice condolence card from Doctor Timm's office," Patricia said.

"Oh, good. No one else called to ask any questions, though? An older gentleman?"

"No. There wasn't much to ask, I guess."

I made three more phone calls and had to stop. There was a limit to how much I can cry in any one day without my soul taking a hit and my body getting dehydrated. I dragged my sorry self over to my couch corner with my notes, a box of tissues, and the shreds of my Travis pillow.

The rest of the calls had been pretty much the same as the first three. The families of the people on Irma's list said things like "To tell the truth, I was kind of relieved when I got the call. She hated being so incapacitated, having to rely on other people to do everything for her. I wish I would have been there when she passed, but it came a little quicker than we expected." And "he'd been getting more and more vague, not sure who we were all the time. Sometimes he'd get angry. I was afraid we were going to have to move him to a new place. Then he didn't wake up one morning." The one that broke my heart was the daughter who worried that her father might have been scared or lonely as he passed because she hadn't been there to hold his hand. They'd all been contacted by Floyd, or at least someone besides me that sounded like it might be Floyd.

The families of the people who had died in the last six months, but weren't on Irma's list had all seemed to have had enough warning to get hospice services and be there with their loved ones as they passed. They got to say their good-byes and surround their person with love. They'd all received condolence cards from Doctor Timm's office, but no phone calls.

People die when people die. There's not always a rhyme or reason to it. Some of them wait until the family all gets there to say good-bye. Some slip off in the night when no one's there. Some tumble out of their chairs at lunch and are dead before they hit the floor. So why did it matter so much that these people died in their sleep that Floyd had called these people's families and that Irma had made this list?

What was Floyd seeing that no one else did and did that get him killed? Did asking these same question get Irma killed, too?

I channeled my inner Tamika and did an internet search for "unexpected deaths in nursing homes."

Among the raft of websites for lawyers who would help you sue a nursing home if you thought your loved one died due to medical error or negligence was a scholarly-looking article on the subject.

In that article, the authors said what I'd observed. Attending physicians at nursing homes are often willing to sign death certificates without even seeing the person after death if the person had been under their treatment. Because of that unnatural deaths of nursing home patients were underreported. At the end of their list of ways people could die unexpectedly in a nursing home was Mercy Killer.

According to the article, mercy killers were usually

employed as caregivers at an institution or in a home, but instead of caring for the people in their charge, they killed them. Different mercy killers that had been caught had given various reasons for what they did, the most prevalent being that they decided the person would be better off dead, that they should be released from their suffering. The article cited several recent cases.

An argument could be made for every one of those names on Irma's list that it was a mercy that they were dead, that they'd been released from pain, that they could be free from their suffering. I pulled my legs up and wrapped my arms around my shins. I would be lying if there hadn't been more than a few times that I'd walked out of Caring Hands saying a little prayer that I wouldn't ever have to live like that.

When Travis died, we'd known for weeks that we were coming to the end. It might have been merciful to him and to me and to Tyler to let him go sooner, but the idea of not having had those last few moments with him felt like a punch in the gut. The thought of someone deliberately taking those moments from us when he was too weak and ill to protect himself had me doubled up on hand-me-down couch as if that punch was real.

I looked at the names on Irma's list and the notes I'd taken. These people hadn't had anyone watching out for them. They were old and sick and fragile and they couldn't protect themselves. Their families were far away and couldn't be with them. It was possible that whoever was doing this truly thought they were doing them a favor. There was no guarantee that alleviating suffering was the only reason whoever it was was doing this, however. They might say it was, but maybe they enjoyed playing God. Maybe they got off on having that kind of power over someone, the power of life and death. It was like a playground bully taken to the nth degree.

I hated bullies. I always had.

Bullies bully until someone stops them. It seemed possible that Floyd and Irma had tried and had paid the ultimate sacrifice for those attempts, but I wasn't weak and I wasn't sick and I certainly wasn't fragile.

This was going to stop.

———

I parked my truck in the Caring Hands lot and hoisted the box loaded with the new craft supplies for the week's projects on my hip. Marty was walking out as I was walking in. He stopped to hold the door open for me. "Thanks. How's your day going?" I asked.

He froze and his mouth dropped open.

"Are you okay?" I asked, not quite sure what I'd said wrong.

Then I realized he wasn't looking at me. He was looking over my shoulder. I turned.

Two cars had pulled into the parking lot and stopped with the vehicles askew, blocking the driveway. One was a Chevy four-door sedan that looked an awful lot like the car that had been parked in front of my house when Rayna and Brady came over. The other was a police vehicle. A police officer should know better than to park so inconsiderately.

I turned back to Marty to tell him as much, but he shoved me to one side, sending me sprawling to the ground, and took off running. Packages of straws and buttons and balloons scattered around me. I sat up in time to see Detective Park emerge from the sedan and sprint across the parking lot to tackle Marty on the lawn of the retirement village right in front of the "Get the Care You Deserve at Caring Hands" sign.

I sat in the midst of my craft supplies, gaping. Park handcuffed Marty and escorted Marty to the police car, saying, "Marty Stubbs, you are under arrest for identity theft and fraud. You have the right to remain silent . . ."

After handing Marty off to the uniformed police officers who did that thing where they push people's heads down as they get in the back seat, Park walked back to me, brushing off his hands. I was glad he wasn't wearing one of his fancy suits. His jeans had a big grass stain on the knee and his button-down shirt was ripped at the sleeve. It would have been a shame to do that to a nice suit. It didn't look so bad on the jeans and the button-down. It gave him a sort of bad-boy vibe.

He extended his hand down to me to help me up. "Sorry about that. I didn't intend for you to get in the middle of it."

"What on earth was it?" I took his hand and hoisted myself to my feet, checking my own jeans for stains and rips. Beyond some dirt that was easily dusted off, I was fine although I'd landed on the exact same spot that I had when Javis and Waylon had sent me flying with their wheelchair demolition derby. That was going to leave a mark. Maybe I could use it as an excuse to get out of yoga next week. Have I mentioned how much I hate Fallen Triangle pose?

Park cocked his head. "We arrested Marty for stealing old folks' identities and setting up fraudulent calls to them."

"No." I frowned. His answer did not line up with the picture I had in my head. "Not Marty. You must have misheard me. It's Gabriel. Gabriel was the one who was lurking around patient rooms and had delivered flowers to them."

He rubbed the back of his neck. "I heard you fine. We looked into Gabriel. It wasn't him."

"Oh," I said. I knelt down to pick up the packages of buttons and put them back in their box, feeling inexplicably disappointed. "So I got it wrong?"

"Don't feel bad. It was looking into Gabriel and what Irma said about all the people they let in and out of their rooms that made me start checking into all the other service people who come in and out so often that nobody notices them." He knelt down next to me and dropped a handful of balloon packages into the box.

"And there was something about Marty that made you decide it was him?" The straws, on the other hand, might need to be replaced. I turned one package around in my hand. It was only a little bent. They'd probably be fine. I could use them as a demo if nothing else.

Park dropped two more packages of buttons into the box. "There was something about Marty's bank accounts that made us decide to investigate further. We set up a sting."

I put the last straw package in the box and stood. "A what?"

"A sting. We made sure a few select people had smart phones that didn't need codes and left around a few other temptations and then we watched." He stood, too, picking up the box.

Tessie's phone. Roland's checkbook. Leaving it out had been deliberate. "I think I almost messed that up for you." I opened the front door for him.

"So I heard. Roland was quite annoyed. Said you should mind your own beeswax." He smiled as he stopped in the lobby near the front desk.

Something still bothered me about what he was telling

me. "But Marty wasn't even here the day Floyd died. Gabriel was." I took the box from him.

Park gave me a funny look. "Marty is an identity thief and a scammer, not a murderer. He didn't have anything to do with Floyd's death."

"But if Marty is the scammer, then Gabriel doesn't have any reason to have killed Floyd." Or Irma. And Brady still wouldn't be fully cleared.

"No. He doesn't. He apparently really does care that much about people's flowers. He actually thought you might be the one stealing information for scams. He said you were loitering in Yvette's room." His face lost its smile. "I appreciate you getting me thinking in the right direction on this one, but you do need to stop poking around."

I took the box from him. "I don't know that I can stop. Brady won't be fully off the hook until someone else is arrested for Floyd's death. And there's something else." I wasn't sure if I was ready to share my theory with him, but I did have his attention.

"What?"

Over his shoulder, I could see Christy twirling a lock of hair and Lillibeth walking through with a garbage can to empty. There were simply too many people around to say what I was thinking. "Not here. Can I meet you some place else?"

Park's eyebrows climbed up his forehead. "Where?"

I huffed out a breath and wiggled my toes inside my boots in a private interpretive dance. "Some place we can talk. Do you know where Espresso Yourself is?"

He nodded.

"Meet me there at four-thirty?"

"See you then."

I made my way to the staff lounge to put away my purse and coat and get my work jacket. As I did, I glanced over at the schedule to see who was on. Okay. I glanced over to see if Malachi was on. We hadn't had a chance to talk since that moment in the basement. My cheeks got hot thinking about what it had been like to kiss him, to kiss anyone really, but especially to kiss Malachi. It had felt like blood had suddenly flowed into body parts that had been dead for a long time.

I took down the clipboard to read the schedule. This week's schedule was on top, but the sheets with the previous weeks' schedules were still there beneath it. There were at least three months' worth of weekly schedules for day, evening, and night shifts. I leafed back to the day that Floyd died to see who was working that shift. Irma had nailed it. Lillibeth, Camila, Malachi, Katina, Isabel, and Darrin. Harvey had died a week or two before that. I dug in my purse for Irma's notebook and found the exact date and slipped the notebook back into my purse. Then I flipped to the day page in the stack of scheduling sheets. Camila. Lillibeth, Francisco, and Margaret had worked that day. I made another quick consult of Irma's notebook to find when Xavier Pinner had died. Isabel, Margaret, Camila, and Heidi. Camila had been working for every one so far. Every single one.

The door started to open and I stepped away from the clipboard, but it was just Malachi. I blew out a breath in relief.

"What are you doing now?" he asked, pausing in the doorway and glancing back over his shoulder.

"Looking at old schedules to see who was working when

the people on Irma's list died to see if I can find a pattern." I pointed at the clipboard.

His eyebrows went up and he closed the door the rest of the way behind him. "And?"

"I'm not quite done, but it looks like Camila was working for every single one," I whispered. "That's a pretty big coincidence, don't you think?

He shook his head. "I know you think there's some kind of conspiracy here, but like we discussed before, old people die, Leah. Old people who are ill die even more often."

"Not before their time," I said. "Not on my watch."

My craft circle had a highly successful first attempt at doing pastel rubbings of leaves. It was a great craft for this group. They still had to use fine motor skills to position the leaves where they wanted them and to hold the pastel to rub it over the paper above the leaves to get the rubbing effect. They were going to make some really lovely greeting card crafts. Yvette and Gladys made three each. Javis made five.

I sighed as I started putting things away. We were a much smaller group than we had been. Javis and Waylon had been banned from being in the same room since the altercation at Spring Fling and Javis had staked his claim to coming to craft class so no Waylon. Floyd and Irma were no longer there either. I'd have to see if I could recruit a few more.

Kendrick poked her head into the room. "Hey, Dionne wants to talk to you."

"Now?" I asked.

"That's what she said."

I looked around at the mess I needed to clean up. "I

can't leave this stuff out. It's not safe. I'll be there as soon as I can."

"It's your funeral," Kendrick said and walked away.

Well, it could be somebody else's funeral if someone decided to eat glue or stick a button up their nose. I went as quickly as I could, loaded things on my cart, and went straight to Dione's office dragging it behind me. "You wanted to see me?"

She glanced up at the clock on her wall. "About fifteen minutes ago. Yes."

I gestured to the cart. "I didn't want to leave the art supplies out. It could cause problems."

She pressed her lips together and then said. "I can see that. Please come in and shut the door."

That didn't sound good, but I did it anyway. The room was small, barely big enough for Dionne's desk and filing cabinets with a couple of extra chairs. I sat in one. "What's going on?" I asked.

She rubbed her chin with her index finger. "It's come to our attention that you are asking a lot of questions and, well, snooping."

"Snooping?" I echoed.

"Yes. Snooping. Looking at things that are none of your business. Asking questions that are not your concern." She tapped her pen against the notepad. "It is important that we respect the privacy of our residents and our employees."

I opened my mouth to protest and then realized I couldn't. I had been snooping.

"You need to stop." She folded her hands neatly on her immaculate desk. "Immediately."

"Some of the things I've noticed have been helpful." Maybe I hadn't figured out who was scamming the residents, but I'd put Detective Park on the right track. He'd said so himself. Of course, he'd also said I should stop.

"I'm aware, but it doesn't balance out issues of privacy and propriety. I'll say this one more time, Leah. It has to stop. Now."

That sounded familiar. Park had said the exact same thing in pretty much the exact same words. "Fine." I stood to leave.

Dionne's shoulders relaxed a little. "I mean it, Leah. If I find out you've continued to meddle in these matters, we will find ourselves someone else to conduct art sessions. Understood?"

"Understood." My face got hot.

Who had ratted me out to Dionne? It had to be Detective Park. He'd already tried to warn me off several times. But reporting me to my boss? That was unconscionable. I stomped to the basement to put away my supplies, not even worrying about the potential axe murderer under the stairs.

I opened the basement door and picked up the box of buttons and balloons from my cart and trotted down the first three steps. That's when something went terribly wrong. My foot hit something and slipped and flew out from under me. I grabbed for the banister and it gave way sending me sailing over the open edge of the stairs to the concrete floor below. As I hit, I heard a crack in my left leg. What felt like an electric shock ran up my leg, there was a moment of numbness and then a wave of pain hit. I don't even remember catching my breath but I'm pretty sure I screamed.

Christy's face appeared at the top of the stairs. "Leah, are you okay?"

I groaned, still trying to make sense of what had happened.

"Leah?!" She saw me on the floor and started to rush down the stairs.

"Stop!" I yelled. "Be careful."

She froze, then took in the missing chunk of banister. Seconds later, she pulled her cell phone out of her pocket and dialed. "Hello. I'm at the Caring Hands Retirement Center and we need an ambulance."

At least they arrived with all the lights and sirens going this time.

SEVENTEEN

I OPENED my eyes to find Rayna sitting next to my gurney in the Emergency Room. She looked more like herself than she had in a while. Her hair was brushed smooth and she had on mascara and lip gloss.

I must have fallen asleep. I'd had a bit too much excitement. The paramedics had had to carry me up the broken basement steps, which had been more than exciting enough. I swear half the staff members had been lined up watching as they'd loaded me into the waiting ambulance like the servants lined up to greet people in a period drama. Once we got to the hospital, they'd shuffled me through X-ray and then given me something for pain. Then I'd fallen asleep as hard and fast as if I'd been unplugged.

"What are you doing here?" I asked as her face swam into focus.

She looked up from her phone. "I'm your emergency contact number, remember?"

I did remember now that she'd mentioned it. We'd been each others' emergency contacts for years. George traveled enough that it made more sense for me to be the second one on Brady's contact form, too, and I really didn't have anyone to put as the emergency on mine besides my friends. Thank goodness they were more reliable than my family.

"So how bad is it?" She pointed at my leg.

"Could be worse. I didn't break anything. My ankle's kind of messed up. The doctor said something about a knee scooter." Good thing Sharon and I had been doing that balance work!

"Lucky."

I shrugged. "That's one way to describe it."

The curtain around my emergency room bay slid open and Malachi stepped in. He wasn't in his usual scrubs. Instead he had on jeans and a T-shirt with a motorcycle logo on it. Worry creased his face. He rushed over to my side.

"Hi there. Are you okay?" Malachi asked. "I came as soon as I got off duty."

"A little less okay physically than I was after Waylon and Javis sent me head over tea kettle," I said. "Way less okay psychologically. I knew those stupid stairs were out to get me."

"At least it wasn't an axe murderer grabbing your ankles," he said, giving my hand a squeeze.

Rayna looked back and forth between us and I realized I hadn't introduced them. "Rayna, this is Malachi, the Physician's Assistant from Caring Hands. Malachi this is my best friend, Rayna."

They shook hands and then an awkward silence fell on the room. "Anybody need a cup of coffee or a bottle of water?" Rayna asked, standing. "I'm terribly thirsty. I'll step out for a minute."

She slid out of the bay, flashing me a thumbs up sign behind Malachi's back as she went.

Malachi turned and slid the curtain shut again. "Subtle."

I laughed. "Usually she's better than that. This is kind of a new circumstance for all of us. I don't generally get gentlemen callers."

"Their loss." He hooked the nearby rolling stool the doctors sat on with his foot and pulled it to the bed and sat down. "What did the doctors say?"

I filled him in.

He lifted the blanket and assessed my ankle. "You did some damage there. You'll probably be off work for a while."

"Maybe for a day or two, but I'll be back soon. I don't need my ankle to crochet baby blankets, after all."

He smiled. "True enough. I can help haul your supplies around."

"Maybe they'll give me a storage area that isn't in the basement." I shuddered. I didn't relish the thought of ever being on those stairs again. The feeling of launching into space like that was not one I'd like to repeat. I'd even more like not to repeat the feeling of landing. "I never want to go down there again."

"I don't blame you. I'll see what I can do to get them to give you a space on the ground floor." He put his hand on top of mine and I got that wonderful settling feeling that he seemed to create in me. "I'm glad you're okay."

The curtain slid back again and Detective Park walked in. "Ms. Glaser," I'm so glad you're okay. I heard about your accident. Mr. Donnelly, good to see you." His tone wasn't glad or good, though, and the expression on his face was worried.

"I didn't think someone falling down some stairs would rise to the level of police involvement," I said with a glance over at Malachi whose hand tightened a bit on mine.

Park shrugged. He was still in his ripped jeans from earlier. Those suits might love him, but the jeans definitely worked. "We had an appointment. When you didn't show up, I checked to see what might be keeping you."

That was right. I'd forgotten. I was furious with him. I tried to push myself to a better sitting position to rant at him, but a jolt of pain went down my leg. I settled for glaring at him from a prone position. "Well, in addition to falling down the stairs, almost getting fired from my job slowed me down."

Both Malachi and Park stiffened, but it was Park who asked, "Why were you almost fired?"

"You should know. I'm assuming you were the one who ratted me out to Dionne." There was a roar in my ears that made it difficult for me to even think.

Park blinked. "Back up, please. What are you talking about?"

"I got called into the administrator's office and told that I would be fired if I didn't stop poking around." So humiliating! I had never been fired from a job before. I had never been called into someone's office for anything other than praise. I was a good girl, God damn it.

"And you think I was the one who told her to do that?" he asked with a head tilt.

"Who else?" I asked. "She used almost your exact words."

He rubbed the back of his neck. "I think it's good advice, but it wasn't me. I feel completely okay with telling you to your face to stay out of this." He rubbed the back of his neck.

"Then who did?" I threw my hands in the air. "And don't rub your neck at me."

He looked up, surprised. "What?"

"That neck thing you do. You rub it when you think something's funny or strange or confusing. I'm not any of those things so don't rub your neck at me."

He stood up straight and dropped his hands to his side. "Didn't you have something you wanted to tell me?"

I hesitated. I wasn't one hundred percent sure I believed him about not ratting me out to Dionne. On the other hand, he'd listened when I told him about Gabriel. Even when my suspicions had turned out to be wrong, he'd paid enough attention to use that information as a stepping stone to finding out what was really happening.

I turned to Malachi. "Could you get me my purse?" I pointed to where it sat in the corner. He handed it to me.

I pulled Irma's notebook out of my purse, and tossed it at Park.

"What's this?" He turned it over in his hands.

"Irma Warren's notebook."

His hand started to creep up to the back of his neck, but he dropped it. "Okay. Why are you giving it to me?"

"There are lists of names in there. Names of people who have died at Caring Hands. People who died in their sleep with no one around. People who were all found by the day shift when one particular person was working."

Malachi made a funny noise.

"What are you saying, Leah?" Park still hadn't opened the notebook. It looked tiny in his hands.

"I'm saying that I think Floyd might have been one of a string of murders at Caring Hands and, if I'm right, the killings started months before Brady had come anywhere near there."

"Leah," Malachi said, a warning tone in his voice.

Park went very still. "Are you saying there's a serial killer at Caring Hands?"

That sounded even more terrifying than it had in my head. All the blood left my face. Everything went cold. Serial killer? Serial killers were things that happened in movies and books with FBI profilers in big cities. Serial killers weren't a thing that happened at nursing homes in medium-sized Central Valley towns. "I'm saying that I don't think the people on that list died natural deaths."

Park turned the notebook over in his hands. "Were their deaths a surprise?"

"Not exactly surprises. They were all pretty ill. The families all knew it was coming, but they didn't expect it quite that soon."

Park glanced over at Malachi and then back to me. "I don't mean to be callous, but isn't pretty normal for people to die at Caring Hands? It seems like a lot of them are waiting for that. Or their families are."

"Maybe that's how whoever is doing this is getting away with it. It all seems like it's in the natural course of things, but it really isn't," I said.

"That's a pretty clever serial killer you're describing."

His words sent another chill up my spine. Serial killer. Somehow mercy killer or angel of mercy didn't sound quite as frightening. "But now that we know what to look for, we can be even more clever."

"We?" His eyebrows climbed halfway up his forehead. "There's no we in this."

I leaned back in the hospital and crossed my arms over my chest. "Do you know why something like this could go on without anyone noticing?"

He sighed. "Why?"

"Because no one's looking out for some of these people. They have family, but they weren't close or the family is far away. They're defenseless."

H nodded slowly. "And somehow it's your job to defend them?"

I felt the color rising up in my cheeks, but pressed on anyway. "If no one else is going to."

"Look. I'm not ignoring this." He held Irma's notebook up. "But I also need to keep within the confines of what the law finds reasonable. From what you're saying, there's no evidence that any of these people were murdered or who might have murdered them."

"So you're not going to do anything?" The frustration rose up inside me so fast I thought I might choke on it.

"I didn't say that." He glanced inside the notebook. "You should probably rest now, though. I'll be in touch."

Rayna came back in with three bottles of water as Park left. "What was he doing here?"

"Not much," I grumbled. Then I yawned.

"Park's right about one thing. You need to get some rest," Malachi said. "Do you need help once you get home?"

"We're good for tonight," Rayna told him and then turned to me. "Tamika's already at your place making sure you can get around and Sharon's bringing take-out over for dinner. One of us will stay in case you need help during the night."

"How'd they get past her security system?" Malachi asked.

"They all have the code," I said.

"Seems like you're pretty well taken care of then." Malachi stood.

"I am. I'm lucky to have such good friends." I smiled over at Rayna.

"True that." He gave my hand a squeeze. "See you in the next couple of days then?"

"Absolutely."

He walked out.

Rayna collapsed into one of the visitor's chairs and fanned herself. "My my my."

———

I spent the first day after my accident enjoying being fussed over and the second one wanting to kill everyone for fussing over me. Apparently, I can't be pleased. Or at least I can't be pleased for long.

Rayna had been right. I had been lucky. I hadn't broken anything, but I'd stretched some ligaments and the like in ways that were "not optimal" according to the Emergency Room doctor. I'd be on a knee scooter for a couple of weeks or so as the tendons in my foot healed, but probably wouldn't suffer any permanent consequences.

"I think I'll go back to work tomorrow," I announced to my friends.

We were sitting on my new-to-me couch, eating pizza.

"Tomorrow?" Tamika shook her head. "You need more time to heal. Why not take tomorrow and then the weekend off?"

"Because I might lose my mind." I set my pizza down. "And because I want to be sure I still have a job. And because there are a few more things I want to check out. "

"Why are you all the sudden worried about keeping your job?" Sharon asked. "They can't fire you for falling."

"I'm worried because I received an official warning from the Caring Hands management. They're putting a note in my file." I picked my pizza back up and took a bite, but it didn't taste as good.

"What did you do?" Sharon asked.

Tamika kicked her. "Ouch. What?" Sharon rubbed at her shin.

Tamika looked from Sharon to me. "What trumped up charges are they leveling against you?" she asked.

I couldn't help it. I laughed. They all had my back in their own ways. "Snooping, apparently."

"Snooping?" Rayna asked. "You mean about Brady?"

"I think this might be much bigger than Brady, Rayna. Way bigger." I paused, not sure how to tell them what I suspected and why. I hated to admit it, but Park's and Malachi's questions had left me feeling not quite as certain as I had been. I decided to let it fly, though. If anybody could help me sort this out, it was these three women. "I think there might be a serial killer at Caring Hands."

There was a collective gasp and then everyone was asking questions at once. I held up my hand to stop them. "At first I thought it was just Floyd and that it might be the flower delivery guy, that he had been getting the information he needed to scam some of the residents when he was delivering flowers and somehow Floyd had caught on to him and Gabriel killed him to cover it up."

"But the person they arrested for the scams wasn't named Gabriel." Sharon looked up. "It was Marty something and he wasn't a florist."

"I know. It pretty much killed that theory. Not only did Gabriel not have a reason to kill Floyd, but Marty wasn't there the day that Floyd died and I'm fairly certain that whoever did it had to be physically in the building."

"Okay. Next theory," Sharon said.

"Tamika helped me do some digging into what I found in Irma's notebook and I think someone who works at Caring Hands might be killing off old people they're supposed to be taking care of." I bit my lip. It sounded crazy, but I was pretty sure it wasn't.

"What? Why?" Rayna shook her head. "Why would anyone do that?"

"They're called Angels of Mercy or Mercy Killers. Apparently, they often think they're doing the right thing, that they're releasing someone from pain and suffering. Of course, sometimes they also get off on the control it gives them. And then there are the ones who like to then try to save the person to get kudos for their heroics." I rattled off what I'd learned.

Sharon leaned forward. "And how is this person doing this?"

"It would be easy to give enough fentanyl to send those fragile old people off without anyone even knowing. A few grains mixed with some other medicine or given with a shot they thought was something else and they'd be gone." I paused. "They probably didn't even know what was happening to them. They trusted the person who was taking care of them."

"And how did you come to this conclusion?" Sharon's arms were crossed over her chest. She clearly did not approve.

"I spent some time calling the next of kin of the people on Irma's list and some time calling the next of kin of the people who had died in the same time frame that weren't on Irma's list." I explained a bit more about the two lists that Tamika and I had made.

"How did you get those names? The next of kin?" Rayna's brow was furrowed.

"I looked them up in their patient files. They keep the inactive ones in the basement by where I keep my art supplies." No need to mention about them suddenly being locked up.

"Do you have permission to look in those files?" Sharon asked.

I was starting to feel like I was being cross-examined. Mindy was right. It wasn't much fun being on this end of a Sharon interrogation. Heat rushed to my cheeks. "Not exactly."

Sharon smacked her forehead. "So you're violating people's privacy and maybe even some HIPAA regulations?"

"Maybe. But if we stop a serial killer, isn't it worth it?" I asked.

Sharon sighed. "So what did you find out?"

"The ones on Irma's list were alone when they died and it happened sooner than people anticipated. The deaths weren't unexpected. The people were seriously ill. They just weren't expected so fast. The other people were either like Effie Shelinger and were fine one second and gone the next with witnesses all around or they'd been going downhill and their families were there when they died," I said.

"And you think this adds up to a serial killer?" Sharon said.

I nodded. "I do and I think it's Camila Diaz."

Sharon held up her hands like a cop stopping traffic. "Hold on a second. I thought you suspected Lillibeth."

I shook my head. "She hasn't been on duty when the people on the list were found, but Camila has. And Lillibeth wants to bring people back to life, not kill them. Plus Camila is always talking about people being in a better place when they're dead and then there are all those pets named after serial killers. I think Floyd was suspicious and started asking questions and Irma, too, and Camila had to get rid of them. Camila pointed out how Irma was as sharp as a tack to me. She knew that Irma would figure it out."

"None of this adds up to anything in court," Sharon said.

And there was the biggest problem. How did we use it to clear Brady? "I know. I'm going to have to find something that will."

"You have to drop this," Rayna said, shaking her head.

"You sound like Detective Park," I grumbled. "I'm pretty sure he's the one who ratted me out to Dionne."

Rayna put her hand on my arm. "Seriously, Leah. I don't want you to lose your job over this. Brady didn't do it and Sharon will be able to prove it."

Sharon nodded. "I have more than enough to create reasonable doubt. I'm sure Park knows that, too. They're not going to arrest him because they don't have anything to make charges against Brady stick."

"But you won't be able to prove Brady is innocent unless we can prove who did do it. You've seen it yourself. People treat him differently now. They will until we find the killer. Besides . . ." I couldn't quite figure out how to say what I was feeling.

"Besides what?" Rayna sighed.

"Somebody needs to stick up for these people." I set my coffee down. Who was I kidding? It wasn't anywhere near as good as a mocha. "They're so vulnerable and trusting. Someone's taking advantage of that for their own satisfaction. Someone who is supposed to be looking out for them."

"And what happens if you lose your job over this?" Rayna asked.

"If I'm right, they won't be able to fire me. I'll be a whistleblower." I looked over at Sharon.

"She might be right about that. I'll check it out. If they

did fire her for exposing something as terrible as a serial killer in their midst, she'd have a hell of a lawsuit. She might never have to work again."

"And if you're wrong?" Rayna asked.

I shrugged. "I'd rather lose my job sticking up for people who can't defend themselves than keep my job at a place that wouldn't want to be sure that the people in their care were safe."

EIGHTEEN

I ROLLED into Caring Hands on Monday on my knee scooter, like a woman with a mission, promptly bashed into a potted plant, and then managed to get to the front desk. I did have a mission, but before I could start on it, I had to figure out where all my supplies were and how to get to them. The closed basement door had yellow tape across it in a crisscross, making it look like a crime scene. I shuddered, feeling the lurch of falling through space again in the pit of my stomach. Even if my stuff was down there, I wasn't going down there ever again.

When I asked about my art supplies, Christy rolled her eyes. "How should I know?" then twirled a lock of hair. Then I knocked on Dionne's door. She did not roll her eyes, but she also wasn't entirely sure where the balloons and buttons and everything else might be.

The residents' business center with the computer was next to Dionne's office. I decided to take a minute to see if I could find out what, if anything, Floyd had been looking for on the computer. Brady had given me the log-in information he'd set up for Floyd.

I stowed my knee scooter to one side and maneuvered into a chair and log in. A landing page popped up. It listed the last time Floyd had used the computer. It was the night before he died.

Now what? I gnawed a little on the side of my finger, then texted Tamika. "How do I find out what someone was looking at on a computer?"

"Look at the History," she texted back a few seconds later.

I clicked the tab and nothing popped up. I texted Tamika. "What if there's nothing there?"

"Then they erased it," she replied.

I sighed. Brady had perhaps done too good a job of teaching Floyd how to use a computer. Whatever he'd found, he hadn't wanted anyone to know he'd found it and I'd bet whatever it was, it had led to his death.

I logged out, mounted back on my trusty steed, and rolled out of the room, only clipping the door jamb slightly and barely missing Malachi who was walking by. "Sorry," I said. "I still haven't figured out exactly how to drive this thing yet. I'm having a lot more sympathy for Irma and her Jazzy Pride."

"You'll get used to it," he assured me. "What were you doing in there?"

I sighed. "Trying to figure out what Floyd might have been looking for on the computer right before he died."

His eyebrows went up. "Any luck?"

"Not really. He'd erased the history. I do know that he was searching there the night before he died. Seems like a pretty big coincidence to me." I started toward the employee lounge and he fell into step beside me.

Malachi opened the door to the lounge for me and I

scooted in after him. My art supplies were stacked neatly on a rolling cart in the corner. "There they are!"

"Oh. I guess I forgot to tell you. I brought them up here before they closed up the basement. I'll help you get them down to the dining hall in a minute." He opened his locker to put in his jacket, shoving it in around the duffel bag that always seemed to be there and a baby doll like the ones Gladys toted around, except this one was bandage-free.

"What are you doing with Gladys's doll?" I asked.

A bit of red touched his cheeks. "I, uh, take the old ones away when she bangs them up too much and bring in a new one and tell her I took the doll to the doctor to get better."

Ohhhhhh. That was Gladys's special secret about her dolls. Most people avoided Gladys. Even her own family. But not Malachi. It wasn't his job. He didn't really even have to notice, but he did anyway and made the effort to help a little old lady. And to help me. No one else had bothered to get my art supplies. They probably hadn't even thought about it. "That's really nice of you."

He turned away from me and shrugged. "It's nothing."

It wasn't, though. I knew that. None of what he did added up to nothing.

———

The balloon button bowls were not nearly as successful as my leaf rubbings had been. The idea was that we would cover a balloon with glue, stick buttons to it, let it dry, then pop the balloon. The buttons would retain the shape of the balloon and be a cute decorative little bowl.

First, I'd nearly passed out blowing up all the balloons because nobody else could get enough air in their lungs to do it. Then the glue dried too fast for Gladys and Miriam to get their buttons stuck to their balloons, but not in the time we needed for Yvette's buttons to retain the balloon's shape when we popped it. We ended up with a bunch of sticky buttons and not much else.

I'd crossed this one firmly off the list of brilliant ideas and stacked the supplies back onto the cart. There was no way I could push the cart and drive my scooter. I'd have to find someone to help me. I started down the hall to see who was at the nurses' station. Camila. A shiver went up my spine. I'd rather do laps on my knee scooter than ask her for help.

Help. Floyd had asked Brady to help him learn how to use the computer. Maybe Floyd had been asking Brady for more help. If the help he needed involved someone who worked here at Caring hands, he wouldn't have left what he wanted help with lying around. He would have hidden it somewhere, the way Irma had hidden her notebook. But where?

The key to finding Irma's notebook had been to look at the world the way she did. Floyd wasn't in a wheelchair, though. He walked around like I did. Well, like I used to before I decided to take the express train to the basement floor. It wasn't a height thing. I needed to try to think like he did. So what did Floyd think about?

The library cart was parked in the hallway outside Gladys's room. Of course! The spy books! Only Brady would have known about those and would be the only one who would know where to look. I pulled out my phone and called Brady. "Hi, Leah. What's up?"

"Brady, when you and Floyd talked about the spy stuff, did he say where he might put a dead drop?"

"Oh, yeah. Out in the courtyard. Over behind the birdcage."

Okayyyyy. "Why there?"

"Well, no one ever went there but us and you can't really see into that corner unless you're right there. Those big orange plants hide you."

True. Very true. "You said there would be a signal between the spies about when to look at the dead drop. Did he make one of those up, too?"

"Sure. He would leave me a note."

A note that someone could have easily torn in half and only left Brady's name for the police to find. "What would the note have said?"

"The cafeteria always serves spaghetti on Tuesday."

No one else would have known what that meant or even that it meant anything besides that maybe Floyd was having trouble keeping his days straight. It certainly wouldn't clue them in to where to look for whatever he might have left for Brady. "Did you look in the dead drop?"

"Yeah. No. He didn't give me the signal."

Except I was pretty sure he had. It just hadn't gotten through. "Where behind the birdcage is the dead drop?"

"There's one of those big brick and cement planters. It has a little overhang. Floyd put a metal box there." He paused. "Leah, do you think he left a message there?"

"I think it's possible, Brady. I'm going to go look."

We hung up. Damn it. Camila was still there at the nurses' station. There was no way she wouldn't see me go by and head out to the courtyard. If she was the one that had killed Floyd and tried to frame Brady for it, she'd see me going. I didn't want to give her any idea that I was on to her. I ducked into Gladys's room to wait her out. If anyone asked, I could say I was going to pluck Gladys's chin hairs. I patted my jacket pocket. The tweezers were still there.

Gladys was sound asleep. It had clearly been her shower day. Her hair was clean and fluffy against her pillow. Her baby doll looked like she'd gone into the shower with her, which made sense with how close Gladys kept her. They probably couldn't pry her out of Gladys's hands and had decided it was easier to let the doll get wet than to upset her. The doll's hair was wet and one of her bandages was loose at the corner. Malachi hadn't been able to give her the new one yet. She'd probably been in the shower when he tried.

Curious about what Gladys was doing to those poor dollies to require this much first aid, I peeled the bandage off the rest of the way to take a peek. Someone had made a very deliberate cut into the doll's arm. It was straight and sure and clean. Professional.

No way could Gladys have made that cut. We don't let the residents have access to anything sharp enough to make a cut like that, even under supervision. Even if she did get hold of something, I doubted she'd have the dexterity to make a cut that clean and sharp considering the arthritis she had in her hands. I'm not even sure I could. It would require a certain amount of force and a strong sure hand. Why, though? Why cut up a little old lady's dolly. I pressed down on one side of the cut, trying to see inside. A corner of white paper peeked out from the cut. Carefully, trying not to rip whatever it was or wake Gladys, I teased it out until I was holding a transdermal Fentanyl patch. An open one, not in its packaging, folded carefully and precisely in half.

I stared at it, my mind racing. How on earth would it have gotten in there? Gladys couldn't have done it. I supposed she could have gotten the patch from someone's garbage. She was always looking through other people's things. But why hide it in her doll? And how? No way was it an accident. Everything about it from the cut on the doll to the way the patch was folded was done with precision, carefully protecting whatever precious grains of the drug that remained.

I shook my head as questions and answers collided. Why did people hide drugs anywhere? To smuggle them. What better way to smuggle fentanyl patches out of Caring Hands then to pretend you were doing a favor for a dottering old lady and getting her a new doll? Not only would no one question it, they'd actually praise you for doing it.

The way I'd praised Malachi. For his kindness. For his care. For his quiet strength.

The way I'd felt when his strong sure hand had touched mine. My face went hot. He'd given me butterflies. The first butterflies I'd let myself feel in years. I'd trusted him. I'd told him private things that I hadn't told anyone else and he'd lied to me, betrayed me.

My heart kicked up a notch, beating a bit faster. Malachi could easily have been the person who reported me to Dionee. He knew more about my investigation than anyone else. I'd thought it was Detective Park trying to get me to stop snooping. I'd been so sure Malachi was on my side, it hadn't occurred to me to suspect him.

Maybe there was another explanation. He hadn't been around on shift for all the deaths in Irma's book, after all. He'd been working night shift before Floyd's death.

Night shift. Just because those people had been found by the day shift in the morning, didn't mean that that was when they had died. He could have easily given them the Fentanyl during the night shift and then faked the records and said he'd checked their vitals and that they were okay. As the Physician's Assistant he had access to everything and no one questioned him working with everyone. It was his job.

Would this be enough to convince Detective Park there was a serial killer at work at Caring Hands and that the serial killer was Malachi? I looked down at the wet doll in my hands. If there had been fingerprints on it, they were long gone. Besides, what would Malachi's fingerprints on Gladys's doll matter? Of course they'd be there. He was the one who'd given her the doll in the first place.

Had Floyd figured this all out? Brady had mentioned Floyd helping Gladys, too. Maybe Floyd had found the patches inside the doll and had put it all together. Maybe the last pieces I needed to convince Detective Park that Malachi was a murderer were in the dead drop behing the Bird of Paradise flowers in the courtyard.

I peeked down the hall. Camila was still there, but Malachi wasn't. I tucked Gladys's baby into the bag on the front of my knee scooter and caromed down the hallway toward the courtyard and Floyd's dead drop, barely avoiding the wall in a couple of spots. My sympathy for Irma's bad scooter driving increased.

I was halfway down the hall when I heard Gladys. "Babyyyyyyy!!!"

She must have woken up and realized she didn't have her doll. I couldn't risk giving the doll back to her. It was evidence.

Ahead, I saw Camila look up from the records she was updating.

"My babyyyyyy!!"

Camila closed the binder she was working in and walked down the hall toward Gladys's room. She shook her head. "Do ye hear the children weeping, O my brothers. Ere the sorrow comes with years? They are leaning their young heads against their mothers, — And that cannot stop their tears."

"That's lovely, Camila," I said, slowing my roll.

"It's from a poem by Elizabeth Barrett Browning," she said. "I love poetry. That's why I named all my pets after poets."

"Poets?" I repeated. Not serial killers?

"Sure. Elizabeth Barrett Browning, Ted Hughes, Aileen Fisher, and, of course, my little Jack K after Jack Kerouac."

Oh, my God. Lizzie B wasn't named after Lizzie Borden. She was named after Elizabeth Barrett Browning. Ted was Ted Hughes, not Ted Bundy. Aileen was Aileen Fisher, not Aileen Wournos. And Jackie K wasn't Jack Kevorkian. He was Jack Kerouac. If I hadn't been so anxious to see what Floyd might have hidden in that dead drop, I might have dropped with relief.

Gladys let out another bellow of "Babbyyyyyyy!"

Camila hurried off down the hall and I scooted toward the courtyard. I put in the code at the double doors to get out of the unit and then down the stretch of hallway to the door to the outdoors. There was a button to push to open it to make it easier for wheelchairs to get through. I pushed it so I could scoot through, then I went as quickly as I could to the corner behind the birdcage.

The hedge here was thick, nearly impenetrable. I turned. I could see the building behind me through the branches, but I didn't think anyone would see me unless they were looking for me. I had cover to poke around. It took me a minute, but I found the ledge around the brick planter and reached my hand underneath, searching for the metal box Floyd might have left there.

"You really are relentless, aren't you?" a deep voice said behind me.

I straightened. Malachi. But I didn't get that warm feeling in my tummy from seeing him that I had before. Now I had a cold pit of dread. "Malachi," I said trying to keep my tone light. Maybe he didn't know why I was here.

He took a step toward me, making me retreat further into the corner. "What are you looking for out here?" he asked. "Are you looking to see if Floyd or Irma left some kind of clue you could follow?"

He thought he was so smart, so clever, so shrewd. He wasn't, though. Two old people figured out who and what he was and now I had, too. "And if I am?"

"Then I'm going to need to take whatever it is from you." He crowded me further into the corner. He shook his head, looking almost regretful. "Why couldn't you leave it alone? Once you managed to get Marty arrested, why couldn't you drop it? For that matter, why go after Marty? What were those old people doing with all that money anyway? Pouring it out into this place? For what? It's not like they're going to get better."

The back of my scooter hit the wall. I couldn't retreat any further so instead I stood straighter. "It won't help you to take it. They'll find out. They'll know to look at you."

"Will they?" He laughed. "So what? All I need is enough time to disappear. I've done it before. It's not so hard when you know how. You just need some money and some papers and I always make sure I have those ready to go. I have a go-bag at my apartment and another here in my locker."

The duffel bag that was always in his locker. Of course.

"All I need is enough time to hit the open road. How long do you think it will take them to find you out here? How long until someone misses you? I mean, no one really needs you for anything, do they?" He pulled a syringe out of his pocket.

That stung. My son would miss me, but how long would it take? Would my friends worry in an hour? A day? How far could he be gone in that time?

"I might not even run. When they do find you, there'll be nothing to tie me to your death. They might step up the investigation, but it won't point to me. If I have to, I'll frame someone else. You've set it up beautifully for me to frame Camila. They won't suspect me. Everyone loves me. You loved me."

He was right. I had. Well, not love exactly. Strongly liked. Maybe even lusted a little. It had never crossed my mind that he was a killer manipulating us all. I looked around for something that I could use a weapon to ward him off. My palms were sweaty against the handles of my knee scooter. I rubbed them against my jacket to dry them. Feeling a familiar small shape, my hand slipped into my pocket and found my tweezers.

"I don't know why Floyd and Irma and you had to make such a fuss anyway. I was doing those people a favor, putting them out of their misery. Just like I was doing you a favor by pretending to be interested you."

I curled my fingers around the tweezers. They weren't much, but they were all I had.

"This really won't be bad, Leah. You'll drift off. Like we said, it's not a bad way to go." He took another step toward me. "Besides, also like you said, you're done. What point is there to you anymore? What use are you?"

All the hairs on my arms and the back of my neck were standing at attention. I wanted to run, but I couldn't. I had to wait and let him come one step closer. He had to be in tweezer range.

I was so not done. I was on a new leg of my journey. Like Brady, I just needed to figure out where that journey was going and how I'd get started on it. I absolutely didn't want to fade away. I wanted to live and damn it, this pretty twisted evil man wasn't going to get in my way. With each breath, clear cold rage ran through me. I felt strong. I felt determined. I felt ready. I felt like Rayna must have felt when she confronted Eva.

Malachi took that one more step toward me, reaching out for me, ready to grab me with one hand and jam that syringe full of fentanyl into me with the other. I wasn't going to let that happen. I wasn't going to drift off anywhere. I was going to fight.

Time switched into slow motion. I pulled the tweezers out of my pocket and jammed them as hard as I could into his arm. He cried out in pain and retreated a step. With the space that gave me, I lifted my knee scooter and swung it in the air as high as I could as if I was cartwheeling my arms into Warrior Two from yoga class. I brought the scooter down hard, grazing his head, but catching him fully on the shoulder. He crumbled to the ground and I hopped over him on one foot, grateful for the balance work Sharon and I had done in yoga class. I was almost out of the corner to freedom when his hand closed around my bad ankle. He yanked and I fell to the concrete, managing to cushion my fall with my shoulder.

"Clever girl," Malachi said as he began to pull me back into the corner. "But not clever enough."

I was horizontal, my hands beneath my shoulders. Malachi had one leg - the bad one. The position felt familiar. It was the part of the Sun Salutation where you lowered yourself from the plank position before you went into Upward Dog: Chaturanga Dandasana. I bent my elbows and, using Malachi as my balance point, I shoved backward with all my strength and kicked him as hard as I could in the face with my good leg, catching him on the chin with the heel of my boot.

He grunted and let go. I scrambled the rest of the way out of the corner, into the open area of the courtyard and screamed. "Help!"

Through the glass I could see Christy walking down the hallway. "Christy!"

She turned, looking confused.

"Christy," I screamed again, waving my hand in the air to catch her attention. Then I asked her to do the one thing I was sure she would do for me. "Call 911!"

I heard Malachi burst out of the hedge behind me, racing to the door, toward Christy, toward his locker with his duffel bag. I twisted around, raised up on one arm, and went into Fallen Triangle pose, Patita Tārāsana. He tripped over my extended leg just like Sierra had tripped over Amelia Nguyen's leg in class. Malachi face-planted hard.

Christy came charging out. "Leah, what are you doing to Malachi?"

"Call 911!" I repeated.

She bent down to help Malachi. "Are you okay?" she asked.

He grabbed her arm. "Did you call them?"

She nodded quickly. "As soon as I saw her trip you like that. She should be arrested for assault!"

"Damn it," he said, shoving her aside. He took off at a run.

———

Malachi didn't make it far. Christy had called 911 and yelled for help before she came out to the courtyard. Of course, she'd thought she was calling 911 to protect Malachi from me, not the other way around, but the outcome was the same.

Lillibeth, Camila, Dionne, and Kendrick had all come running when they heard all the shouting, slowing Malachi down in the process as they tried to see if he was okay and make sure I hadn't hurt him.

"Stop Malachi!" I yelled. "He's the murderer! He killed Floyd! And Irma!"

They all turned to look at me, stunned. Five sets of eyes opened wide and mouths formed into little o's. Malachi lowered his shoulder and plowed through them like a linebacker through an offensive line, but it was too late. The police, including Detective Park, had already arrived.

I explained what I knew as quickly and as concisely as I could with as few flourishes as possible. Interpretive dance was entirely out of the question. My leg hurt. A lot.

Detective Park helped me up into the building and to one of the chairs in the lobby. As he listened, his hand crept toward his neck, but then he snatched it back down in his lap and took notes instead. He spoke in a low voice into his radio and a few minutes later, a uniformed officer walked a handcuffed Malachi past us.

As they went past, Malachi lunged at me. "You stupid

dried up old hag. I can't believe you thought I would actually be interested in you and your miserable, pathetic life. Your time's over. You know, I only pretended to like you so I would know what you were finding out while you were sticking your big ugly nose into everything."

Park shoved Malachi back before he could make contact with me. He turned to me and said, "I've called the paramedics. They're on their way. I have to take him in, but I'll be in touch."

NINETEEN

IT WAS seven-thirty p.m. and I was on my couch with my crocheting in my lap, right where I'd been when Rayna had called me to tell me that Brady had been taken in for questioning by the police. This time it didn't feel quite so lonely. Mainly because Tamika, Sharon, Rayna, and their spouses were all there, making dinner for me and generally fussing over me. Detective Park was over talking to Tamika, getting some of the information she'd found for me.

"Mom! You're a total bad ass!" Tyler crowed, plopping down on the couch next to me. I could still see remnants of the initial worry fading from the depths of his eyes, but mostly I was glad that he was looking at me as a hero rather than a victim.

"Well, maybe not a total bad ass, but at least a partial one." I couldn't help smiling.

"Nuh uh. That cop guy over there." He gestured with his thumb toward Detective Park. "He says you're the one who figured out who it was, found the evidence, and subdued him. That sounds total bad ass to me."

It didn't sound too shabby to me either.

"Thank you, Leah," Brady said, sitting down next to Tyler. "I don't know if anyone would have every figured out what had really happened to Floyd and all those other people if you hadn't. Nobody might have ever believed I was innocent and who knows how many more people Malachi would have killed." His voice broke a little on that last sentence. I reached out and took his hand and gave it a squeeze.

The doorbell rang and Sharon answered it. Eva stood on the other side, a casserole dish in her hands, shifting from foot to foot. "I, uh, brought lasagna."

Sharon looked over her shoulder at me and I nodded. She stepped aside to let Eva in. She gave me a little wave before going over to set her dish down on a table that was already groaning with food.

Rayna saw her and straightened as if she'd been hit with a hot glue gun.

Eva's head bowed. "I . . . I'm really sorry."

Rayna's eyes went wide. "You're what?"

Eva lifted her head and set her shoulders. "I'm sorry. I shouldn't have posted that stuff about Brady. I . . . I'd like to find some way to make it up to you."

Rayna leaned over to get a look at me. I shrugged. She turned back to Eva. "Okay, then. Would you like a glass of wine?"

Eva slumped in relief. "Yes. Please."

The two walked toward the kitchen.

"I'll stay home for the weekend to help while you get on your feet," Tyler gestured toward my leg with its bulky brace around it. Malachi had done some more damage to it.

"You don't have to do that, Ty. I'm fine. I can take care of myself."

"I think you proved that. Maybe let me do it because I

want to? You've always been there for me. I want to start repaying the favor." He smiled. "Plus I want to kick Brady's ass in League of Legends. I need payback."

I hugged him. I had to admit it. I'd done a pretty fine job of mothering. The two boys wandered away and Detective Park sat down next to me on the other side on the couch. "Ms. Glaser."

It sounded awfully formal considering the setting and what we'd been through together. "I think you can probably call me Leah."

"Okay. Then maybe I can be Daniel?" He leaned back on the couch.

I smiled. "Sure."

"I wanted to let you know what we've found out. Floyd had a series of print-outs of images in that metal box he'd hidden in the planter. They were all images of the man we know as Malachi Donnelly. That wasn't the name associated with the photos, though. I'm not sure how he managed to find them." He shook his head.

I had a guess. "Brady showed him how to do a reverse image search."

"Makes sense." He looked around at the buzz of friends around the room. "I guess I should go. You have plenty of people looking after you."

"I do. Thank you, but you don't have to leave. Have something to eat. There's plenty." It might be wise to have someone taste Eva's lasagna before the rest of us did.

He hesitated. "I wish we'd been looking out for you a little sooner. There's no easy way to say this, but someone — we're assuming Malachi — sabotaged those stairs at Caring Hands."

That had not been what I'd expected to hear. The shock

of it made my skin go very hot and then intensely cold. My lips felt rubbery, but I managed to squeak out a "what?"

"We found some glass beads like the ones you used in those suncatchers at the bottom of the stairs and the banister had been sawn through in two places so that if anyone leaned on it, it would collapse."

Glass beads. That would explain what had made my foot slip out from under me and the sawn through post would explain why the banister had collapsed beneath me.

The memory of falling flashed through me again in a shiver, but the steady look in Daniel's eyes held me. It wasn't the same sense of calm that Malachi had been able to create. This was something different. Something new.

"From what we've been able to find out, you were nearly the only person to go up and down the stairs on a regular basis."

"How do you even know all that? Do the Monterey police investigate every time someone falls down the stairs?" I asked.

"No. But we tend to notice when someone falls down the stairs at a place where people have been murdered." He shifted and suddenly our faces were quite close. "One more thing. Just so you know, you are not a dried-up old hag. Not at all."

A flush bloomed all the way up to my scalp and I oh-so-casually tucked my hair behind my ear. "Thank you."

He stood. "See you soon?"

I nodded and he disappeared into the throng of friends and family that jammed my little house.

I PULLED into Judy Gordon's driveway, parked, dragged out my knee scooter, rolled up to the front door, and rang the bell. It took her a while to answer, but she got there eventually.

"Leah," she said, touching her hand to her chest and smiling. "I wasn't expecting you."

"I know." I pushed past her and wheeled back to her sunroom without taking off my shoes. The portrait I'd done of Sugar Pop was prominently displayed.

I took the check she'd written to me that I'd never managed to cash in all the excitement and ripped it into tiny pieces, then dropped them to the floor. Without another word, I took Sugar Pop's portrait off the wall, tucked it under my arm, and wheeled out.

THE END

Thanks for reading my book *Women of a Certain Rage!* I hope you enjoyed Leah's story! Rayna's will be coming soon in *She Looks Good for Her Rage*. You can read on for a short sneak-peek!

RAYNA

I was standing at my kitchen sink, staring at my own reflection in the darkened window when I heard the first scream.

I don't sleep well under the best of circumstances and this was definitely not the best of circumstances. I'd woken up at four-thirty (four twenty-seven to be exact) and tried like hell to go back to sleep. I'd shut my eyes and done my deep breathing. I'd tried to empty my brain of thought, but my to-do list paraded through instead. Not because it was important. More because it wasn't.

Oh, sure. George and Brady would notice if dinner didn't hit the table at some point in the evening or if their laundry wasn't folded and put away or if bills weren't paid or the recycling wasn't sorted or any of the things that seemed to fill most of my days. None of it felt crucial, though.

"Jack! Jack! Where are you?"

It was a woman's voice. High-pitched and shrill. Panicked.

"Jackkkkk!"

It had to be our neighbor three doors down, Monique Bradley. Her two-year-old Jack was one of those busy little boys who constantly seemed about to fall from some place he shouldn't have been climbing or to get stuck in something he shouldn't have been crawling into or to eat something that wasn't food. I snorted. My oldest had been the same way. Life had felt like a constant battle to keep him alive. His little brother Brady? He'd been a dream baby. Fat and content and cooing. Boy, had things changed.

"Jackkkkk!"

Wow. Truly panicked. I grabbed a sweater out of the coat closet and slipped my feet into some sandals and went to see if I could help.

Monique ran from one set of bushes to another, looking under them. Her crossover SUV sat in the driveway with all of the doors and back hatch open. The front door of her house hung open, too, and the porch lights were on.

I got to Monique at the same as Cassidy, the young woman who rented the apartment above the Bradley's garage, ran up. "What is it? What's happening?"

Monique whirled around, eyes wide. "Have you seen Jack?"

Cassidy shook her head. "No. Of course not. What's going on?"

Monique sank down on her front steps and put her face in her hands. "He's gone. Jack is gone."

Eileen Rendahl is a national-bestselling award-winning author of mystery, thriller, urban fantasy, romantic comedy, and romantic suspense. She also writes as Kristi Abbott, Lillian Bell, and Eileen Carr. If you think you're confused, imagine what it's like inside her head.

She has had many jobs and lived in many cities and feels unbelievably lucky to be where she is now and to be doing what she's doing.

For more information, visit www.EileenRendahl.com.

www.ingramcontent.com/pod-product-compliance
Lightning Source LLC
Chambersburg PA
CBHW021147160726
47994CB00001B/105